PRIMEVAL AND OTHER TIMES

OLGA TOKARCZUK

PRIMEVAL AND OTHER TIMES

translated from the Polish by Antonia Lloyd-Jones

TWISTED SPOON PRESS

PRAGUE

ISBN 978-80-86264-35-6

This publication has been funded by the
Book Institute – the ©POLAND Translation Program

INSTYTUT KSIĄŻKI

©POLAND

PRIMEVAL AND OTHER TIMES

THE TIME OF PRIMEVAL

Primeval is the place at the centre of the universe.

To walk at a brisk pace across Primeval from north to south would take an hour, and the same from east to west. And if someone wanted to go right round Primeval, at a slow pace, taking a careful, considered look at everything, it would take him a whole day, from morning to evening.

To the north the border of Primeval is the road from Taszów to Kielce, busy and dangerous, because it arouses the anxiety of travel. The Archangel Raphael protects this border.

To the south the town of Jeszkotle marks the border, with its church, old people's home and low-rise tenements surrounding a muddy marketplace. The town presents a threat because it arouses the desire to possess and be possessed. The Archangel Gabriel guards Primeval on the town side.

From south to north, from Jeszkotle to the Kielce road runs the Highway, with Primeval lying on either side of it.

On the western border of Primeval there are wet riverside meadows, a bit of forest, and a manor house. Next to the manor house there's a stud farm, where a single horse costs as much as the whole of Primeval. The horses belong to the squire, and the meadows to the parish priest. The danger on the western border is of sinking into conceit. The Archangel Michael guards this border.

To the east the border of Primeval is the White River, which separates its territory from Taszów's. Then the White River turns towards a mill, while the border runs on alone, through common land, between alder bushes. The danger on this side is foolishness, arising from a desire to be too clever. Here the Archangel Uriel guards the border.

At the centre of Primeval God has raised a large hill, onto which each summer the maybugs swarm down, so people have named it Maybug Hill. For it is God's business to create, and people's business to name.

From the north-west the Black River runs south, joining the White River below the mill. The Black River is deep and dark. It flows through the forest, and the forest reflects its shaggy face in it. Dry leaves sail along the Black River, and careless insects fight for life in its eddies. The Black River tangles with tree roots and washes away at the forest. Sometimes whirlpools form on its dark surface, for the river can be angry and unbridled. Every year in late spring it spills onto the priest's meadows and basks there in the sunshine, letting the frogs multiply by the thousand. The priest battles with it all summer, and every year it benignly lets itself be sent back to its course towards the end of July.

The White River is shallow and sprightly. It spills down a wide channel in the sand and has nothing to hide. It is transparent and the sun is reflected in its limpid, sandy bottom. It looks like a great shining lizard. It swishes between the poplar trees, winding its way capriciously. It is hard to predict its capers. One year it might make an island out of a clump of alder trees, only to move far away from them for decades after. The White River flows through copses, meadows, and common land. It shines sandy and gold.

Below the mill the rivers merge. First they flow close beside each other, undecided, overawed by their longed-for intimacy, and then they fall into each other and get lost in one another. The river that flows out of this melting pot by the mill is no longer either the White or the Black, but it is powerful and effortlessly drives the mill wheel that grinds the grain for bread. Primeval lies on both the Black and White rivers and also on a third one, formed out of their mutual desire. The river arising from their confluence below the mill is called The River, and flows on calm and contented.

THE TIME OF GENOWEFA

In the summer of 1914, two of the Tsar's brightly uniformed soldiers came for Michał on horseback. Michał saw them approaching from the direction of Jeszkotle. The torrid air carried their laughter. Michał stood on the doorstep in his floury coat and waited, though he knew what they would want.

"Who are you?" they asked in Russian.

"My name is Mikhail Jozefovich Niebieski," he answered, just as he should answer, in Russian.

"Well, we've got a surprise for you."

He took the document from them and showed it to his wife. All day she cried as she got him ready to go to war. She was so weak from crying, so weighed down, that she couldn't cross the threshold to see her husband off to the bridge.

When the flowers fell from the potato plants and little green fruits set up in their place, Genowefa found that she was pregnant. She counted the months on her fingers and came to the first haymaking at the end of May. It must have happened then. Now she mourned the fact that she hadn't had the chance to tell Michał. Maybe her daily growing belly was a sort of sign that Michał would come home, that he was bound to come home. Genowefa ran the mill herself, just as Michał had done. She oversaw the workmen and wrote out receipts for the peasants who brought in the grain. She listened out for the rush of the water driving the millstones and the roar of the machinery. Flour settled on her hair and eyelashes, so as she stood at the mirror each evening she saw an old woman in it. Then the old woman undressed before the mirror and inspected her belly. She got into bed, but despite the pillows and woollen socks she couldn't get warm. And as a person always enters sleep feet first, like water, she couldn't sleep for hours. So she had a lot of time for prayer. She started with "Our Father," then "Hail Mary," and kept her favourite, dreamy prayer to her guardian angel until last. She asked him to take care of Michał, for at war a man might need more than one guardian angel. After that her praying would pass into images of war — they were sparse and simple, for Genowefa knew no other world but Primeval, and no other wars but the brawls in the marketplace on Saturdays when the drunken men came out of Szlomo's bar. They would yank at each other's coat tails, tumble to the ground and roll in the mud, soiled, dirty and wretched. So Genowefa imagined the war like a fight in the mud, puddles and litter, a fight in which everything is settled at once, in one fell swoop. Therefore she was surprised the war was taking so long.

Sometimes when she went shopping in town she overheard people's conversations.

"The Tsar is stronger than the German," they'd say, or "The war'll be over by Christmas."

But it wasn't over by Christmas, or by any of the next four Christmases.

Just before the holidays Genowefa set off to go shopping in Jeszkotle. As she was crossing the bridge she saw a girl walking along the river. She was poorly dressed and barefoot. Her naked feet plunged boldly into the snow, leaving small, deep prints. Genowefa shuddered and stopped. She watched the girl from above and found a kopeck for her in her bag. The girl looked up and their eyes met. The coin fell into the snow. The girl smiled, but there were no thanks or warmth in that smile. Her large white teeth appeared, and her green eyes shone.

"That's for you," said Genowefa.

The girl crouched down and daintily picked the coin out of the snow, then turned and went on her way without a word.

Jeszkotle looked drained of all colour. Everything was black, white and grey. There were small groups of men standing in the marketplace, discussing the war — cities destroyed, their citizens' possessions scattered about the streets, people running from bullets, brother searching for brother. No one knew who was worse — the Russki or the German. The Germans poison people with gas that makes their eyes burst. There'll be famine in the run-up to harvest time. War is the first plague, bringing the others in its wake.

Genowefa stepped round a pile of horse manure that was melting the snow in front of Szenbert's shop. On a plywood board nailed to the door was written:

PHARMACY
Szenbert & Co
sells only stocks of
top quality
Laundry soap
Washing blue
Wheat and rice starch
Oil, candles, matches
Insecticide powder

She suddenly felt weak at the words "insecticide powder." She thought of the gas the Germans were using that made people's eyes burst. Do cockroaches feel the same when you sprinkle them with Szenbert's powder? She had to take several deep breaths to stop herself from vomiting.

"Yes, Madam?" said a young, heavily pregnant woman in a sing-song voice. She glanced at Genowefa's belly and smiled.

Genowefa asked for some kerosene, matches, soap and a new scrubbing brush. She drew her finger along the sharp bristles.

"I'm going to do some cleaning for the holidays. I'm going to scrub the floors, wash the curtains and scour the oven."

"We have a holiday coming too, the Dedication of the Temple. You're from Primeval, aren't you, Madam? From the mill? I know you."

"Now we know each other. When's your baby due?"

"In February."

"Mine too."

Mrs Szenbert began to arrange bars of grey soap on the counter.

"Have you ever wondered why we silly girls are giving birth when there's a war on?"

"Surely God . . ."

"God, God . . . He's just a good accountant with an eye on the debit as well as the credit column. There has to be a balance. One life is wasted, another is born . . . Expecting a son, I shouldn't doubt?"

Genowefa picked up her basket.

"I need a daughter, because my husband's gone to the war and a boy grows up badly without a father."

Mrs Szenbert came out from behind the counter and saw Genowefa to the door.

"We all need daughters. If we all started having daughters at once there'd be peace on earth."

They both burst out laughing.

THE TIME OF MISIA'S ANGEL

The angel saw Misia's birth in an entirely different way from Kucmerka the midwife. An angel generally sees everything in a different way. Angels perceive the world not through the physical forms which it keeps producing and then destroying, but through the meaning and soul of those forms.

The angel assigned to Misia by God saw an aching, caved-in body, rippling into being like a strip of cloth — it was Genowefa's body as she gave birth to Misia. And the angel saw Misia as a fresh, bright, empty space, in which a bewildered, half conscious soul was just about to appear. When the child opened her eyes, the guardian angel thanked the Almighty. Then the angel's gaze and the human's gaze met for the first time, and the angel shuddered as only a bodiless angel can.

The angel received Misia into this world behind the midwife's back: it cleared a space for her to live in, showed her to the other angels and to the Almighty, and its incorporeal lips whispered: "Look, look, this is my sweet little soul." It was filled with unusual, angelic tenderness, loving sympathy — that is the only feeling angels harbour. For the Creator has not given them instincts, emotions or needs. If they did have them, they would not be spiritual creatures. The only instinct angels have is the instinct for sympathy. The only feeling angels have is infinite sympathy, heavy as the firmament.

Now the angel could see Kucmerka washing the child in warm water and drying her with a soft flannel. Then it gazed into Genowefa's eyes, reddened with effort.

The angel observed events like flowing water. It wasn't interested in them as such, they didn't intrigue it, because it knew where they were flowing from and to, it knew their start and finish. It could see the current of events that were like and unlike each other, close to each other in time and distant, resulting one from another or completely independent of each other. But that meant nothing to it either.

For an angel, events are something like a dream, or a film with no beginning or end. Angels are unable to get involved in them, they don't need them for anything. A human being learns from the world, learns from events, learns knowledge about the world and about himself, is reflected in events, defines his own limits and potential, and names things for himself. An angel doesn't have to source anything from the outside, but has knowledge through itself, it contains everything there is to know about the world and about itself within itself — that is how God has made it.

An angel doesn't have an intellect like the human one, it doesn't draw conclusions or make judgements. It doesn't think logically. To some people an angel would seem stupid. But from the start an angel carries within it the fruit of the tree of knowledge, pure wisdom that can only be enriched by simple intuition. It is a mind devoid of reasoning, and so devoid of mistakes and the fear they produce, an intellect without the prejudices that come from erroneous perception. But like all other things created by God, angels are volatile. That explains why Misia's angel was so often not there when she needed it.

When it wasn't there, Misia's angel would turn its gaze away from the terrestrial world and look at the other angels and other worlds, higher and lower, assigned to each thing on Earth, each animal and plant. It could see the vast ladder of existences, the extraordinary structure and the Eight Worlds contained within it, and it could see the Creator embroiled in creation. But anyone who thought Misia's angel was gazing at the countenance of the Lord would be wrong. The angel could see more than a man, but not everything.

Mentally returning to other worlds, the angel had difficulty focusing attention on Misia's world, which, like the world of other people and animals, was dark and full of suffering, like a murky pond overgrown with duckweed.

THE TIME OF CORNSPIKE

The barefoot girl to whom Genowefa gave a kopeck was Cornspike.

Cornspike turned up in Primeval in July or August. People gave her this name because she gathered ears of corn left over after the harvest and roasted them for herself over a fire. Then in autumn she stole potatoes, and once the fields were empty in November, she spent her time at the inn. Sometimes someone stood her a shot of vodka, sometimes she got a slice of bread and lard. But people are unwilling to give something for nothing, for free, especially at an inn, so Cornspike started whoring. A little tipsy and warmed up by the vodka, she would go outside with the men and give herself to them for a ring of sausage. And as she was the only woman in the district who was young and easy, the men hung around her like dogs.

Cornspike was big and buxom. She had fair hair and a fair complexion that the sun hadn't ruined. She brazenly looked everyone straight in the face, even the priest. She had green eyes, one of which wandered slightly to the side. The men who took Cornspike in the bushes always felt uneasy afterwards. They'd button up their flies and go back into the fug inside the tavern with flushed faces. Cornspike never wanted to lie on her back in an honest way. She'd say: "Why should I lie underneath you? I'm your equal."

She preferred to lean against a tree or the wooden wall of the inn and fling her skirt over her shoulders. Her bottom would shine in the darkness like the moon.

This was how Cornspike learned the world.

There are two kinds of learning, from the inside and from the outside. The first is regarded as the best, or even the only kind. And so people learn through distant journeys, watching, reading, universities and lectures — they learn from what is happening outside them. Man is a stupid creature who has to learn. So he tacks knowledge onto himself, he gathers it like a bee, gaining more and more of it, putting it to use and processing it. But the thing inside that is "stupid" and needs learning doesn't change.

Cornspike learned by absorbing things from the outside to the inside.

Knowledge that is only grown on the outside changes nothing inside a man, or merely changes him on the surface, as one garment is changed for another. But he who learns by taking things inside himself undergoes constant transformation, because he incorporates what he learns into his being.

So by taking the stinking, dirty peasants from Primeval and the district into herself, Cornspike became just like them, was drunk just like them, frightened by the war just like them, and aroused just like them. What's more, by taking them into herself in the bushes behind the inn, Cornspike also took in their wives, their children, and their stuffy, stinking wooden cottages around Maybug Hill. In a way she took the entire village into herself, every pain in the village, and every hope.

Such were Cornspike's universities. Her diploma was her growing belly.

Mrs Popielska, the squire's wife, heard about Cornspike's fate and had her brought to the manor. She glanced at that large belly.

"You're going to give birth any day. How do you intend to support yourself? I'll teach you to sew and to cook. You'll even be able to work in the laundry. Who knows, if everything turns out well, you'll be able to keep the baby."

But when the squire's wife saw the girl's alien, insolent look, as it boldly travelled across the paintings, furniture and upholstery, she hesitated. And when this gaze moved across the innocent faces of her sons and daughter, she changed her tone.

"It is our duty to help our neighbours in need. But our neighbours must want help. I provide this sort of help. I run a shelter in Jeszkotle. You can hand in the child there, it's clean and very nice there."

The word "shelter" grabbed Cornspike's attention. She looked at the squire's wife. Mrs Popielska gained in confidence.

"I distribute food and clothing before the harvest. People

don't want you here. You bring confusion and depravity. You are a loose woman. You should go away from here."

"Aren't I free to be where I want?"

"All this is mine, these are my lands and forest."

Cornspike revealed her white teeth in a broad smile.

"All yours? You poor, skinny little bitch . . ."

Mrs Popielska's face stiffened. "Get out," she said calmly.

Cornspike turned around, and now the sound of her bare feet could be heard slapping against the parquet floor.

"You whore," said Mrs Franiowa, the char at the manor, whose husband had been crazy about Cornspike that summer, and slapped her in the face.

As Cornspike reeled her way across the coarse gravel in the drive, the carpenters on the roof whistled at her. So she lifted her skirt and showed them her bare behind.

Outside the park she stopped and stood wondering where to go.

On the right she had Jeszkotle, and on the left the forest. She felt drawn to the forest. As soon as she went in among the trees she was aware that everything smelled different, stronger and sharper. She walked towards an abandoned house in Wydymacz, where she sometimes spent the night. The house was the remains of a burned-down hamlet, and now the forest had grown over it. Swollen from the weight she was carrying and the heat, her feet could not feel the hard pinecones. By the river she felt the first, alien pain flooding her body. Gradually panic was starting to take hold of her. "I'm going to die, now I'm going to die, because there's no one to help me," she thought in terror. She stopped in the middle of the Black River and refused to take another step. The cold water washed at her legs and lower body. From the water she saw a hare, who was quick to hide under a fern. She envied it. She saw a fish, weaving among the tree roots. She envied it. She saw a lizard that slithered under a stone. And she envied it too. She felt another pain, stronger this time, more terrifying. "I'm going to die," she thought, "now I'm simply going to die. I'll start to give birth and no one will help me." She wanted to lie down in the ferns by the river, because she needed coolness and darkness, but, in defiance of her entire body, she walked onwards. The pain came back a third time, and now she knew she did not have much time left.

The tumbledown house in Wydymacz consisted of four walls and a bit of roof. Inside lay rubble overgrown with nettles. It stank of damp. Blind snails trailed along the walls. Cornspike picked some large burdock leaves and made herself a bed with them. The pain kept coming back in more and more impatient waves. When at moments it became unbearable, Cornspike realised that she had to do something to push it out of her, throw it out onto the nettles and burdock leaves. She clenched her jaw and began to push. "The pain will come out the way it went in," she thought, and sat down. She pulled up her skirt. She couldn't see anything in particular, just the wall of her belly and her thighs. Her body was still taut and locked up in itself. Cornspike tried to peep inside herself there, but her belly got in her way. So with hands trembling from the pain, she tried to feel the spot where the child should come out of her. Her fingertips could feel her swollen vulva and her rough pubic hairs, but her groin couldn't feel the touch of her fingers. She was touching herself like something alien, like an object.

The pain intensified and muddled her senses. Her thoughts were torn like decaying fabric. Her words and ideas were falling apart and soaking into the ground. Tumescent from giving birth, her body had taken total control. And as the human body thrives on images, they flooded Cornspike's semi-conscious mind.

It seemed to Cornspike as if she were giving birth in a church, on the cold stone floor, just in front of an icon. She could hear the soothing drone of the organ. Then she imagined she was the organ, and she was playing, she had all sorts of sounds inside her, and whenever she wanted she could emit them all at once. She felt mighty and omnipotent. But at once her omnipotence was shattered by a fly, the common buzzing of a large purple fly just above her ear. The pain hit Cornspike with new force. "I'm going to die, I'm going to die," she moaned. "I'm not going to die, I'm not going to die," she moaned a moment later. Sweat clogged her eyelids and stung her eyes. She began to sob. She propped herself up on her arms and desperately began to push. And after this effort she felt relief. Something splashed and sprang out of her. Cornspike was open now. She fell back on the burdock leaves and sought the child among them, but there was nothing there except warm water. So Cornspike gathered her strength and began to push again. She closed her eyes tight and pushed. She took a breath and pushed. She cried and stared upwards. Between the rotten beams she could see a cloudless sky. And there she saw her child. The child got up hesitantly and stood on its legs. It was looking at her as no one had ever looked at her before: with vast, inexpressible love. It was a little boy. He picked up a twig from the ground and it changed into a little grass snake. Cornspike was happy. She lay down on the leaves and fell into a sort of dark well. Her thoughts returned, and calmly, gracefully, floated across her mind. "So the house has a well. So there's water in the well. I'm living in the well, because it's cool and damp in there. Children play in wells, snails regain their sight and grain ripens. I'll have something to feed the child on. Where is the child?"

She opened her eyes, terrified, and felt that time had stopped. That there was no child.

The pain came again, and Cornspike began to scream. She screamed so loud the walls of the tumbledown house shook, the birds were startled, and the people raking hay in the meadows looked up and crossed themselves. Cornspike had a choking fit and swallowed the scream. Now she was screaming to the inside, into herself. Her scream was so mighty that her belly moved. Cornspike felt something new and strange between her legs. She raised herself on her arms and looked her child in the face. The child's eyes were painfully tight shut. Cornspike pushed once more and the child was born. Trembling with effort, she tried to take it in her arms, but her hands couldn't reach the image her eyes could see. In spite of this she heaved a sigh of relief and let herself slip away into the darkness.

When she awoke, she saw the child beside her — shrunken and dead. She tried to set it to her breast. Her breast was bigger than it, painfully alive. There were flies circling above it.

All afternoon Cornspike tried hard to encourage the dead child to suck. Towards evening the pain returned and Cornspike delivered the afterbirth. Then she fell asleep again. In her dream she fed the child not on milk but on water from the Black River. The child was an incubus that sits on a person's chest and sucks the life out of him. It wanted blood. Cornspike's dream was becoming more and more disturbed and oppressive, but she couldn't wake up from it. In it a woman appeared, as large as a tree. Cornspike could see her perfectly, every detail of her face, her hairstyle and her clothing. She had curly black hair, like a Jew, and a wonderfully expressive face. Cornspike found her beautiful. She desired her with her entire body, but it wasn't the desire she already knew, from the bottom of her belly, from between her legs; it flowed from somewhere inside her body, from a point above her belly, close to her heart. The mighty woman leaned over Cornspike and stroked her cheek. Cornspike looked into her eyes at close range, and saw in them something she had never known before and had never even thought existed. "You are mine," said the enormous woman, and caressed Cornspike's neck and swollen breasts. Wherever her fingers touched Cornspike, her body became blessed and immortal. Cornspike surrendered entirely to this touch, spot after spot. Then the large woman took Cornspike in her arms and cuddled her to her breast. Cornspike's cracked lips found the nipple. It smelled of animal fur, camomile and rue. Cornspike drank and drank.

A thunderbolt crashed into her dream and all of a sudden she saw that she was still lying in the ruined cottage on the burdock leaves. There was greyness all around her. She didn't know if it was dawn or dusk. For the second time lightning struck somewhere very close by, and seconds later a downpour tumbled from the sky that drowned out the next peal of thunder. Water poured through the leaking roof beams and washed the blood and sweat off Cornspike, cooled her burning body, watered and fed her. Cornspike drank water straight from the sky.

When the sun emerged, she crawled out in front of the cottage and began to dig a hole, then pulled some tangled roots from the ground. The ground was soft and yielding, as if wanting to help her with the burial. She laid the baby's body in the uneven hole.

She spent a long time smoothing the ground over the grave, and when she raised her eyes and looked around, everything was different. It was no longer a world consisting of objects, of things, phenomena that exist alongside each other. Now what Cornspike saw had become one single mass, one great animal or one great person, who took on many forms, to burgeon, to die and be born again. Everything around Cornspike was one single body, and her body was a part of this great body — enormous, omnipotent, unimaginably mighty. In every movement, in every sound its power showed through, which by sheer will could create something out of nothing and change something into nothing. Cornspike's head began to spin and she leaned back against a low ruined wall. Simply looking intoxicated her like vodka, muddled her head and aroused laughter somewhere in her belly.

Everything seemed just the same as ever: beyond the small green meadow bisected by the sandy road was the pine forest, with hazel bushes growing densely along its edges. A light breeze was stirring the grass and leaves, a grasshopper was singing somewhere and flies were buzzing. Nothing more. And yet now Cornspike could see how the grasshopper was joined to the sky, and what was keeping the hazel bushes by the forest path. She could see more than that too. She could see the force that pervades everything, she could understand how it works. She could see the contours of other worlds and other times, stretched out above and below ours. She could also see things that cannot be described in words.

THE TIME OF THE BAD MAN

The Bad Man appeared in the forests of Primeval before the war, though there may have been someone like him living in those woods forever.

First, in spring they found the half decomposed body of Bronek Malak in Wodenica, whom everyone thought had gone to America. The police came from Taszów, examined the site and took the body away on a cart. The policemen came to Primeval several times more, but nothing happened as a result.

No murderer was found. Then someone dropped a hint that he had seen a stranger in the forest. He was naked, and hairy like a monkey, flitting among the trees. Then others remembered that they had found strange tracks and marks in the forest too — a footprint on a sandy path, a hole dug in the ground, discarded animal carcasses. Someone had heard howling in the forest, a half-human, half-animal wail.

So people began to tell stories of where the Bad Man came from. They said that before the Bad Man became the Bad Man, he was an ordinary peasant who committed a terrible crime, though no one knew exactly what.

Regardless of what the crime was about, his conscience gnawed at him and wouldn't allow him a moment's rest, and so, tormented by its voice, he ran away from himself, until he found solace in the woods. He trudged about the forest and finally lost his way. He thought he saw the sun dancing in the sky, and that was what made him lose direction. He reckoned the road north would definitely take him somewhere. But then he lost faith in the road north and headed east, believing that to the east the forest would finally end. But as he was going east, he was overcome by doubts again. He stopped in confusion, unsure of his direction. So he changed his plan and decided to go south, but he lost faith in the road south too, and duly headed west. Then it turned out he had returned to the spot he had started from — at the very centre of the great forest. So on the fourth day he lost faith in all the points of the compass. On the fifth day he stopped trusting his own reason. On the sixth day he forgot where he had come from and why he had come to the forest, and on the seventh day he forgot his own name.

And ever since he had become like the animals in the forest. He lived on berries and mushrooms, then started hunting small animals. Each successive day wiped larger and larger pieces from his memory — the Bad Man's mind was becoming smoother and smoother. He forgot words, because he didn't use them. He forgot how he was to pray each evening. He forgot how to kindle a fire and how to make use of it. How to do up the buttons on his coat and how to lace his boots. He forgot the songs he had known since childhood, and then his entire childhood. He forgot the faces of the people dearest to him, his mother, wife and children, he forgot the taste of cheese, roast meat, potatoes and potato soup.

This forgetting went on for many years, and finally the Bad Man was nothing like the man who had come to the forest any more. The Bad Man was not himself, and had forgotten what it meant to be himself. Hair started growing on his body, and from eating raw meat his teeth became strong and white, like an animal's teeth. Now his throat emitted hoarse noises and grunts.

One day the Bad Man saw an old fellow in the forest gathering brushwood and felt the human being was alien to him, revolting even, so he ran up to the old man and killed him. Another time he attacked a peasant driving a carthorse. He killed him and the horse. He devoured the horse, but didn't touch the man — a dead person was even more repulsive than a live one. Then he killed Bronek Malak.

One time the Bad Man accidentally reached the edge of the forest and got a view of Primeval. The sight of the houses stirred a sort of vague emotion in him, which included regret and rage. Just then a terrible wail was heard in the village, like the howling of a wolf. The Bad Man stood at the edge of the forest for a while, then turned around and tentatively leaned his hands against the ground. To his amazement he discovered that this way of moving about was much more comfortable and much faster.

His eyes, now closer to the ground, could see more and better. His as yet weak sense of smell could pick up the odours of the ground better. One single forest was better than all the villages, all the roads and bridges, cities and towers. So the Bad Man went back into the forest forever.

THE TIME OF GENOWEFA

The war caused chaos in the world. The forest at Przyjmy burned down, the Cossacks shot the Cherubins' son, there weren't enough men, there was no one to reap the fields, and there was nothing to eat.

Squire Popielski from Jeszkotle packed his belongings on carts and disappeared for several months. Then he came back. The Cossacks had looted his house and cellars. They had drunk his hundred-year-old wines. Old Boski, who saw it happen, said one wine was so old that they had sliced it with a bayonet like jelly.

Genowefa oversaw the mill while it was still working. She got up at dawn and supervised everything. She checked no one was late for work. Then, once everything was running in its rhythmical, noisy way, she felt the sudden surge of a wave of relief, warm as milk. Everything was safe, so she went home and made breakfast for the sleeping Misia.

In spring 1917, the mill stopped working. There was nothing to mill — people had eaten up all their stores of grain. Primeval lacked its familiar noise. The mill was the motor that drove the world, the machinery that set it in motion. Now all that was audible was the rushing of the River. Its strength went to waste. Genowefa walked about the empty mill and cried. She wandered like a ghost, like a white, floury lady. In the evenings she sat on the steps of her house and gazed at the mill. She dreamed about it at night. In her dreams the mill was a ship with white sails, the kind she had seen in books. Inside its wooden hulk it had enormous, grease-coated pistons that went back and forth. It puffed and panted. Heat belched from its interior. Genowefa desired it. She awoke from these dreams sweating and anxious. As soon as it was light, she got up and sewed her tapestry at the table.

During the flu epidemic of 1918, when the village boundaries were ploughed up, Cornspike came to the mill. Genowefa saw her circling it, staring in at the windows. She looked exhausted. She was thin and seemed very tall. Her fair hair had gone grey and covered her shoulders like a dirty shawl. Her clothes were torn.

Genowefa watched her from the kitchen, and when Cornspike peered in at the window, she withdrew. She was afraid of Cornspike. Everyone was afraid of Cornspike. Cornspike was mad, maybe sick too. She talked nonsense and swore. Now, as she circled the mill she looked like a hungry bitch.

Genowefa glanced at the icon of the Virgin Mary of Jeszkotle, crossed herself and went outside.

Cornspike turned towards her and Genowefa felt a shudder. What a terrible look that Cornspike had in her eyes.

"Let me into the mill," she said.

Genowefa went back inside for the key. Without a word she opened the door.

Cornspike went into the cool shade ahead of her, and instantly fell to her knees to gather up the scattered, single grains and heaps of dust that had once been flour. She scooped up the grains with her slender fingers and stuffed them into her mouth.

Genowefa followed her every step of the way. From above, Cornspike's stooping figure looked like a heap of rags. Once she had eaten her fill of grain, she sat down on the ground and began to cry. The tears flowed down her dirty face. Her eyes were closed and she was smiling. Genowefa felt a lump rise to her throat. Where was she living? Did she have any family? What had she done at Christmas? What had she eaten? She could see how frail her body was now, and remembered Cornspike from before the war. In those days she was a buxom, beautiful girl. Now she looked at her bare, wounded feet with toenails as tough as an animal's claws. She reached out a hand to touch the grey hair. Just then Cornspike opened her eyes and looked straight into Genowefa's eyes, not even into her eyes but straight into her soul, into her very centre. Genowefa withdrew her hand. They were not the eyes of a human being. She ran outside and felt relief as she saw her house, the hollyhocks, Misia's little dress twinkling among the gooseberry bushes, and the curtains. She fetched a loaf of bread from indoors and went back to the mill.

Cornspike emerged from the darkness of the open door with a bundle full of grain. She was looking at something behind Genowefa's back, and her face brightened.

"Sweetie-pie," she said to Misia, who had come up to the fence.

"What happened to your child?"

"It died."

Genowefa handed her the loaf of bread at arm's length, but Cornspike came very close to her, and as she took the loaf, she pressed her lips to Genowefa's mouth. Genowefa recoiled and jumped back. Cornspike burst out laughing. She put the loaf into her bundle. Misia began to cry.

"Don't cry, sweetie-pie, your daddy's on his way home to you," muttered Cornspike and walked off towards the village.

Genowefa wiped her lips on her apron until they darkened. That evening she found it hard to sleep. Cornspike couldn't be wrong. Cornspike could tell the future, everyone knew about it. And from the next day Genowefa started waiting. But not as she had done until now. Now she waited from one hour to the next. She put the potatoes under the eiderdown so they wouldn't go cold too quickly. She made the bed. She poured water into a basin for shaving. She laid Michał's clothes over a chair. She waited as if Michał had gone to Jeszkotle for tobacco and was coming straight back.

And so she waited all summer and autumn, and winter. She didn't go far from home, and she didn't go to church. In February, Squire Popielski came back and gave the mill some work. Where he got the grain for milling nobody knew. As manager and assistant, the squire recommended a man called Niedziela from Wola. Niedziela was quick and reliable. He bustled about between the top and bottom of the mill, shouting at the peasants. He wrote the number of bags milled in chalk on the wall. Whenever Genowefa came to the mill, Niedziela moved about even faster and shouted even louder, while stroking his sparse whiskers, which were nothing like Michał's bushy moustache.

She was reluctant to go up there. Only on truly essential matters — if there was a mistake in the grain receipt, or if the machinery stopped.

Once, when she was looking for Niedziela, she saw the boys carrying the sacks. They were naked to the waist, and their upper bodies were coated in flour, like big pretzels. The sacks were shielding their heads, so they all looked identical. She could not see in them the young Serafin or Malak, but just men. The naked torsos riveted her gaze and made her feel anxious. She had to turn and look away.

One day Niedziela arrived with a Jewish boy. The boy was very young. He didn't look more than seventeen. He had dark eyes and black curly hair. Genowefa saw his lips — large, with a finely drawn line, darker than any she had seen before.

"I've taken on another one," said Niedziela, and told the boy to join the porters.

Genowefa talked to Niedziela absent-mindedly, and when he went off, she found an excuse to linger. She saw the boy take off his linen shirt, fold it carefully and hang it over the stair rail. She was moved when she saw his naked rib cage — slim, but muscular, and his swarthy skin, under which his blood was pulsating and his heart was beating. She went home, but from then on she often found a reason to go down to the gate, where the sacks of grain or flour were received and collected. Or she came at dinner time, when the men came down to eat. She looked at their flour-dusted shoulders, sinewy arms and their linen trousers, damp with sweat. Involuntarily her gaze sought out one among them, and when it found him, she felt a hot flush as the blood rushed to her face.

That boy, that Eli — as she heard him being called — aroused fear in her, anxiety and shame. At the sight of him her heart began to pound and her breathing became faster. She tried to watch coolly and indifferently. His dark, curling hair, strong nose and strange, dark lips. The dark, hairy atrium of his armpit as he wiped the sweat from his face. He swayed as he walked. Several times he met her gaze and was startled, like an animal that has come too close. Finally they bumped into each other in the narrow doorway. She smiled at him.

"Bring a sack of flour to my house," she said.

From then on she stopped waiting for her husband.

Eli put the sack down on the floor and took off his linen cap.

He crumpled it in his whitened hands. She thanked him, but he didn't leave. She saw that he was chewing his lip.

"Would you like some fruit juice?"

He said yes. She handed him a mug and watched him drink. He lowered his long, girlish eyelashes.

"I'd like to ask you a favour . . ."

"Yes?"

"Come and chop some wood for me this evening, could you?"

He nodded and left.

She waited all afternoon. She did up her hair and looked at herself in the mirror. Then, once he had come, as he was chopping the wood, she brought him some buttermilk and bread. He sat down on the chopping block and ate. Without knowing why, she told him about Michał at the war. He said: "The war's over now. Everyone's coming back."

She gave him a bag of flour. She asked him to come the next day, and the next day she asked him to come again.

Eli chopped wood, cleaned the stove, and did some minor repairs. They rarely talked, and always on trivial subjects. Genowefa watched him furtively, and the longer she looked at him the more her gaze grew attached to him. Finally she could not bear not to look at him. She devoured him with her gaze. At night she dreamed she was making love with a man, and it was not Michał, or Eli, but a stranger. She would wake up feeling dirty. She would get up, fill the basin with water and wash her entire body. She wanted to forget the dream. Then she would watch through the window as the workmen came down to the mill. She would see Eli furtively looking in at her windows. She would hide behind the curtain, angry with herself because her heart was thumping as if she had been running. "I won't think about him, I swear," she would decide, and get down to work. At about noon she would go and see Niedziela, always by some chance meeting Eli on the way. Amazed by her own voice, one day she asked him to come by.

"I've baked you a bun," she said, and pointed at the table.

He timidly took a seat and put his cap down in front of him. She sat opposite, watching him eat. He ate cautiously and slowly. White crumbs remained on his lips.

"Eli?"

"Yes?" He looked up at her.

"Did you like it?"

"Yes."

He stretched his hand out across the table towards her face. She recoiled abruptly.

"Don't touch me," she said.

The boy lowered his head. His hand went back to the cap. He said nothing. Genowefa sat down.

"Tell me, where did you want to touch me?" she asked quietly.

He raised his head and stared at her. She thought she could see flashes of red in his eyes.

"I'd have touched you here," he said, pointing to a spot on his neck.

Genowefa ran her hand down her neck, feeling the warm skin and blood pulsing beneath her fingers. She closed her eyes.

"And then?"

"Then I would have touched your breasts . . ."

She sighed deeply and threw her head back.

"Tell me where exactly."

"Where they are softest and hottest . . . Please . . . let me . . ."

"No," she said.

Eli got up and stood in front of her. She could smell the scent of sweet bun and milk on his breath, like the breath of a child.

"You're not allowed to touch me. Swear to your God you won't touch me."

"You whore," he croaked, and threw his crumpled cap to the floor. The door slammed behind him.

Eli came back that night. He knocked gently, and Genowefa knew it was him.

"I forgot my cap," he whispered. "I love you. I swear I won't touch you until you want me to."

They sat down on the floor in the kitchen. Streams of red heat lit up their faces.

"It has to become clear if Michał is alive. I am still his wife."

"I'll wait, but tell me, how long?"

"I don't know. You can look at me."

"Show me your breasts."

Genowefa slipped her nightdress off her shoulders. Her naked breasts and belly shone red. She could hear Eli catch his breath.

"Show me how much you want me," she whispered.

He unbuttoned his trousers and Genowefa saw his swollen member. She felt the bliss from her dream, which was the crowning moment of all her efforts, glances and rapid breathing. This bliss was beyond all control, it could not be restrained. What had appeared now was terrifying, because nothing could ever be any more. It had already come true, flowed over, ended and begun, and from then on everything that happened would be dull and loathsome, and the hunger that would awaken would be even more powerful than ever before.

Squire Popielski was losing his faith. He hadn't stopped believing in God, but God and all the rest of it were becoming rather flat and expressionless, like the etchings in his Bible.

For the squire, everything seemed to be all right when the Pełskis came by from Kotuszów, when he played whist in the evenings, when he had conversations about art, when he visited his cellars and pruned the roses. Everything was all right when the wardrobes smelled of lavender, when he sat at his oak desk with his pen with the gold holder in his hand, and in the evening his wife massaged his tired shoulders. But as soon as he went out, drove away from home somewhere, even to the dirty marketplace in Jeszkotle or the local villages, he entirely lost his physical immunity to the world.

He saw the crumbling houses, rotting fences, and time-worn stones cobbling the main street, and thought: "I was born too late, the world is coming to an end. It's all over." His head ached and his sight was growing weak — to the squire it all seemed darker, his feet were frozen and an indeterminate pain ran right through him. Everything was empty and hopeless. And there was no helping it. He would go home to his manor house and hide in his study — that stopped the world from collapsing for a while.

But the world collapsed anyway. The squire discovered this for himself when he saw his cellars on returning after his hasty escape from the Cossacks. Everything in them had been destroyed, smashed, chopped, burned, trampled, and spilled. He surveyed the losses as he waded up to his ankles in wine.

"Chaos and destruction, chaos and destruction," he whispered.

Then he lay down on the bed in his plundered home and wondered: "Where does evil come from in this world? Why does

God allow evil to happen, if He is so good? Or maybe God is not good?"

The changes taking place in the country provided a remedy for the squire's depression.

In 1918 there was a great deal to do, and nothing is as good a cure for grief as activity. For the whole of October the squire gradually geared himself up for social action, until in November the depression left him and he found himself on the other side of it. Now for a change he hardly slept at all and had no time to eat. He ran about the country, made trips to Kraków and saw it as a princess awoken from sleep. He organised elections for the first parliament, founded several associations, two parties, and the Małopolski Union of Fish Pond Owners. In February the next year, when the Small Constitution was enacted, Squire Popielski caught cold and ended up in his room again, in bed, with his head turned towards the window — in other words, in the place where he had started.

His recovery from pneumonia was like coming back from a distant journey. He read a lot and began to write a memoir. He wanted to talk to someone, but everyone around him seemed banal and uninteresting. So he ordered books to be brought up to his bed from the library and ordered new ones by post.

Early in March he went out on his first walk about the park, and saw an ugly, grey world again, full of decay and destruction. National independence didn't help, nor did the constitution. On a path in the park he saw a red, child's glove sticking out of the melting snow, and for some strange reason the sight of it sank deep into his memory. Dogged, blind regeneration. The apathy of life and death. The inhuman machinery of life.

Last year's efforts to rebuild everything anew had come to nothing.

The older Squire Popielski became, the more terrible the world seemed to him. A young man is busy with his own blooming, pushing forwards and extending the boundaries: from his childhood bed to the walls of the room, the house, the park, the city, the country, the world, and then, in his manhood, comes a time of fantasising about something even greater. The turning point occurs at about forty. Youth in its intensity, in its full force, tires itself out. One night or one morning a man crosses a boundary, reaches his peak and takes his first step downwards, towards death. Then the question arises: should he descend proudly with his face turned towards the darkness, or should he turn around towards what was, keep up an appearance and pretend it isn't darkness, but just that the light in the room has been extinguished?

Meanwhile the sight of the red glove emerging from under the dirty snow convinced the squire that the greatest deception of youth is optimism of any kind, a persistent faith in the idea that something will change or improve, or that there is progress in everything. So now the vessel had broken inside him, full of the despair he had always carried within him like hemlock. The squire looked around him and saw suffering, death and decay, which were as widespread as dirt. He crossed the whole of Jeszkotle and saw the kosher abattoir, the rotten meat on hooks, a frozen beggar outside Szenbert's shop, a small funeral cortege following a child's coffin, low clouds over low houses on the marketplace, and the gloom that was invading from all directions, already infesting everything. It was like a gradual, continual self-immolation, in which human destinies, whole lives are thrown into the consuming flames of time.

On his way back to the manor house he passed the church, so he dropped in there, but found nothing inside. He saw an icon of the Virgin Mary of Jeszkotle, but there was no God in the church capable of restoring the squire's hope.

THE TIME OF THE VIRGIN MARY OF JESZKOTLE

Enclosed in the icon's decorative frame, the Virgin Mary of Jeszkotle had a limited view of the church. She hung in a side nave, so she couldn't see the altar, or the stoup at the entrance. A pillar shielded her view of the pulpit. All she could see were the people arriving — individuals who dropped in at the church to pray, or else whole strings of them as they glided up to the altar for communion. During mass she saw dozens of people's profiles — men's and women's, old people's and children's. The Virgin Mary of Jeszkotle was the pure will to provide help for the sick and the weak. She was a strength inscribed into the icon by a divine miracle. When people turned their faces towards her, when they moved their lips, pressed their hands to their bellies or folded them at the level of their hearts, the Virgin Mary of Jeszkotle gave them strength and the power to recover. She gave to it everyone without exception, not out of mercy, but because that was her nature — to give the power to recover to those who needed it. What happened thereafter was for the people to decide. Some allowed this strength to take effect within them, and those ones got better. Then they came back with votive offerings, miniatures of the healed parts of the body cast in silver, copper, or even gold, and with beads and necklaces with which they decked the icon.

Others let the power trickle out of them, as out of a leaking vessel, and it soaked into the ground. And then they lost their faith in miracles.

So it was with Squire Popielski, who appeared before the icon of the Virgin Mary of Jeszkotle. She saw him kneel down and try to pray. But he couldn't, so he stood up angrily and looked at the valuable votive offerings and the bright colours of the holy painting. The Virgin Mary of Jeszkotle saw that he was greatly in need of good, helpful strength for his body and soul. And she gave it to him, she filled him with it and immersed him in it. But Squire Popielski was as watertight as a crystal ball, so the good strength flowed off him onto the cold church floor and set the church in a gentle, barely palpable tremble.

THE TIME OF MICHAŁ

Michał came back in the summer of 1919. It was a miracle, because in a world where war has pushed every kind of law beyond its limits, miracles often occur.

Michał spent three months getting home. The place he had set off from was on virtually the other side of the globe — Vladivostok, a city on the coast of a foreign sea. So he had broken free of the ruler of the East, the king of chaos, but as whatever exists beyond the boundaries of Primeval is blurred and fluid as a dream, Michał was no longer thinking of that as he stepped onto the bridge.

He was sick, emaciated, and dirty. His face was covered in black stubble, and there were swarms of lice revelling in his hair. The threadbare uniform of a beaten army hung on him as on a stick, without a single button. Michał had swapped the shining buttons with the imperial eagle for bread. He also had a fever, diarrhoea, and the tormenting feeling that the world he had set out from no longer existed. Hope came back to him as he stood on the bridge and saw the Black and White Rivers merging together in a never-ending wedding. The rivers were still there, the bridge was still there, and so was the stone-crushing heat.

From the bridge Michał saw the white mill and the red geraniums in the windows.

Outside the mill a child was playing, a little girl with thick plaits. She must have been three or four years old. White hens were earnestly tripping around her. A woman's hands opened the window. "The worst is going to happen," thought Michał. Reflected in the moving windowpane, the sun dazzled him for a moment. Michał headed for the mill.

He slept all day and all night, and in his sleep he counted all the days of the past five years. His tired, fuddled mind lost its way and wandered in the labyrinths of sleep, so Michał had to start his count all over again. During this time Genowefa took a close look at the uniform, stiff with dust, touched the sweat-soaked collar, and plunged her hands in the pockets that smelled of tobacco. She caressed the buckles of the rucksack but did not dare to open it. Then the uniform hung on the fence, so that everyone who walked past the mill was bound to see it.

Michał awoke the next day at dawn and examined the sleeping child. He gave precise names to what he saw:

"She has thick, brown hair. She has dark eyebrows, a dark complexion, small ears, a small nose, all children have small noses, her hands are plump and childish, but you can see the fingernails, they're round."

Then he went up to the mirror and examined himself. He was a stranger to himself.

He walked around the mill and stroked the great stone wheel as it turned. He gathered flour dust in his hand and tasted it with the tip of his tongue. He plunged his hands in the water, ran his finger along the fence boards, sniffed the flowers, and set the wheel of the chaff-cutter in motion. It creaked and cut off a swathe of crushed nettles.

Behind the mill he walked into the tall grass and peed.

When he came back into the room he mustered the courage to look at Genowefa. She wasn't asleep. He gazed at her.

"Michał, no man has touched me."

THE TIME OF MISIA

Like every person, Misia was born broken into pieces, incomplete, in bits. Everything in her was separate — looking, hearing, understanding, feeling, sensing, and experiencing. Misia's entire future life would depend on putting it all together into a single whole, and then letting it fall apart.

She needed someone who would stand before her and be a mirror for her, in which she was reflected as a whole.

Misia's first memory was the sight of the ragged man on the road to the mill. Her father staggered as he walked, and then often cried at night, nestling against her mother's breasts. So Misia treated him as her equal.

From then on she felt there was no difference between adult and child in anything that really mattered. Child and adult — they were transitory states. Misia watched closely to see how she herself was changing and how the other people around her were changing, but she didn't know where it was all heading, what the aim of these changes was. In a cardboard box she kept mementoes of herself, her little self and then the bigger one — knitted baby bootees, a tiny cap as if made to fit a fist, not a child's head, a little linen top, and her first little dress. Then she placed her six-year-old foot next to the knitted bootee and felt a sense of the fascinating laws of time.

Since her father's return, Misia had started to see the world. Before then everything had been blurred and out of focus. Misia could not remember herself from before her father's return, as if she hadn't existed at all. She remembered individual objects. The mill had seemed enormous to her then, a monolithic mass with no beginning or end, no top or bottom. Afterwards she saw the mill differently, with her reason. It had meaning and form. It was the same with other things. Once, when Misia had thought "river," it had meant something cold and wet. Now she could see that the river flowed to and from somewhere, and that the same river existed before and after the bridge, and that there were other rivers . . . Scissors — once they were a strange, complicated tool, difficult to make work, which Mama put to magical use. Ever since her father had sat down at the table, Misia could see that the scissors were a simple mechanism with two blades. She made something similar out of two flat sticks. Then for a long time she tried seeing things as they had formerly been again, but her father had changed the world forever.

THE TIME OF MISIA'S GRINDER

People think they live more intensely than animals, than plants, and especially than things. Animals sense that they live more intensely than plants and things. Plants dream that they live more intensely than things. But things last, and this lasting is more alive than anything else.

Misia's grinder came into being because of someone's hands combining wood, china and brass into a single object. The wood, china and brass made the idea of grinding materialise. Grinding coffee beans to pour boiling water on them afterwards. There is no one of whom it could be said that he invented the grinder, because creating is merely reminding yourself of what exists beyond time, in other words, since time began. Man is incapable of creating out of nothing — that is a divine skill.

The grinder has a belly made of white china, and in the belly an opening, in which a small wooden drawer collects the fruits of its labour. The belly is covered with a brass hat, with a handle ending in a bit of wood. The hat has a closing hole, into which the rattling coffee beans are poured.

The grinder was made in some factory workshop, and then ended up at someone's house, where every morning it ground coffee. Hands held it, warm and alive. They pressed it to someone's breasts, where under calico or flannel a human heart was beating. Then the impetus of war transferred it from a safe shelf in the kitchen to a box with other objects, into valises and sacks, into train carriages, in which people pushed ahead in panic-stricken flight from violent death. Like every other thing, the grinder absorbed all the world's confusion: images of trains under fire, idle rivulets of blood, and abandoned houses, as a different wind played with their windows every year. It absorbed the warmth of human bodies going cold and the despair of abandoning the familiar. Hands touched it, and they all brushed it with an immeasurable quantity of thoughts and emotions. The grinder accepted them, because all kinds of matter have this capacity — to arrest whatever is fleeting and transitory.

Michał had found it far away in the East, and had hidden it in his army rucksack as a spoil of war. That evening when the soldiers stopped for the night he had sniffed its drawer — it smelled of safety, coffee, home.

Misia took the grinder outside to the bench in front of the house and turned the handle. Then the grinder ran lightly, as if it were playing with her. Misia watched the world from the bench, and the grinder turned and ground empty space. But one day Genowefa tipped a handful of black beans into it and told it to grind them. Then the handle no longer turned as smoothly. The grinder choked, and slowly, systematically, began to work and to creak. The playing was over. There was so much gravity in the grinder's work that no one would have dared to stop it now. It became nothing but grinding. And then the grinder, Misia and the whole world were united by the odour of freshly ground coffee.

If you take a close look at an object, with your eyes closed to avoid being deceived by the appearances that things exude around themselves, if you allow yourself to be mistrustful, you can see their true faces, at least for a moment.

Things are beings steeped in another reality, where there is no time or motion. Only their surface can be seen. The rest, hidden elsewhere, defines the significance and meaning of each material object. A coffee grinder, for example.

The grinder is just such a piece of material infused with the concept of grinding.

Grinders grind, and that is why they exist. But no one knows what the grinder means in general. Perhaps the grinder is a splinter off some total, fundamental law of transformation, a law without which this world could not go round or would be completely different. Perhaps coffee grinders are the axis of reality, around which everything turns and unwinds, perhaps they are more important for the world than people. And perhaps Misia's one single grinder is the pillar of what is called Primeval.

Late spring was the most loathsome time of year for the parish priest. Around Saint John's Day, the Black River brazenly flooded his meadows.

The priest was by nature impetuous and touchy about his dignity, so when he saw something of so little substance, so sluggish, so non-descript and vacuous, so elusive and cowardly taking away his meadows, he was filled with rage.

With the water, shameless frogs immediately appeared, naked and revolting, always climbing on top of one another and mindlessly copulating, emitting hideous noises as they did so. The devil must have had a voice like that: screeching, wet, hoarse with lust, and trembling with insatiable desire. And with the frogs, water snakes appeared in the priest's meadows, slithering and writhing in such a vile way that the priest instantly felt unwell. At the very thought that such a long, slimy body might touch his boot he felt a shudder of disgust and a stab of cramp in his stomach. The image of the snake would sink into his memory for a long time after, ravaging his dreams. There were also fish in the flooded areas, and to these the priest had a better attitude. The fish could be eaten, so they were good, God's gift.

The river flooded the meadows for at most three short nights. After the invasion it rested, reflecting the sky in itself. It went on lolling about like that for a month. Under the water, all month long the lush grass rotted, and if it was a hot summer, a smell of rot and decay floated over the meadows.

From Saint John's Day, every day the priest came to see the black river water flooding Saint Margaret's daisies, Saint Roch's bluebells, and Saint Clare's herbs. Sometimes it seemed to him as if the innocent blue and white heads of the flowers, up to their necks in water, were calling out to him for help. He could hear their reedy little voices, like the tinkling of the hand bells during the Elevation. There was nothing he could do for them. His face went red as he clenched his fists helplessly.

He prayed. He began with Saint John, patron saint of all waters. But in this prayer the priest often felt that Saint John was not listening to him, that he was more concerned about the equation of day and night and the bonfires lit by the young, about vodka, about the conduct of garlands tossed into the water, and nocturnal rustling in the bushes. He even had a grudge against Saint John, who every year, regularly allowed the Black River to flood his meadows. He was even quite offended by Saint John because of it. So he started praying to God Himself.

The next year, after the biggest flood, God said to the parish priest: "Separate the river from the meadows. Bring in lots of earth and build a protective embankment to keep the river in its channel." The priest thanked the Lord and started organising the construction of an embankment. For two weeks he thundered from the pulpit that the river was destroying God's gifts, and called for a concerted fight against the element in the following order: one man from each homestead would carry earth and build the embankment two days a week. Thursday and Friday were assigned to Primeval, Monday and Tuesday to Jeszkotle, and Wednesday and Saturday to Kotuszów.

On the first day appointed for Primeval, only two peasants turned up for work, Malak and Cherubin. The enraged priest got in his sprung chaise and drove round all the cottages in Primeval. It turned out Serafin had a broken finger, the young Florian had been conscripted, the Chlipałas had just had a baby, and Światosz had a hernia.

So the priest achieved nothing. Feeling discouraged, he went back to the presbytery.

That evening at prayer he sought God's advice again. And God replied: "Pay them." The priest was slightly confused by this answer. As however the parish priest's God was sometimes very like him, He immediately added: "Give at most ten groszy for a day's work, because otherwise the game won't be worth the candle. The entire hay crop isn't worth more than fifteen zlotys."

So once again the priest drove his chaise to Primeval and hired several brawny peasants to build the embankment. He took on Józek Chlipała, whose son had just been born, Serafin with his broken finger, and two more farmhands.

They only had one cart, so the work went slowly. The priest was worried the spring weather would foil his plans. He urged the peasants on as much as he could. He, too, rolled up his cassock but, mindful of his good leather boots, he just ran among the peasants, prodding the sacks and whipping the horse. Next day only Serafin with his broken finger came to work. Once again the angry priest drove his chaise round the entire village, but it turned out the workmen either weren't at home, or had been laid low by illness.

That was a day when the priest hated all the peasants from Primeval — they were lazy, indolent, and greedy for money. He ardently excused himself before the Lord for this feeling unworthy of His servant. Again he asked God for advice. "Raise their wages," God told him, "give them fifteen groszy for a day's work, and even though you won't have any profit from this year's hay, you will make up the loss next year." This was wise council. The work went ahead.

First of all, sand was brought on carts from beyond Górka, then the sand was loaded into jute sacks and the river was lined with them like a dressing, as if it were wounded. Only then was it all covered in earth, and grass was sown on top.

The parish priest joyfully examined his own work. Now the river was completely separated from the meadow. The river could not see the meadow. The meadow could not see the river.

The river no longer tried to tear free of its appointed place. It flowed along peaceful and pensive, impenetrable to the human gaze. Along its banks the meadows went green, and then flowered with dandelions.

In the priest's meadows the flowers never stop praying. All those Saint Margaret's daisies and Saint Roch's bluebells pray, and so do the common yellow dandelions. Constant prayer makes the bodies of the dandelions become less and less material, less and less yellow, less and less solid, until in June they change into subtle seed clocks. Then God, moved by their piety, sends warm winds that take the seed-clock souls of the dandelions up to heaven.

The same warm winds brought the rains on Saint John's Day. The river swelled centimetre by centimetre. The parish priest could not sleep or eat. He ran along the weir and the meadows by the river and watched. He measured the water level with a stick and muttered curses and prayers. The river took no notice of him. It flowed in a broad channel, whirled in eddies and washed up against the insecure banks. On the twenty-seventh of June the priest's meadows started soaking up water. The parish priest ran along the new embankment with his stick and watched in despair as the water easily got into the chinks, rose along paths known only to itself, and penetrated the embankment. The next night the waters of the Black River destroyed the sand dyke and flooded the meadows, as every year.

On Sunday from the pulpit the priest compared the river's

exploits to the work of Satan, saying that every day, hour by hour, just like the water, Satan puts pressure on a man's soul. That in this way a man is forced to make a constant effort to put up barriers. That the slightest neglect of daily religious duties weakens the barrier and that the tenacity of the tempter is comparable with the tenacity of the water. That sin trickles, flows and drips onto the wings of the soul, and the enormity of evil keeps flooding a man until he falls into its whirlpools and goes to the bottom.

After this sermon the priest went on feeling agitated for a long time, and could not sleep. He could not sleep for hatred of the Black River. He told himself it is impossible to hate a river, a stream of turbid water, not even a plant, not an animal, just a geographical feature. How was it possible for him, a priest, to feel something so absurd? To hate a river.

And yet it was hatred. The priest wasn't even bothered about the sodden hay, but he was bothered by the mindlessness and blunt obstinacy of the Black River, its impalpability, selfishness and limitless vacuity. When he thought about it like that, hot blood pulsed in his temples and ran round his body faster. It began to carry him away. He would get up and dress, regardless of the time of night, and then leave the presbytery and go into the meadows. The cold wind sobered him up. He smiled to himself and said: "How can I get angry at a river, a common dip in the ground? A river is just a river, nothing more." But once he was standing on its bank, it all came back. He was filled with disgust, revulsion, and rage. He would gladly have buried it in earth, from its source to its mouth. And he looked around to make sure no one could see him, then tore off an alder branch and lashed the shameless, rounded hulk of the river.

"Go away. If I see you, I can't sleep," Genowefa told him.

"And if I don't see you, I can't live."

She gazed at him with her light grey eyes and again he felt her touch the very centre of his soul with that look of hers. She put down her buckets and brushed a strand of hair from her brow.

"Bring the buckets and come down to the river with me."

"What will your husband say?"

"He's at the manor."

"What will the workmen say?"

"You're helping me."

Eli grabbed the buckets and followed her down the stony track.

"You've grown into a man," said Genowefa without turning round.

"Do you think about me when we don't see each other?"

"I think about you whenever you think about me. Every day. I dream about you."

"Oh God, why don't you end it?" Eli abruptly put the buckets down on the path. "What sin have I or my fathers committed? Why must I suffer so?"

Genowefa stopped and looked at her feet.

"Don't blaspheme, Eli."

For a while they said nothing. Eli picked up the buckets and they went onwards. The path widened, so now they could walk abreast of each other.

"We won't be seeing each other any more, Eli. I'm pregnant. I'm going to have the child in autumn."

"It ought to be my child."

"It has all become clear and sorted itself out . . ."

"Let's run away to the city, to Kielce."

". . . Everything pushes us apart. You're young, I'm old. You're a Jew and I'm a Pole. You're from Jeszkotle, I'm from Primeval. You're single, and I'm married. You're mobile, I'm fixed to the spot."

They stepped onto the wooden pier, and Genowefa started removing the laundry from the buckets and plunging it into the cold water. The dark water rinsed out the light soapsuds.

"It was you that led me astray," said Eli.

"I know."

She put down the laundry, and for the first time leaned her head against his shoulder. He could smell the fragrance of her hair.

"I fell in love with you as soon as I saw you. Instantly. Love like that never ends," she said.

"What is love?"

She didn't answer.

"I can see the mill from my windows," said Eli.

THE TIME OF FLORENTYNKA

People think madness is caused by a great, dramatic event, some sort of suffering that is unbearable. They imagine you go mad for some reason — because of being abandoned by a lover, because of the death of someone you love, or the loss of a fortune, a glance at the face of God. People also think madness strikes suddenly, all at once, in unusual circumstances, and that insanity falls on a person like a net, fettering the mind and muddling the emotions.

But Florentynka had gone mad in the normal course of things, you could say for no reason at all. Long ago she might have had reasons for madness — when her husband drowned in the White River while drunk, when seven of her nine children died, when she had miscarriage after miscarriage, when she got rid of the ones she didn't miscarry, and the two times when she almost died as a result, when her barn burned down, when the two children left alive deserted her and disappeared into the world.

Now Florentynka was old, and had all her experiences behind her. Skinny as a rake and toothless, she lived in a wooden cottage by the Hill. Some of her cottage windows looked onto the forest, and others onto the village. Florentynka had two cows left which fed her, and also fed her dogs. She had a small orchard full of maggoty plums, and in summer some large hydrangea bushes bloomed in front of her house.

Florentynka went mad without anyone noticing. First her head ached and she couldn't sleep at night. The moon was disturbing her. She told the neighbours it was watching her, that its vigilant gaze came through the walls and windowpanes, and its glowing light left traps for her in the mirrors, windowpanes, and reflections in water.

Then, in the evenings, Florentynka started going outside and waiting for the moon. It rose above the common, always the same, though in a different form. Florentynka shook her fist at it. People saw this fist raised at the sky and said: she's gone mad.

Florentynka's body was small and thin. After her period of non-stop child-bearing she was left with a round belly which now looked comical, like a loaf of bread stuffed under her skirt. After this time of child-bearing womanhood she did not have a single tooth left, true to the saying: "One child — one tooth." Everything costs something. Florentynka's breasts — or rather what time does with a woman's breasts — were long and flat.

They nestled against her body. Their skin was like tissue paper for wrapping the decorations after Christmas, and the fine blue veins were visible through it — a sign that Florentynka was still alive.

And those were days when women died sooner than men, mothers sooner than fathers, wives sooner than husbands, because they had always been the vessels that secreted mankind. Children hatched out of them like chicks from eggs. Then the egg had to find a way to glue itself back together. The stronger the woman, the more children she bore, and so the weaker she became. In the forty-fifth year of life, freed from the endless round of child-bearing, Florentynka's body reached its own particular nirvana of sterility.

Ever since Florentynka had gone mad, cats and dogs had started frequenting her yard. Soon people began to treat her as a refuge for their consciences, and instead of drowning the kittens or puppies, they tossed them under the hydrangea bushes. At Florentynka's hands, the two feeder-cows nourished a whole pack of animal foundlings. Florentynka always treated animals with respect, as she did people. In the morning she said "good day" to them, and whenever she put down a bowl of milk for them, she never forgot to say "bon appetit." What's more, she never called them just "dog" or "cat," because it sounded as if she were talking about objects. She said "Mr Dog" and "Mr Cat," like Mr Malak or Mr Chlipała.

Florentynka didn't regard herself as a lunatic at all. The moon was persecuting her, like any normal persecutor. But one night something strange happened.

As usual when there was a full moon, Florentynka took her dogs and went out onto the hillside to curse the moon. The dogs lay down around her in the grass, and she shouted into the sky:

"Where is my son? How did you seduce him, you fat, silver toad? You beguiled my old man and dragged him into the water! I saw you in the well today, I caught you red-handed — you poisoned our water . . ."

A light went on in the Serafins' house and a man's voice shouted into the darkness.

"Shut up, you mad woman! We're trying to sleep."

"So go to sleep, sleep yourselves to death. Why on earth were you born if you're only going to sleep?"

The voice fell silent, and Florentynka sat on the ground and stared at the silvery face of her persecutor. It was furrowed with wrinkles, rheumy-eyed, with marks left by some sort of cosmic cowpox. The dogs lay on the grass, and the moon was reflected in their dark eyes too. They sat quietly, and then the old woman laid a hand on the head of the big shaggy bitch. Just then she saw in her mind a thought that wasn't hers, not even a thought, but the outline of a thought, an image, an impression. This something was alien to her thinking, not just because — as she sensed — it came from outside, but because it was completely different: monotone, distinct, deep, sensual, scented.

In it were the sky and two moons, one beside the other. There was a river — cold and joyful. There were houses — alluring and awful all at once. The line of the forest — a sight full of strange excitement. On the grass lay sticks, stones, and leaves filled with images and memories. Beside them, like paths, ran scent trails full of meanings. Under the ground ran warm, live corridors. Everything was different. Only the outlines of the world remained the same. Then with her human reason Florentynka realised that people were right — she had gone mad.

"Am I talking to myself?" she asked the bitch, who was resting her head on her knees.

She knew she was.

They went home. Florentynka poured the remains of the evening's milk into bowls. She, too, sat down to eat. She wetted a piece of bread in the milk and chewed it with her toothless gums. As she ate she stared at one of the dogs, trying to say something to him through pure images. She emitted a thought, "imagining" something like: "I am, and I am eating." The dog raised its head.

So that night, whether because of the persecutor-moon or her madness, Florentynka learned how to talk to her dogs and cats. The conversations relied on emitting images. What the animals imagined was not as concise and specific as human speech. It did not include thoughts, but it did have things seen from the inside, without the human distance that brings a sense of alienation. It made the world seem more friendly.

Most important for Florentynka were the two moons from the animals' images. It was astonishing to find that animals saw two moons, and people only one. Florentynka could not understand it, so finally she stopped trying to. The moons were different; in a way they were even opposed to each other, but also identical at the same time. One was soft, rather damp, and tender. The other was hard as silver, shining and jingling merrily. So Florentynka's persecutor had a dual nature, and this very feature made it even more of a threat to her.

THE TIME OF MISIA

When she was ten years old, Misia was the smallest girl in her class, and so she sat in the front bench. As she walked between the benches, the teacher always stroked Misia's head.

On her way home from school Misia collected things her

dollies needed: horse chestnut shells for plates, acorn tops for cups, and moss for pillows.

But once she got home, she couldn't decide what she wanted to play. On the one hand she was drawn to the dolls, to changing their dresses, and feeding them dishes that were invisible, but which did actually exist. She was drawn to wrapping their stiff bodies in baby quilts and telling them simple, rag-doll stories for bedtime. Then, once she had picked them up, she'd suddenly feel disheartened. They weren't Karmilla, Judyta, or Bobaska any more. Misia's eyes saw flat eyes painted onto pink faces, reddened cheeks and mouths that were permanently sealed, for which no food could exist. Misia turned over the thing she had once regarded as Karmilla and gave it a spanking. She could feel she was hitting sawdust covered in material. The doll didn't complain or protest. So Misia sat her with her pink face to the window-pane and stopped bothering with her. She went to rummage in her Mama's dressing table.

It was wonderful to sneak into her parents' bedroom and sit before the two-winged mirror that could even show things that were normally invisible — shadows in the corners, the back of your own head . . . Misia tried on the beads and rings, opened the little bottles and spent ages fathoming the mystery of lipstick. One day, when she was feeling especially disappointed with her Karmillas, she raised the lipstick to her mouth and painted it blood-red. The red of the lipstick set time in motion, and Misia saw herself in a few dozen years, just as she would die. She furiously wiped the lipstick off her mouth and went back to the dolls. She took their coarse, sawdust-stuffed paws in her hands and clapped them together soundlessly.

But she always went back to her mother's dressing table. She'd try on her silk camisoles and high-heeled shoes. She'd make herself a floor-length dress out of a lacy petticoat. She'd look at her reflection in the mirror, and suddenly think she looked funny. "Wouldn't it be better to make a ball dress for Karmilla?" she'd think, and excited by this idea, go back to the dolls.

One day, at the crossroads between her Mama's dressing table and the dolls, Misia found a drawer in the kitchen table. In the drawer there was everything. The entire world.

First of all, the photographs were kept here. One of them showed her father in a Russian uniform with a pal. They were standing with their arms around each other, like good friends. Her father had a moustache from ear to ear. In the background a fountain was playing. Another one showed her Papa's and Mama's heads. Mama was in a white veil, and Papa had the same black moustache. Misia's favourite picture was one of her mother with her hair cut short, wearing a headband. Mama looked like a real lady in it. Misia had her own photo in here too. She was sitting on a bench in front of the house with the coffee grinder on her knees. Above her head the lilac was in bloom.

Secondly, the most valuable object in the house, as far as Misia was concerned, was in here — the "moonstone," as she called it. Her father had once found it in a field, and he said it was different from all normal stones. It was almost perfectly round, and there were tiny crumbs of something very shiny embedded in its surface. It looked like a Christmas tree decoration. Misia would put it to her ear and wait for a sound, a sign from the stone. But the stone from heaven was silent.

Thirdly, there was an old thermometer with a broken mercury tube inside, so the mercury could move freely about the thermometer, not restricted by any scale, regardless of the temperature. One time it would stretch out in a stream, and then freeze, rolled in a ball like a frightened animal. One time it would look black, and another time it would be black, silvery, and white all at once. Misia loved playing with the thermometer with the mercury shut inside it. She thought the mercury was a living creature. She called it Sparky. Whenever she opened the drawer she said softly:

"Hello, Sparky."

Fourthly, old, broken, unfashionable costume jewellery was thrown into the drawer, all those trashy purchases no one can resist: a snapped chain whose gold paint has come off, exposing the grey metal, a fine filigree brooch made of horn, depicting Cinderella, with the birds helping her to pick the peas out of the ashes. Between pieces of paper shone the glassy stones of forgotten rings from the fair, earring clasps, and glass beads of various shapes. Misia marvelled at their simple, useless beauty. She would look into the window through the green eye of the ring, and the world became different. Beautiful. She could never decide what sort of world she would prefer to live in: green, ruby, blue, or yellow.

Fifthly, among the other things in here lay a switchblade, hidden from children. Misia was afraid of the knife, though sometimes she imagined she could use it. In defence of her father, for instance, if someone tried to do him harm. The knife looked innocent. It had a dark red ebonite handle, in which the blade was treacherously concealed. Misia had once seen her father release it with barely a flick of his finger. The mere "click" it gave sounded like an attack and made Misia shudder. That was why she reckoned she shouldn't even touch the knife by accident. She left it in its place, deep in the right-hand corner of the drawer, under the holy pictures.

Sixthly, on top of the knife lay some small holy pictures collected over the years, which the priest used to hand out to the children on his way round the parish. All of them showed either the Virgin Mary of Jeszkotle or the little Lord Jesus in a skimpy shirt, grazing a lamb. The Lord Jesus was chubby and had fair curly hair. Misia loved this sort of Lord Jesus. One of the pictures showed a bearded God the Father sprawling on a blue throne. God was holding a broken staff, and for a long time Misia didn't know what it was. Then she realised that this Lord God was holding a thunderbolt, and began to be afraid of Him.

There was a little medallion knocking around among the pictures. It wasn't an ordinary medallion. It was made out of a kopeck. On one side the image of the Virgin Mary had been die-cast, and on the other an eagle was spreading its wings.

Seventhly, there were some small, neatly shaped pig bones rattling about in the drawer that were used to play a throwing game. Misia kept an eye on her mother whenever she made aspic out of pig's feet to make sure she didn't throw away the bones. The shapely little bones had to be cleaned properly, then dried out on the stove. Misia liked holding them in her hand — they were light, and they looked so similar to each other, just the same, even from different pigs. How can it be, wondered Misia, that all the pigs that are killed for Christmas or Easter, all the pigs in the world have exactly the same little dice bones inside them? Sometimes Misia imagined the live pigs, and felt sorry for them. At least there was a bright side to their death — the dice bones were left after them.

Eighthly, old, used Volta batteries were stored in the drawer. At first Misia didn't touch them at all, just like the switchblade. Her father said they might still be charged with energy. But the notion of energy shut inside a small, flat box was extremely appealing. It reminded her of the mercury trapped in the thermometer. Though you could see the mercury, but not this energy.

What did energy look like? Misia took a battery and weighed it in her hand for a while. Energy was heavy. There must be a lot of energy in such a little box. It must be packed in there like a cabbage for pickling, and pressed down with a fingertip. Then Misia touched the yellow wire with her tongue and felt a gentle tingling — it was the remains of the invisible electrical energy coming out of the battery.

Ninthly, Misia found various medicines in the drawer, and knew it was absolutely forbidden to put them in her mouth. Mama's tablets were in there, and Papa's ointment. Misia had particular respect for her Mama's white pills in a small paper bag. Before Mama took them, she was angry and irritated, and suffered from headaches. But afterwards, once she had swallowed them, she calmed down and began to play patience.

And yes, tenthly there were cards in there for playing patience and rummy. On one side they all looked the same — a green plant design, but when Misia turned them over, a gallery of portraits was revealed. She spent hours examining the faces of the kings and queens. She tried to fathom the relationships between them. She suspected that as soon as the drawer was closed they started holding long conversations with each other, maybe even quarrelling about their imaginary kingdoms. She liked the Queen of Spades the best. She thought her the most beautiful and the saddest. The Queen of Spades had a bad husband. The Queen of Spades didn't have any friends. She was very lonely. Misia always looked for her in her mother's patience rows. She also looked for her whenever Mama told fortunes. But Mama spent too long staring at the laid-out cards. Misia got bored when there was nothing happening on the table, and then she went back to rummaging in the drawer, inside which lay the entire world.

In Cornspike's cottage in Wydymacz there lived a snake, an owl, and a kite. These creatures never got in each other's way. The snake lived by the hearth in the kitchen, and Cornspike put out a bowl of milk for him there. The owl sat in the loft, in an alcove where a window had been bricked in. He looked like a statuette. The kite kept to the roof beams, at the highest point in the house, but his real home was the sky.

Cornspike took longest to tame the snake. Every day she put out milk for him, gradually moving the bowl closer to the inside of the house. One day the snake crawled up to her feet. She picked him up, and she won him over with her warm skin, which smelled of grass and milk. The snake wound around her arm, and his golden pupils gazed into Cornspike's clear eyes. She gave him the name Goldie.

Goldie fell in love with Cornspike. Her warm skin heated the snake's cold heart and cold body. He desired her odours and the velvet touch of her skin, with which nothing on earth could compare. Whenever Cornspike picked him up, he felt as if he, a common reptile, were changing into something completely different, into something extremely important. As gifts he brought her the mice he hunted, lovely milky pebbles from the riverside, and bits of bark. Once he brought her an apple, and the woman raised it to her face, laughing, and her laughter was fragrant with abundance.

"You tempter," she would say to him endearingly.

Sometimes she threw him a piece of her clothing, and then Goldie would wind his way into the dress and savour the remains of Cornspike's aroma. He would wait for her on every path, wherever she went, following her every move. During the day she let him lie on her bed. She carried him round her neck like a silver chain, tied him around her hips and wore him instead of a bracelet, and at night, as she slept, he watched her dreams and furtively licked her ears.

Goldie suffered when the woman made love with the Bad Man. He could sense that the Bad Man was alien to both people and animals. At those times he burrowed in the leaves or looked the sun straight in the eye. Goldie's guardian angel lived in the sun. Snakes' guardian angels are dragons.

One day Cornspike went through the meadows to pick herbs by the River with the snake around her neck. There she ran into the parish priest. The priest saw them and recoiled in terror.

"You sorceress!" he cried, waving his stick. "Keep away from Primeval and Jeszkotle, and my parishioners. Do you go walking about with the devil around your neck? Haven't you heard what the Scriptures say? What the Lord God said to the serpent? 'And I will put enmity between thee and the woman, she shall bruise thy head, and thou shalt bite her heel.'"

Cornspike burst out laughing and raised her skirt, showing her naked underbelly.

"Get away! Get away, Satan!" cried the priest and crossed himself several times.

In the summer of 1927 a sprig of masterwort grew in front of Cornspike's cottage. Cornspike observed it from the moment it put a thick, fat, stiff shoot out of the earth. She watched as it slowly developed its large leaves. It grew all summer, from day to day, and from hour to hour, until it reached the roof of the cottage and opened its ample canopies above it.

"What now, my fine fellow?" Cornspike said to it ironically. "You've pushed yourself so far, you've climbed so high into the sky that now your seeds are going to germinate in the thatch, not in the ground."

The masterwort was about two metres high and had such mighty leaves that they took away the sunlight from the plants around it. Towards the end of summer no other plant was capable of growing beside it. On Saint Michael's Day it bloomed, and for a few hot nights Cornspike could not sleep for the bittersweet aroma that pervaded the air. The sharp edges of the plant's mighty, sinewy body bounced off the silver moonlit sky. Sometimes a breeze rustled in the canopies, and the overblown flowers showered down. The rustling noises alerted Cornspike to raise herself on an elbow and listen closely to the plant living. The whole room was full of seductive aromas.

And one night, when Cornspike had finally fallen asleep, a young man with fair hair stood before her. He was tall and powerfully built. His arms and thighs looked as if they were made of polished wood. The glow of the moon illuminated him.

"I've been watching you through the window," he said.

"I know. The smell of you disturbs the senses."

The young man came inside the room and stretched both hands out to Cornspike. She snuggled in between them and pressed her face to the hard, powerful chest. He lifted her slightly so that their mouths could find each other. From under half-closed eyelids Cornspike saw his face — it was rough like the stem of a plant.

"I have desired you all summer," she said into a mouth tasting of sweets, candied fruits, and the earth when rain is going to fall.

"And I you."

They lay down on the floor and brushed against each other like grasses. Then the masterwort planted Cornspike on his hips and took root in her rhythmically, deeper and deeper, pervading her entire body, penetrating its inner recesses, and drinking up its juices. He drank from her until morning, when the sky became grey and the birds began to sing. Then a shudder shook the masterwort, and his hard body froze still, like timber. The canopies began to rustle and dry, prickly seeds showered down on Cornspike's naked, exhausted body. Then the fair-haired youth went back outside, and Cornspike spent all day picking the aromatic grains from her hair.

THE TIME OF MICHAŁ

Misia had always been lovely, from the first time he saw her outside the house, playing in the sand. He fell in love with her at once. She fitted perfectly in the small devastated space in his soul. He gave her the coffee grinder he had brought from the East as a war trophy. With the grinder he surrendered himself into the little girl's hands, to be able to start everything anew.

He watched as she grew, as her first teeth fell out, and in their place new ones appeared — white, too large for her little mouth. With sensuous pleasure he watched the nightly unplaiting of her braids and the slow, sleepy motions of her hairbrush. Misia's hair was at first chestnut, then dark brown, and it always had red lights, like blood, like fire. Michał wouldn't let it be cut, even when, matted with sweat, it stuck to her pillow during illness. That was the time the doctor from Jeszkotle said Misia might not survive. Michał fainted. He slipped off his chair and fell on the floor. It was clear what Michał's body was saying by this fall — if Misia died, he would die, too. Just like that, literally, without a doubt.

Michał didn't know how to express what he felt. It seemed to him that anyone who loves is constantly giving. So he was always giving her little surprises, seeking out shiny stones for her in the river, carving little pipes out of willow, blowing eggs, folding birds out of paper, and buying toys in Kielce — he did whatever might please a little girl. But he cared most of all about big things, of the kind that are permanent, and also beautiful, of the kind time communes with, rather than man. These things were meant to stop time for his love forever. And to stop time for Misia forever. Thanks to them, their love would be eternal.

If Michał had been a powerful ruler, he would have constructed a huge building for Misia on a mountaintop, beautiful and indestructible. But Michał was just an ordinary miller, so he bought Misia clothes and toys, and made her paper birds.

She had the most dresses of all the children in the neighbourhood. She looked as beautiful as the young ladies from the manor house. She had real dolls, bought in Kielce, dolls that blinked, and when turned on their backs they let out a squeal that was meant to sound like a baby crying. She had a wooden pram for them, two prams even — one was made out of a dismantled kennel. She had a two-storey doll's house and several teddy bears. Wherever Michał went, he always thought of Misia, and always missed her. He never raised his voice to her.

"If you'd only smack her on the bottom once," said Genowefa peevishly.

The very thought that he might hit this trusting little body caused Michał to feel weak, in the same way that had once ended in him fainting. That was why Misia often ran from her angry mother to her father. She would hide in his flour-whitened jacket like a little animal. He would stop in his tracks, amazed over and over again at her pure, unsullied trust.

When she started going to school, every day he took a short break from his work in the mill to go out onto the bridge and see her coming back. Her small figure would emerge by the poplars — the sight of her restored everything Michał had lost since Misia had left that morning. Then he would look over her exercise books and help with her lessons. He also taught her Russian and German. He guided her little hand across all the letters of the alphabet. He sharpened her pencils.

Then something began to change, in 1929. By then Izydor had been born, and the rhythm of life had changed. One day Michał saw both of them, Misia and Genowefa, as they were hanging out the washing, both the same height, in white headscarves, and the underclothes on the lines — tops, brassieres, and petticoats, one set just a little smaller than the other, women's clothes. For a moment he wondered whose the smaller ones were, and when he realised, he felt disconcerted, like a young boy. Until now the petite size of Misia's clothes had aroused his affection. Now, as he looked at the lines of washing, he was filled with anger at the idea that time could run so fast. He would have preferred not to see that underwear.

At the same time, maybe a little later, one evening before falling asleep, in a drowsy voice Genowefa told him Misia had already started her periods. Then she nodded off, cuddling up to him and sighing in her sleep like an old woman. Michał couldn't fall asleep. He lay and stared into the darkness. When he finally got to sleep, he had a dream, bizarre and disjointed.

He dreamed he was walking along a border, and on both sides grew corn, or maybe tall, yellow grass. He could see Cornspike going along it. She was holding a sickle, and using this sickle to cut spikes of grass.

"Look," she said to him. "They're bleeding."

He leaned forward, and indeed, on the cut blades of grass he saw drops of blood welling up. It seemed to him unnatural and dreadful. He began to feel afraid. He wanted to get out of there, but when he turned around, he saw Misia in the grass. She was wearing her school uniform, lying there with her eyes closed. He knew she had died of typhoid.

"She's alive," said Cornspike. "But it's always the case that at first you die."

She leaned over Misia and said something into her ear. Misia woke up.

"Come on, let's go home." Michał took his daughter by the hand and tried to pull her after him.

But Misia was different, as if she hadn't yet gained consciousness. She wasn't looking at him.

"No, Papa, I have so many things to do. I'm not coming."

Then Cornspike pointed at her lips.

"Look, she's not moving her lips when she speaks."

Michał understood in the dream that Misia had been touched by a sort of death, an incomplete death, but just as paralysing as real death.

THE TIME OF IZYDOR

November 1928 was rainy and windy. And so it was the day Genowefa gave birth to her second child.

As soon as Kucmerka the midwife had rushed over, Michał took Misia to the Serafins. Serafin put a bottle of vodka on the table, and soon the other neighbours arrived. They all wanted to drink to Michał Niebieski's offspring.

At the same time Kucmerka was heating water and preparing

the sheets. Moaning monotonously, Genowefa was pacing the length of the kitchen.

At the same time in the autumn firmament Saturn was spreading out in Sagittarius like a great iceberg. Mighty Pluto, the planet that helps to cross all manner of borders, was lodged in Cancer. That night he took Mars and the delicate Moon in his arms. Within the harmony of the eight heavens, the sensitive ears of the angels picked up a clattering sound like the noise of a cup falling and smashing to smithereens.

At the same time Cornspike had just swept the room and squatted down in the corner over a bundle of last year's hay. She had begun to give birth. It took a few minutes. She bore a large, beautiful baby. The room was filled with the scent of masterwort.

At the same time at the Niebieskis', when the little head appeared, Genowefa started having complications. She fainted. The terrified Kucmerka opened the window and shouted into the darkness:

"Michał! Michał! People!"

But the gale drowned her voice, and Kucmerka realised she would have to manage on her own.

"You're a weakling, not a woman!" she shouted at the swooning Genowefa to give herself courage. "Fit for dancing, not child bearing. You'll smother the child, you'll smother it . . ."

She slapped Genowefa's face.

"Christ Almighty, push! Push!"

"A daughter? Son?" raved Genowefa and, brought round by pain, began to push.

"Son, daughter, what's the difference? Come on, again, again . . ."

The child plopped into Kucmerka's hands and Genowefa fainted again. Kucmerka attended to the child. It began to whine softly.

"Daughter?" asked Genowefa, coming round.

"Daughter? Daughter?" the midwife mocked her. "You're a wimp, not a woman."

The breathless women entered the house.

"Go and tell Michał he has a son," Kucmerka ordered them. They gave the child the name Izydor. Genowefa was in a bad way. She had a fever and couldn't feed the baby. She kept shouting things in her delirium, saying they had switched her child for another. When she came to, she immediately said: "Give me my daughter."

"We have a son," Michał answered her.

Genowefa spent a long time examining the baby. It was a boy, large and pale. He had thin eyelids, with small blue veins showing through them. His head looked too big, too solid. He was very restless, crying and squirming at the slightest sound, and screaming so hard that it was impossible to quieten him. He was woken by the floor creaking or the clock ticking.

"It's because of the cow's milk," said Kucmerka. "You must start feeding him."

"I haven't got any milk, I haven't got any milk," groaned Genowefa in despair. "We must find a wet nurse quickly."

"Cornspike has given birth."

"I don't want Cornspike," said Genowefa.

A wet nurse was found in Jeszkotle. She was a Jew. One of her twins had died. Michał had to go and fetch her twice a day by horse and cart.

Even when fed on woman's milk, Izydor went on crying. For nights on end Genowefa would carry him in her arms, to and fro, about the kitchen and the living room. She also tried going to bed and ignoring the crying, but then Michał got up and very quietly, to avoid disturbing Misia's sleep, wrapped the baby in a blanket and took him outside, under the starry sky. He would take his son to the Hill or along the Highway towards the forest. The child would be calmed by the rocking motion and the scent of the pine trees, but as soon as Michał came home and crossed the threshold, he would start to cry again.

Sometimes, pretending to be asleep, through half-open eyes Michał would watch his wife as she stood over the cradle and gazed at the child. She looked at him coldly and dispassionately, as if at a thing, an object, not a human being. As if sensing this gaze, the child would cry even louder, even more mournfully. Something was going on in the heads of mother and child, Michał didn't know what, but one night Genowefa whispered to him confidentially:

"That's not our child. That's Cornspike's child. Kucmerka told me 'daughter,' I remember that. Then something must have happened, Cornspike could have beguiled Kucmerka, because when I woke up it was a son."

Michał sat down and lit the lamp. He saw his wife's tear-stained face.

"Genowefa, you can't think like that. That's Izydor, our son. He looks like me. And we wanted a son, didn't we?"

Something of this short, nocturnal conversation remained in the Niebieskis' house. Now they both watched the child. Michał sought similarities. Genowefa surreptitiously checked her son's fingers, examined the skin on his back and the shape of his ears. And the older the child got, the more proof she found for the idea that he was not their offspring.

On his first birthday Izydor still didn't have a single tooth. He could hardly sit up and hadn't grown much. It was clear that all his growth was going to his head — though his face remained small, Izydor's head was growing, lengthways and widthways from the line of his brow.

In the spring of 1930 they took him to Taszów, to the doctor.

"It might be hydrocephalus, and the child will most probably die. There's no cure for it."

The doctor's words were a magic spell that awoke the love in Genowefa that had been frozen by suspicions.

Genowefa loved Izydor the way you love a dog or a crippled, helpless small animal. It was the purest human compassion.

THE TIME OF SQUIRE POPIELSKI

Squire Popielski had a good time for business. Every year he acquired one more fish pond. The carp in these ponds were huge and fat. When their time came, they crowded into the net of their own accord. The squire loved to walk along the dikes, circling right round them, gazing into the water, and then into the sky. The abundance of fish soothed his nerves, and the ponds allowed him to get a grip on the sense of it all. The more ponds, the more sense. Busy with the ponds, Squire Popielski's mind had a lot to do: he had to plan, ponder, count, create, and devise. He could think about the ponds the whole time, and then his mind didn't wander off into cold, dark areas that dragged him down like a quagmire.

In the evenings the squire devoted his time to his family. His wife, as slim and fragile as a reed, would shower him in a hail of problems, trivial and unimportant, as it seemed to him. About the servants, the banquet, the children's school, the car, money, the shelter. In the evening she sat with him in the living room and drowned the music from the radio with her monotonous voice. Once the squire had been happy when she massaged his back. Now once an hour his wife's slender fingers turned a page of the book she had been reading for a year. The children were growing, and the squire knew less and less about them. The presence of his oldest daughter, with her disdainfully pouting lips, made him feel uncomfortable, as if she were someone alien, or even hostile to him. His son had become reticent and timid, and never sat on his knees or tugged his moustache any more. His youngest son, the pampered favourite, tended to be wayward and had fits of rage.

In 1931 the Popielskis and their children went to Italy. On returning from the holiday Squire Popielski knew he had found his passion — in art. He started collecting albums about painting, and then spent more and more time in Kraków, where he bought pictures. Moreover, he often invited artists to the manor, held discussions with them, and drank. At dawn he would take the entire company to his ponds and show them the olive-green hulks of the enormous carp.

The next year Squire Popielski fell violently in love with Maria Szer, a young painter from Kraków, a representative of futurism. As happens in sudden loves, meaningful coincidences started appearing in his life, chance common acquaintances, and the necessity for sudden journeys. Thanks to Maria Szer, Squire Popielski fell in love with modern art. His lover was like futurism: full of energy, crazy, though in certain matters stone cold sober. She had a body like a statue — smooth and hard. Strands of her fair hair stuck to her brow as she worked on an enormous canvas. She was the opposite of the squire's wife. Beside her, his wife was like an eighteenth-century classical landscape: full of details, harmonious, and painfully static.

In the thirty-eighth year of his life Squire Popielski felt as if he had discovered sex. It was wild, crazy sex, like modern art, like Maria Szer. By the bed in her studio stood an enormous mirror, which reflected the entire transformation of Maria Szer and Squire Popielski into a woman and a man. It reflected the rumpled bedding and the sheepskins, and the naked bodies smeared in paint, and the grimaces on their faces, and their naked breasts, and their bellies, and their backs with smudged lipstick streaks.

On his way back to the manor from Kraków in his new car, Squire Popielski would elaborate plans to escape to Brazil, or to Africa with his Maria, but once he crossed the threshold he was happy to find everything in its place, safe and permanent, reliable.

After six months of madness Maria Szer informed him that she was leaving for America. She said everything was new there, full of vigour and energy, and that there you could create your own life, like a futurist painting. After her departure Squire Popielski caught a strange illness with lots of symptoms, which to simplify matters was called arthritis. For a month he lay in bed, where he could surrender to suffering in peace.

He lay there for a month, not so much out of pain or weakness, as because the facts he had been trying to forget for the past few years were back — that the world was ending, and reality was disintegrating like rotten wood, matter was being eaten away from underneath by mould, it was happening quite senselessly and was meaningless. The squire's body had given up — it too was disintegrating. The same thing had happened to his will. The time between making a decision and taking action kept bloating and becoming unendurable. Squire Popielski's throat was swollen and stifled. It all meant that he was still alive, that various processes were still going on in his body, his blood was flowing, and his heart was beating. "It has caught up with me," thought the squire, and from his bed he tried to fix his vision on something, but his vision had become sticky: it wandered about the furniture, landing on them like a fly. Plip! It landed on a pile of books that the squire had had brought to him but hadn't read. Plip! a bottle of medicine. Plip! a stain on the wall. Plip! the view of the sky through the window. He found it tiring to look into people's faces. They seemed so mobile, so volatile. It took a lot of vigilance to look into them, but Squire Popielski didn't have the strength for vigilance, so he averted his gaze.

Squire Popielski had a crushing, ghastly feeling that the world, and everything that was good and bad in it, was passing him by: love, sex, money, thrills, distant voyages, beautiful pictures, intelligent books, wonderful people — all this was gliding past. The squire's time was slipping away. Then in sudden despair he felt a desire to break free and rush off somewhere. But where, and what for? He fell onto the pillows and choked back his unwept tears.

And once again the spring brought him some hope of salvation. Once he had started to walk, admittedly on a cane, he stood by his favourite pond and asked himself the first question: Where do I come from? He stirred anxiously. Where did I come from, where is my beginning? He went home and made an effort to force himself to read — about the ancient world and prehistory, about excavations and Cretan culture. About anthropology and heraldry. But all this knowledge took him nowhere, so he asked himself a second question: What can a person actually know? And what are the benefits of acquired knowledge? And can you know something fully? He thought and thought, and on Saturdays he discussed the matter with Pełski, who came to play bridge. Nothing resulted from these discussions and reflections. With time he no longer felt like opening his mouth. He knew what Pełski would say, and he knew what he himself would say. He felt as if they were always talking about the same thing, repeating their questions, as if they were playing roles, like moths coming closer to a lamp and then shying away from the obvious truth that might burn them. So finally he asked himself a third question: What should a person achieve, how should he live, what should he do, and what not? He read Machiavelli's *The Prince*, and books by Thoreau, Kropotkin, and Kotarbiński. All summer he read so much that he hardly ever left his room. Worried by this, one evening his wife went up to his desk and said:

"They say that rabbi from Jeszkotle is a healer. I went to see him and I asked him to come and visit us. He agreed."

The squire smiled, disarmed by his wife's naivety.

The conversation did not turn out the way he had imagined it. Along with the rabbi came a young Jew, because the rabbi could not speak Polish. Squire Popielski had no wish to confide his sufferings in this bizarre couple. So he asked the old man his three questions, though to tell the truth, he wasn't counting on an answer. The young man with sidelocks translated the clear, lucid Polish sentences into the rabbi's tortuous, throaty language. Then the rabbi surprised the squire.

"You collect questions. That's good. I have one more, final question for your collection: Where are we heading? What is the goal of time?"

The rabbi stood up. In parting he offered the squire his hand in a very well-bred manner. Moments later he made another strange remark from the doorway, and the boy translated:

"The time for some tribes is coming to an end. Therefore I will give you something that should now become your property."

The squire was amused by the Jew's mysterious and solemn tone. For the first time in months he ate his dinner with an appetite and made fun of his wife.

"You're resorting to all manner of sorcery to cure me of my arthritis. Evidently the best medicine for ailing joints is an old Jew who answers a question with a question."

For dinner there was carp in aspic.

Next day the boy with sidelocks came to see the squire and brought him a large wooden box. Intrigued, the squire opened it. Inside there were some compartments. In one lay an old book with a Latin title: *Ignis fatuus, or an instructive game for one player.*

In the next compartment, which was lined in velvet, lay a birch-wood octagonal die. On each face it had a different number of spots, from one to eight. Squire Popielski had never seen a die like this one before. In the remaining compartments lay some little brass figurines of people, animals, and objects. Underneath he found a piece of cloth, folded over and over and frayed at the edges. More and more amazed by this bizarre present, he unfolded the cloth on the floor, until it took up almost the entire empty space between his desk and the bookcases. It was a sort of game, a sort of ludo in the form of a huge, circular labyrinth.

THE TIME OF DIPPER THE DROWNED MAN

The Drowned Man was the soul of a peasant called Dipper. Dipper had drowned in the pond one August, when the vodka he had drunk thinned his blood too much. He was on his way back by cart from Wola when his horses were suddenly startled by moon shadows and overturned the cart. The peasant had fallen into the shallow water, and the horses had gone off in confusion. The water at the edge of the pond was warm, thanks to the August sunshine, and Dipper felt good lying in it. When the warm water got into the drunken Dipper's lungs, he groaned, but he didn't sober up.

Trapped in his drunken body, his intoxicated soul, a soul that hadn't been absolved, with no map of the road onwards to God, remained like a dog by the body going cold in the bulrushes.

Such a soul is blind and helpless. It keeps stubbornly returning to the body, because it knows no other form of existence. Yet it pines for the land it comes from, where it once used to be and from which it has been expelled into the material world. It remembers it, reminisces, laments and pines, but it does not know how to get back there. It is carried on waves of despair. Then it abandons the now rotting corpse and tries to find the way on its own. It wanders about crossroads and wayside inns and tries to cadge rides by the highways. It takes on various forms. It enters into animals and things, sometimes even barely conscious people, but it never manages to settle anywhere. In the material world it is an outcast, and nor does the spirit world want it either. For to enter the spirit world it needs a map.

After this hopeless wandering the soul returns to the body or to the place where it left the body. But for it the cold, dead body is what the charred remains of a house are for a living person. The soul tries to get the dead heart and the dead, lifeless eyelids moving, but it hasn't enough strength or determination. In keeping with divine order, the dead body says: No. Thus the person's body becomes a hated home, and the site of the body's death the soul's hated prison. The Drowned Man's soul rustles in the reeds, simulates shadows and sometimes borrows a shape from the mist, thanks to which it tries to make contact with people. It can't understand why people avoid it, why it strikes terror in them.

So in its confusion Dipper's soul thought that it was still Dipper.

In time, a sort of disappointment and dislike of everything human was born in Dipper's soul. Some remains of old, human or even animal thoughts were tangled in it, some memories and images. So it believed it would re-enact the moment of disaster, the moment of Dipper's or someone else's death, and that this would help it to become free. That was why it wanted so badly to startle some other horses, overturn a cart and drown a person. So from the soul of Dipper the Drowned Man was born.

The Drowned Man chose as his headquarters a forest pond with a dike and a little bridge, and also the entire forest called Wodenica, and the meadows from Papiernia all the way to Wydymacz, where the mist could be especially dense. Mindless and vacant, he roamed his estates. Only sometimes, when he met a man or an animal, was he animated by a sense of anger. Then his enduring took on meaning. He would do his best at any price to cause whatever creature he encountered some evil, lesser or greater, but an evil.

The Drowned Man was always discovering his own potential anew. At first he thought he was weak and defenceless, that he was something like a flurry of wind, a light haze or a puddle of water. Then he discovered that he could move faster than anyone could imagine, just by thought alone. He thought about a place, and at once he could be there, in a flash. He also discovered that the mist obeyed him, and that he could control it as he wished. He could take strength from it, or a shape, he could move entire clouds of it, block out the sun with it, blur the horizon and extend the night. The Drowned Man realised that he was the King of the Mist, and from then on that was how he started to think of himself — the King of the Mist.

The King of the Mist felt best under water. For years on end he lay under its surface on a bed of silt and rotting leaves. From under the water he watched the changing seasons and the movements of the sun and the moon. From under the water he saw the rain, the leaves falling in autumn, the dances of summer dragonflies, people bathing, and the orange feet of wild ducks. Sometimes something woke him from this sleep-non-sleep, sometimes not. He never wondered about it. He just endured.

THE TIME OF OLD BOSKI

Old Boski spent his entire life on the manor house roof. The manor house was large, and its roof enormous — full of slants, slopes, and edges. And entirely covered in beautiful wooden shingle. If you were to straighten out the manor house roof and spread it on the ground, it would cover the entire field that Boski owned.

Boski left the cultivation of this land to his wife and children — he had three girls and a boy, Paweł, handsome and capable. Each morning Old Boski went up onto the roof and replaced the rotting or mouldering shingles. His work had no end. Nor did it have a beginning, because Boski did not start from a specific spot and did not move in a specific direction. On his knees he examined the wooden roof metre by metre, shifting here and there.

At noon his wife brought him his dinner in a double pot. In one container there was rye soup, in the other potatoes, or buckwheat with fried crackling and buttermilk, or cabbage and potatoes. Old Boski didn't come down for dinner. He was handed the double pot on a rope in the bucket in which the wooden shingles went up.

Boski ate, and as he chewed he looked at the world around him. From the manor roof he saw meadows, the Black River, the roofs of Primeval, and tiny human figures, so small and fragile that Old Boski fancied blowing on them and sweeping them off the world like refuse. At this thought he would stuff another helping of food into his mouth, and on his weather-beaten face a grimace would appear that may have been a smile. Boski liked this moment of each day, when he imagined people being blown about in all directions. Sometimes he imagined it slightly differently: his breath became a hurricane, tearing the roofs off houses, knocking over trees and cutting down orchards. Water would flood into the plains, and people would hurry to build boats to save themselves and their property. Craters would appear in the earth, from which pure fire would burst forth. Steam would blast into the sky from the battle between fire and water. Everything would shake in its foundations and finally cave in like the roof of an old house. People would stop mattering — Boski would destroy the entire world.

He swallowed his mouthful and sighed. The vision evaporated. Now he rolled himself a cigarette and looked closer, at the manor courtyard, the park and the moat, the swans and the pond. He would stare at the carriages driving up, and later the cars. From the roof he saw ladies' hats and gentlemen's bald patches, he saw the squire coming home from a horseback ride and the squire's wife, who always took tiny little steps. He saw the young lady, fragile and delicate, and her dogs, which inspired terror in the village. He saw the eternal traffic of lots of people, their greeting and parting gestures and facial expressions, people coming in and going out, talking to each other and listening.

But what did they matter to him? He would finish smoking his roll-up, and his gaze would stubbornly return to the wooden shingles, to settle on them like a freshwater mussel, to savour and feed on them. And at once he would be thinking how to trim and cut them — and so his dinner break came to an end.

His wife would fetch the double pot, which he let down on the rope, and go home across the meadows to Primeval.

Old Boski's son Paweł wanted to be someone "important." He was afraid that if he didn't start to take action soon, he would become as "unimportant" as his father and would spend his whole life putting shingles on a roof. So when he turned sixteen, he got out of the house where his ugly sisters reigned supreme and found himself a job in Jeszkotle working for a Jew named Aba Kozienicki, who traded in wood. At first Paweł worked as an ordinary woodcutter and loader, but Aba must have liked him, because he soon entrusted him with the responsible job of marking and grading the tree trunks.

Even in grading wood Paweł Boski always looked to the future — the past didn't interest him. The very thought that you could shape the future, and have an influence on what would happen, excited him. Sometimes he wondered how it all comes about. If he had been born in the manor as a Popielski, would he have been the same as he was now? Would he have thought the same way? Would he still have liked Misia, the Niebieskis' daughter? Would he still have wanted to be a paramedic, or would he have aimed higher — doctor, university professor?

One thing the young Boski was sure of — knowledge. Knowledge and education were wide open to everyone. Of course it was easier for others, all those Popielskis and such like. And it wasn't fair. But on the other hand he, too, could learn, though it would take greater effort, because he had to earn a living and help his parents.

So after work he went to the district library and borrowed books. The district library was poorly stocked. It lacked encyclopaedias and dictionaries. The shelves were full of things like *The Kings' Daughters* and *Without a Dowry* — books for women.

At home he hid the library books from his sisters in his bed. He didn't like them touching his things.

All three sisters were big, solid, and coarse. Their heads looked small. They had low brows and thick fair hair, like straw. The prettiest of them was Stasia. When she smiled, her white teeth flashed in her tanned face. She was a bit disfigured by her awkward, waddling feet. The middle one, Tosia, was already engaged to a farmer from Kotuszów, and Zosia, large and strong, was supposed to be leaving any day for domestic service in Kielce, the big city. Paweł was glad they were leaving home, though he disliked his home as much as he disliked his sisters.

He hated the dirt that got into the cracks in the old wooden cottage, into the floors and under his fingernails. He hated the stench of cow's manure that permeated his clothing when he went into the barn. He hated the smell of potatoes being steamed for the pigs — it pervaded the entire house and everything inside it, his hair and skin. He hated the boorish dialect in which his parents spoke and which sometimes pushed its way onto his own tongue. He hated the cloth, the raw wood, the wooden spoons, the holy pictures from the church fête, and his sisters' fat legs. Sometimes he managed to gather this hatred somewhere in the area of his jaws, and then he felt a great strength in himself. He knew he would have everything he desired, that he would push forwards and no one would be able to stop him.

THE TIME OF THE GAME

The labyrinth drawn on the cloth consisted of eight circles, or spheres, called Worlds. The closer to the middle, the denser the labyrinth seemed to be, and the more blind alleys and back streets leading to nowhere there were in it. And vice versa — the outer spheres gave the impression of being brighter and more spacious, and here the paths of the labyrinth seemed wider and less chaotic, as if inviting you to wander. The sphere that represented the centre of the labyrinth — the darkest and most tangled one — was called the First World. By this World someone's unskilled hand had drawn an arrow in copying pencil and written: "Primeval." "Why Primeval?" wondered Squire Popielski. "Why not Kotuszów, Jeszkotle, Kielce, Kraków, Paris, or London?" A complex system of little roads, intersections, forks and fields led deviously towards a single passage into the next circular zone, called the Second World. In comparison with the tangle at the centre, here there was a bit more space. Two exits led to the Third World, and Squire Popielski soon realised that in each World there would be twice as many exits as in the previous one. With the tip of his fountain pen he carefully counted all the exits from the final sphere of the labyrinth. There were 128 of them.

The small book entitled *Ignis fatuus, or an instructive game for one player* was simply an instruction manual for the game written in Latin and in Polish. The squire flicked through it page by page, and found it all very complicated. The manual described in turn each possible result of throwing the die, each move, each pawn-figurine, and each of the Eight Worlds. The description seemed incoherent and full of digressions, until finally it occurred to the squire that here he had the work of a lunatic.

The game is a sort of journey, on which now and then choices keep appearing, the first words read. *The choices make themselves, but sometimes the player is under the impression that he is making them consciously. This may frighten him, because then he will feel responsible for where he ends up and what he encounters.*

The player sees his journey like cracks in the ice — lines that split, turn, and change direction at a dizzy pace. Or like lightning in the sky that seeks a way for itself through the air in a manner that is impossible to predict. The player who believes in God will say: "divine judgement," "the finger of God" — that omnipotent, powerful extremity of the Creator. But if he doesn't believe in God, he will say: "coincidence," "accident." Sometimes the player will use the words "my free choice," but he is sure to say this more quietly and without conviction.

The game is a map of escape. It starts at the centre of the labyrinth. The aim is to pass through all the spheres and break free of the fetters of the Eight Worlds.

Squire Popielski leafed through the complicated description of the pawns and opening strategies for the Game, until he came to the description of the First World. He read:

In the beginning there was no God. There was no time or space. There was just light and darkness. And it was perfect.

He had a feeling he knew those words from somewhere.

The light moved within itself and flared up. A pillar of light tore into the darkness and there it found matter that had been immobile forever. It struck it with full force, until it awoke God in it. Still unconscious, still unsure what He was, God looked around Him, and as He saw no one apart from Himself, He realised that He was God. And unnamed for Himself, incomprehensible to Himself, He felt the desire to know Himself. When He looked closely at Himself for the first time, the Word came forth — it seemed to God that knowing was naming.

And so the Word rolls from the mouth of God and breaks into a thousand pieces that become the seeds of the Worlds. From this time on the Worlds grow, and God is reflected in them as in a mirror. And as He examines His reflection in the Worlds, He sees Himself more and more, knows Himself better and better, and this knowledge enriches Him, and thus it enriches the Worlds, too.

God comes to know Himself through the passage of time, because only that which is elusive and changeable is most similar to God. He comes to know Himself through the rocks that emerge hot out of the sea, through the plants in love with the sun, through generations of animals. When man appears, God experiences a revelation, and for the first time He is able to name in Himself the fragile line of night and day, the subtle boundary, from which light starts to be dark and dark light. From then on He looks at Himself through the eyes of people. He sees thousands of His own faces and tries them on like masks and, like an actor, for a while becomes the mask. Praying to Himself through the mouths of people, He discovers contradiction in Himself, for in the mirror the reflection can be real, and reality can pass into the reflection.

"Who am I?" asks God, "God or man, or maybe both one and the other at once, or neither of them? Was it I that created people, or they Me?"

Man tempts Him, so He creeps into the beds of lovers, and there He discovers love. He creeps into the beds of old people, and there He finds transience. He creeps into the beds of the dying, and there He finds death.

"Why shouldn't I give it a try?" thought Squire Popielski. He went back to the beginning of the book and set out the brass figurines in front of him.

Misia noticed that the tall, fair-haired boy from the Boski family was always looking at her in church. Then, when she came out after mass, he would be standing outside looking at her again, and he kept on looking. Misia could feel his gaze on her, like an uncomfortable piece of clothing. She was afraid to move freely or breathe deeply. He made her feel awkward.

So it was all winter, from Midnight Mass to Easter. When it started getting warmer, each week Misia came to church more lightly dressed, and felt Paweł Boski's gaze on her even more strongly. At Corpus Christi this gaze touched her bare nape and exposed arms. To Misia it felt very soft and pleasant, like stroking a cat, like feathers, like dandelion fluff.

That Sunday Paweł Boski came up to Misia and asked if he could walk her home. She agreed.

He talked the entire way, and what he said amazed her. He said she was dainty, like a luxury Swiss watch. Misia had never thought of herself as dainty before. He said her hair was the colour of the dearest type of gold. Misia had always thought she had brown hair. He also said her skin had a fragrance of vanilla. Misia didn't dare admit she had just baked a cake.

Everything in Paweł Boski's words discovered Misia anew. Once she reached home she couldn't get down to any work. However, she wasn't thinking about Paweł, but about herself: "I am a pretty girl. I have small feet, like a Chinese woman. I have beautiful hair. I smile in a very feminine way. I smell of vanilla. A person might long to see me. I am a woman."

Before the holidays Misia told her father she would no longer be going to college in Taszów and that she had no head for calculations and calligraphy. She was still friendly with

Rachela Szenbert, but their conversations were different now. They walked along the Highway to the forest together. Rachela urged Misia not to drop school. She promised to help her with arithmetic. And Misia told Rachela about Paweł Boski. Rachela listened, as a friend would, but she was of a different opinion.

"I'm going to marry a doctor or someone like that. I won't have more than two children so I won't ruin my figure."

"I'm only going to have a daughter."

"Misia, do stay on until graduation."

"I want to get married."

Along the same road Misia went for walks with Paweł. By the forest they held hands. Paweł's hand was big and hot. Misia's was small and cold. They turned off the Highway down one of the forest roads, and then Paweł stopped, and with that big, strong hand he drew Misia close to him.

He smelled of soap and sunlight. At this point Misia became rather weak, submissive and limp. The man in the white starched shirt seemed enormous. She barely reached up to his chest. She stopped thinking. It was dangerous. She came to her senses once her breasts were already bare and Paweł's lips were roaming across her belly.

"No," she said.

"You have to marry me."

"I know."

"I'm going to ask for your hand."

"Good."

"When?"

"Soon."

"Will he agree? Will your father agree?"

"There's nothing to agree. I want to marry you and that's all."

"But . . ."

"I love you."

Misia tidied her hair and they went back to the Highway, as if they had never left it.

THE TIME OF MICHAŁ

Michał did not like Paweł. He may have been good looking, but that was all. Whenever Michał looked at his broad shoulders, strong legs in breeches, and shining boots, he felt painfully old and shrunken like a dried-up apple.

Paweł came to their house very often now. He would sit at the table and fold one leg over the other. With her tail tucked under, the bitch Dolly would sniff his polished boots and their tops made of dog skin. He talked about the business he was doing with Kozienicki in the timber trade, about the school for paramedics where he had enrolled, and about his great plans for the future. He looked at Genowefa and smiled the whole time, giving a close, thorough view of his even white teeth. Genowefa was delighted. Paweł brought her small gifts. With a blush on her face she would put the flowers in a vase, as the cellophane rustled on a box of chocolates.

"How naive women are," thought Michał.

He got the impression that his Misia had been written into Paweł Boski's ambitious life plans, like an object. With complete calculation: because she was the only daughter, virtually an only child, because Izydor didn't really count. Because she was going to have a fine dowry, because she was from a wealthier family, because she was so different, elegant, beautifully dressed, delicate.

As if by the way, Michał sometimes spoke in his wife's and daughter's presence of old Boski, who had said maybe a hundred or two hundred words in his life and spent all his time on the manor house roof, and of Paweł's sisters, who were plain and mediocre.

"Old Boski is a decent fellow," Genowefa would say.

"So what, no one's responsible for his siblings," added Misia, looking meaningfully at Izydor. "There's someone like that in every family."

Michał would pretend to be reading the newspaper as his daughter dressed up to go dancing with Paweł on Sunday afternoons. She would spend about an hour preening before the mirror. He saw her fill in her eyebrows with her mother's dark pencil and carefully paint her lips in a furtive way. He saw her standing sideways before the mirror to check the effect of her brassiere, and putting a drop of violet scent behind her ear, her first perfume that she had begged for as a seventeenth birthday present. He said nothing as Genowefa and Izydor looked out of the window after her.

"Paweł has mentioned marriage to me. He said he'd like to propose now," said Genowefa one such Sunday.

Michał refused even to hear her out.

"No. She's still too young. Let's send her to Kielce, to a better school than the one in Taszów."

"She doesn't want to study at all. She wants to get married. Can't you see that?"

Michał shook his head.

"No, no, no. It's still too soon. What does she want a husband and children for? She should enjoy life . . . Where are they going to live? Where's Paweł going to work? He's still at school too, isn't he? No, they've got to wait."

"Wait for what? Until they have to get married in a hurry, urgently?"

That was when Michał thought of the house, that he would build his daughter a big, comfortable house on good land. That he would plant an orchard for it and provide it with cellars and a garden. A big house, so Misia would not have to leave, so they could all live there together. There would be enough rooms in it for everyone, and their windows would look out in all four directions. And it would be a house with foundations made of sandstone and walls made of real brick, which would be kept warm from the outside by the best timber. And it would have a ground floor, a first floor, a loft and cellars, a glazed porch, and a balcony for Misia, so she could watch the procession coming across the fields at Corpus Christi from it. In this house Misia would be able to have lots of children. There would also be a servant's room, because Misia should have domestic help.

Next day he ate his dinner early and went all round Primeval looking for a site for the house. He thought of the Hill. He thought about the common by the White River. All the way he calculated that building such a house would take at least three years, and would delay Misia's marriage by that time.

THE TIME OF FLORENTYNKA

On Easter Saturday Florentynka went off to church with one of her dogs for the blessing of the food. Into her basket she put a jar of the milk that fed her and her dogs, because that was all she had in the house. She covered the jar in fresh horseradish leaves and periwinkles.

In Jeszkotle baskets full of the food to be blessed for the Easter Sunday meal are placed on the side altar of the Virgin Mary of Jeszkotle. It is the woman who should take care of the food — both its preparation and its blessing. God-the-man has more important matters in his head: wars, catastrophes, conquests, and distant journeys . . . Women take care of the food.

So people brought their baskets to the side altar of the Virgin Mary of Jeszkotle and waited on benches for the priest to come and sprinkle holy water. Each person sat at a distance from the next and in silence, because on Easter Saturday the church is dark and hushed like a cave, like a concrete air-raid shelter.

Florentynka went up to the side altar with her dog, whose name was Billygoat. She put her basket down among the other baskets. In the others there was sausage, cake, horseradish with cream, colourful painted eggs, and beautiful white bread. Ah, how hungry Florentynka was, and how hungry her dog was.

Florentynka gazed at the picture of the Virgin Mary of Jeszkotle and saw a smile on her smooth face. Billygoat sniffed at someone's basket and pulled a piece of sausage out of it.

"Here you hang and smile, good Lady, while the dogs eat your gifts," said Florentynka in a hushed tone. "Sometimes it's hard for a person to understand a dog. You, good Lady, surely understand animals and people equally. Surely you even know the thoughts of the moon . . ."

Florentynka sighed.

"I'm going to pray to your husband, and you mind my dog."

She tied the dog to the railing in front of the miraculous icon, among the baskets, over which crocheted napkins had been thrown.

"I'll be back in a moment."

She found herself a place in the front row among the dressed-up women from Jeszkotle. They moved away from her a little and glanced at each other knowingly.

Meanwhile the sacristan, who was meant to keep order in the

church, went up to the side altar of the Virgin Mary of Jeszkotle. First he noticed something moving, but for some time his eyes could not make sense of what they were seeing. When he realised that a hideous great mangy dog had just been rummaging around in the baskets full of food to be blessed, he staggered in indignation and the blood rushed to his face. Horrified by this sacrilege, he leaped forward to drive away the impudent animal. He grabbed the string, and with hands trembling in dismay, undid the knot. Just then he heard a quiet woman's voice coming from the icon:

"Leave that dog alone! I'm minding him for Florentynka from Primeval."

THE TIME OF THE HOUSE

The foundations were dug in a perfect square. Its sides corresponded to the four points of the compass.

First Michał, Paweł Boski and the workmen built the walls out of stone — that was the underpinning — and then out of wooden beams.

Once they had enclosed the cellars, they started talking about the place as a "house," but only once they had built the roof and crowned it with a garland did it become a house for good and proper. For a house starts to exist as soon as its walls enclose a bit of space within them. It is this enclosed space that is the soul of the house.

They spent two years building the house. They hoisted the garland onto the roof in the summer of 1936. They took a photo of themselves in front of the house.

The house had several cellars. One of them had two windows,

and this one was meant to be the basement and the summer kitchen in one. The next cellar had one window — they designated it the closet, laundry, and potato store. The third one had no windows at all — this was to be a storage space in case of need. Under this third one Michał ordered another, fourth little cellar to be dug, small and cold — for ice and goodness knows what else.

The ground floor was high, on stone underpinnings. The way into the ground floor was up steps with a wooden balustrade. There were two entrances. One was from the road, via the porch straight into a large hallway, which led into the rooms. The second entrance led through a vestibule into the kitchen. The kitchen had a large window, and against the wall opposite stood the kitchen stove made of sky-blue tiles that Misia chose in Taszów. The stove was finished with brass fittings and rails. There were three doors in the kitchen: into the biggest room, under the stairs, and into a small room. The ground floor was a ring of rooms. If you opened all the doors, you could walk around it in a circle.

From the hallway a staircase led up to the first floor, where the next four rooms were waiting to be finished.

Above all this there was yet another storey — the loft, which was reached via some narrow, wooden stairs. The loft fascinated little Izydor, because it had windows looking in all four directions.

The outside of the house was covered in boards laid like fish scales. This was old Boski's idea. Old Boski also laid the roof, just as beautiful as the manor house roof. In front of the house there was a lilac tree. It was already growing there before the house existed. Now it was reflected in the windowpanes. A bench was placed under the lilac. People from Primeval stopped there to admire the house. No one in the area had ever built such a fine house before. Squire Popielski also came on horseback and clapped Paweł Boski on the shoulder. Paweł invited him to the wedding.

On Sunday Michał went to fetch the parish priest to come and bless the house. The priest stood on the porch and looked around approvingly.

"What a beautiful house you have built for your daughter," he said.

Michał shrugged.

Finally they began to bring in the furniture. Old Boski made most of it, but there were also pieces brought by horse and cart from Kielce, such as a large grandfather clock, a dresser for the living room, and a round oak table with carved legs.

Misia's eyes grew sad when she looked at the house's surroundings — flat, grey earth covered in dry grass of the kind that grows on fallow ground. So Michał bought a lot of trees for Misia. And in the course of a single day around the house he established something that would one day be an orchard, with apple trees, pears, plums, and walnuts. At the very centre of the orchard he planted twin rennet apples, the tree that grows the fruit that tempted Eve.

THE TIME OF MRS PAPUGA

Stasia Boska lived alone with her father after her mother's death, and after her sisters had gone to live with their husbands and Paweł had married Misia.

It was hard living with old Boski. He was always dissatisfied and quick tempered. Sometimes he thrashed her with something heavy if she was late with his dinner. Then Stasia would go among the currants, crouch among the bushes and cry. She tried to cry quietly, to avoid enraging her father even more.

When Boski found out from his son that Michał Niebieski had bought land to build a house for his daughter, he couldn't sleep. A few days later he scraped together all his savings and bought some land too, right next to Michał's.

He decided to build a house there for Stasia. He spent a long time thinking about it, as he sat on the manor house roof. "If Michał Niebieski can put up a house for his daughter, why can't I, Boski, do the same?" he reflected. "Why shouldn't I build a house, too?"

And Boski started building a house.

He marked out a rectangle on the ground with a stick, and next day began to dig the foundations. Squire Popielski gave him a holiday. It was the first holiday old Boski had ever had. Then Boski fetched large and smaller rocks from the neighbourhood, white chunks of limestone that he arranged evenly in the excavated pits. It took a month. Paweł came to see Boski and lamented over the excavated pits.

"What are you doing, Papa? Where will you get the money? Don't make a fool of yourself by building some henhouse under my nose."

"Big-headed already, are you? I'm building your sister a house."

Paweł knew there was no way of convincing his father, so finally he fetched the planks for him by horse and cart.

Now the houses were rising almost in parallel. One was big and shapely, with large windows and spacious rooms. The other was small, pressed to the ground, hunched, with tiny windows. One stood on an open space, with the forest and River behind it. The other was wedged in between the Highway and the Wola Road, hidden in the currant bushes and wild lilac.

While Boski was busy building the house, Stasia had more peace. By noon she had to feed the animals, and then she got down to making the dinner. First she went to the field, and from the sandy earth she dug up some potatoes. She dreamed she might find treasure under the bushes, jewels wrapped in a rag or a tin full of dollars. Later on as she peeled the small potatoes, she would imagine she was a healer, the potatoes were the sick people who had come to her, and she was removing their illness and cleansing their bodies of all foul matter. Then as she tossed the peeled potatoes into the boiling water she would imagine she was brewing an elixir of beauty, and as soon as she drank it, her life would change once and for all. Some doctor or lawyer from Kielce would see her on the Highway, shower her in gifts and fall in love with her like a princess.

That was why making the dinner took so long.

Imagining is essentially creative; it is a bridge reconciling matter and spirit. Especially when it is done intensely and often. Then the image turns into a drop of matter, and joins the currents of life. Sometimes along the way something in it gets distorted and changes. Therefore, if they are strong enough, all human desires come true — but not always entirely as expected.

One day, when Stasia went outside to pour away the dirty water, she saw a strange man. And it was just as in her dreams. He came up to her and asked the way to Kielce, and she replied. A few hours later he came back and ran into Stasia again, this time with a yoke across her shoulders, so he helped her and they talked for longer. He was not actually a lawyer or a doctor, but a postal worker, employed to install the telephone line from Kielce to Taszów. Stasia found him jolly and self-confident. He arranged to meet her for a walk on Wednesday and for some fun on Saturday. And the amazing thing was that old Boski liked him. The newcomer was called Papuga.

From then on Stasia's life started taking a different course. She bloomed. She spent time in Jeszkotle and went shopping at Szenbert's, and everyone saw Papuga driving her there in a chaise. In the autumn of 1937 Stasia fell pregnant, and at Christmas they were married and she became Mrs Papuga. The modest wedding reception was held in the one room of the newly completed cottage. The next day old Boski put up a wooden wall across the room, and in this way he divided the house in two.

In the summer Stasia gave birth to a son. By now the telephone line went far beyond the boundaries of Primeval. Papuga only appeared on Sundays, when he was tired and demanding. His wife's endearments irritated him, and he was annoyed at having to wait so long for his dinner. Then he only came every other Sunday, and at All Saints he didn't turn up at all. He said he had to visit his parents' graves, and Stasia believed him.

As she waited for him with the Christmas Eve supper, she saw her reflection in the windowpane, which the night had made into a mirror, and realised Papuga had gone for good.

THE TIME OF MISIA'S ANGEL

As Misia was giving birth to her first child, the angel showed her Jerusalem.

Misia was lying in bed in her bedroom between white sheets, amid a scent of floors scrubbed with lye, shielded from the sun by grosgrain lily-pattern curtains. The doctor from Jeszkotle was there, and a nurse, and Genowefa, and Paweł, who kept sterilising all sorts of instruments, and the angel, whom no one could see.

Everything was muddled in Misia's head. She was tired. The pains came suddenly, and she couldn't cope with them. She drifted into a sleep, a half-sleep, a waking dream. She imagined she was as tiny as a coffee bean and was falling into the funnel of a grinder as vast as the manor house. Down she fell into the black abyss, and landed in the grinding machinery. It hurt. Her body was being turned into dust.

The angel could see Misia's thoughts and felt for her body, though it could not understand what the pain was really like. So for a brief moment it took Misia's soul away to a completely different place, and showed her Jerusalem.

Misia saw vast stretches of a tawny desert that undulated as if it were in motion. In a gentle depression in this sea of sand lay a city. It was circular. Around it there were stone walls, in which stood four gates. The first gate was the Milk Gate, the second Honey, the third Wine, and the fourth Olive Oil. From each gate a single road led into the middle. Along the first oxen were being driven, along the second lions were being led, along the third falcons were being carried, and along the fourth people were walking. Misia found herself in the middle of the city, where on a cobbled marketplace stood the Saviour's house. She was standing outside his door.

To her surprise, someone knocked from the inside, and Misia asked: "Who's there?" "It's me," replied a voice. "Come in," she said. Then the Lord Jesus came out to her and hugged her to his chest. Misia could smell the scent of the cloth in which he was dressed. The Lord Jesus and the entire world loved her.

But at this point Misia's angel, who was paying close attention all the time, took her from the arms of the Lord Jesus and threw her back into her child-bearing body. Misia sighed and gave birth to a son.

During the first autumn full moon Cornspike dug up the roots of herbs — soapwort, comfrey, coriander, chicory, and marshmallow. There were lots of them growing by the ponds in Primeval. So Cornspike would take her daughter with her, and they would walk by night through the forest and village.

One day as they were passing Maybug Hill, they saw a hunched female figure surrounded by dogs. The silver moonlight was making the tops of all their heads white.

Cornspike headed towards the woman, pulling Ruta after her. They went up to the old woman. The dogs began to growl anxiously.

"Florentynka," said Cornspike softly.

The woman turned to face them. Her eyes were faded, as if rinsed out. Her face was like a shrivelled apple. A skinny grey plait lay on her thin shoulders.

They sat on the ground next to the old woman. They started gazing, as she was, at the great, round, self-satisfied face of the moon.

"He took my children, he fooled my old man, and now he's muddled my senses," complained Florentynka.

Cornspike sighed heavily and stared into the face of the moon.

One of the dogs suddenly began to howl.

"I had a dream," said Cornspike. "The moon knocked at my windows and said: 'You haven't got a mother, Cornspike, and your daughter hasn't got a grandmother, is that right?' 'Yes,' I replied. And then he said: 'In the village there is a good, lonely woman, whom I once wronged, I don't even know why any more. She hasn't any children or grandchildren. Go to her and tell her to forgive me. I am old now and I have a weak mind.' That's what he said. And then he added: 'You'll find her on the Hill, that's where she curses me, every month when I appear to the world in my complete form.' Then I asked him: 'Why do you want her to forgive you? What do you need a human being's forgiveness for?' And he replied: 'Because human suffering carves dark furrows on my face. One day I'll be extinguished by human pain.' That's what he told me, so here I am."

Florentynka stared piercingly into Cornspike's eyes.

"Is that the truth?"

"It is. The pure truth."

"He wanted me to forgive him?"

"Yes."

"And for you to be my daughter, and her my granddaughter?"

"That's what he told me."

Florentynka raised her face to the sky and something shone in her pale eyes.

"Granny, what's the big dog's name?" asked little Ruta.

"Billygoat."

"Billygoat?"

"Yes. Give him a pat."

Ruta cautiously held out her hand and put it on the dog's head.

"He's my cousin. He's very wise," said Florentynka, and Cornspike saw tears running down her wrinkled cheeks.

"The moon is just a mask for the sun. He puts it on when he comes out at night to keep an eye on the world. The moon has a short memory, he can't remember what happened a month ago. He gets everything mixed up. Forgive him, Florentynka."

Florentynka sighed deeply.

"I forgive him. Both he and I are old, why should we have to quarrel?" she said quietly. "I forgive you, you old fool!" she shouted into the sky.

Cornspike began to laugh, laughing louder and louder, until the dogs woke up and leaped to their feet. Florentynka started laughing, too. She stood up, spread her arms, and raised them into the sky.

"I forgive you, Moon. I forgive you for all the wrong you have done me!" she cried, loud and shrill.

Suddenly, from out of nowhere, from over the Black River a breeze sprang up and ruffled the old woman's grey locks. A light came on in one of the houses and a man's voice shouted:

"Shut up, woman! We're trying to sleep."

"So go to sleep, sleep yourselves to death!" shouted Cornspike over her shoulder in reply. "Why on earth were you born if you're only going to sleep?"

THE TIME OF RUTA

"Don't go to the village, or you'll get into trouble," Cornspike would say to her daughter. "Sometimes I think they're all drunk there — they're so slow and lumbering. They only liven up when something goes wrong."

But Ruta felt drawn to Primeval. There was a mill there, and a miller and his wife, there were poor farmhands, there was Cherubin, who pulled teeth with pincers. There were children running about, just like her. Or at least they looked the same. And there were houses with green shutters, and white linen drying on the fences, which was the whitest thing in Ruta's world.

As she walked through the village with her mother, Ruta could feel everyone looking at them. The women shaded their eyes from the sun, and the men furtively spat. Her mother took no notice, but Ruta was afraid of their glances. She tried to keep as close to her mother as she could, squeezing her big hand as tightly as possible.

In the evenings, in summer, when the bad people were already sitting at home busy with their own affairs, Ruta liked to go to the edge of the village and gaze at the solid grey cottages and the bright smoke from their chimneys. Later, once she had grown a bit, she felt brave enough to creep right up to their windows and peep inside. At the Serafins' there were always small children crawling about the floorboards. Ruta could watch them for hours, as they stopped over a little bit of wood, tasted it on their tongues, and turned it over in their chubby paws — she watched as they put various objects in their mouths and sucked them, as if it were candy, or crawled under the table and spent ages staring in wonder at the wooden table sky.

Finally the people would put their children to bed, and then Ruta would inspect all the things they collected: dishes, pots, knives and forks, curtains, holy pictures, clocks, tapestries, flowers in pots, frames with photos, patterned oilskin tablecloths, bedspreads, baskets, all those little objects that make people's houses unique. She knew all the objects in the village and she knew whom they belonged to. Only Florentynka had white net curtains. The Malaks had a set of nickel cutlery. Young Miss Cherubin crocheted beautiful cushions. At the Serafins' there was a huge picture on the wall of Jesus teaching from a boat. Only the Boskis had green bedspreads with roses on them, and later, when their house right by the forest was almost ready, they started bringing real treasures into it.

Ruta took a liking to this house. It was the biggest and the most beautiful. It had a sloping roof with a lightning conductor and windows in the roof, it had a real balcony and a glazed porch, and there was also a second, kitchen entrance. Ruta found herself a place to sit in a large lilac tree, from where she could watch the Boskis' house in the evenings. She saw a soft, new carpet being laid in the biggest room, as gorgeous as the floor of an autumn forest. She was sitting in the lilac when the big grandfather clock was carried in, with its heart swinging this way and that, measuring out the time — the clock must have been a living creature, because it moved of its own accord. She saw the toys belonging to the little boy, Misia's first son, and then the cradle that was bought for the next child.

And only once she was familiar with each thing, right down to the smallest object in the Boskis' new house, did she turn her attention to the boy her own age. The lilac tree wasn't tall enough to let her see what the boy was doing in his room in the loft. She knew he was Izydor and that he wasn't like other children. She didn't know if that was good or bad. He had a big head and his mouth hung open, letting saliva dribble onto his chin. He was as tall and thin as a reed in the pond.

One evening Izydor caught Ruta by the foot as she sat in the lilac tree. She pulled free of him and ran away. But a few days later she came back, and he was waiting for her. She made room for him next to her among the branches. They sat there all evening and didn't say a word. Izydor watched life going on in his new home. He saw people moving their lips, without hearing what they were saying. He saw them wandering in confusion from room to room, into the kitchen and into the pantry. He saw little Antek crying soundlessly.

Ruta and Izydor liked being silent together in the tree.

Now they started meeting every day. They would disappear from people's sight. They would go through a hole in the fence into Malak's field and walk down the Wola Road towards the forest. Ruta picked plants from the roadside verge: carob pods, goosefoot, oregano, and sorrel. She shoved them under Izydor's nose for him to sniff.

"You can eat this. And this. This one, too."

From the road they watched the Black River, a shining fissure right down the middle of the green valley. Then they passed a milkcap copse, dark, smelling of mushrooms, and went into the forest.

"Let's not wander off too far," protested Izydor at first, but then he put himself entirely in Ruta's hands.

It was always warm and soft in the forest, like in the velvet-lined box where Michał's medal was kept. Wherever you lay down, the bed of pine needles on the forest floor would sag gently, making a hollow that fitted the body perfectly. Above was the sky, overtopped by the tips of the pine trees. It was fragrant.

Ruta had lots of ideas. They played hide-and-seek and tag, pretended to be trees and made various figures out of twigs, sometimes as small as a hand, sometimes large, taking up a patch of the forest. In summer they found whole clearings yellow with chanterelles and examined sedate mushroom families.

Ruta loved fungi more than plants and animals. She described how the real mushroom kingdom is hidden under the earth, where the sun doesn't reach. She said that only mushrooms that are condemned to death or exiled from the kingdom as a punishment come out onto the earth's surface. Here they perish from the sun, at the hand of man, or trodden by animals. The real underground mushroom spawn is immortal.

In the autumn Ruta's eyes became yellow and piercing like a bird's, and then she would go mushroom hunting. She would say even less than usual, and Izydor thought she seemed absent. She knew all the spots where the spawn came out onto the earth's surface, where it extended its tentacles into the world. When she found a penny bun or a birch bolete, she lay down next to it on the ground and spent a long time examining it before venturing to pick it. But Ruta loved amanitas best of all. She knew all their favourite glades. There were the most amanitas in the birch wood on the other side of the Highway. That year, when the divine presence was especially clearly felt in all Primeval, the amanitas appeared at the beginning of July and covered the birch glades in their red caps. Ruta skipped among them, but being careful not to destroy them. Then she lay down in between them and peeped under their red dresses.

"Watch out, they're poisonous," Izydor warned her, but Ruta laughed.

She showed Izydor various amanitas, not just red ones, but white, greenish, or the kind that imitate other mushrooms, horse mushrooms for example.

"My Mama eats them."

"You're lying, they're deadly poison," said Izydor resentfully.

"They don't hurt my Mama. I'll be able to eat them one day, too."

"All right, all right. Watch out for the white ones. They're the worst."

Ruta's courage impressed Izydor. But just looking at the mushrooms wasn't enough for him. He wanted to know more about them. In Misia's cookbook he found a whole chapter devoted to them. On one page there were drawings of edible mushrooms, and on another inedible and poisonous ones. Next time he took the book to the forest under his sweater and showed Ruta the drawings. She didn't believe it.

"Read what's written here," he said, pointing to the caption under the amanita. "*Amanita muscaria*. Fly agaric."

"How do you know that's written there?"

"I put the letters together."

"What's that letter?"

"A."

"A? Is that all? Just a?"

"That's em."

"Em."

"And that sort of half em is en."

"Teach me to read, Izydor."

So Izydor taught Ruta to read. First from Misia's cookbook, then he brought an old calendar. Ruta quickly caught on to learning, but she also got bored quickly. By the autumn Izydor had taught her almost as much as he knew himself.

One day, as he was waiting for her in the milkcap copse, leafing through the calendar, a large shadow fell across the white pages. Izydor looked up and was horrified. There behind Ruta stood her mother. She was bare-footed and large.

"Don't be afraid of me. I know you very well," she said.

Izydor didn't reply.

"You're a clever boy." She knelt down beside him and touched his head. "You have a good heart. You'll go far in your journeys."

Swiftly and surely she pulled him towards her and hugged him to her breast. Izydor was paralysed by numbness or fear, and stopped thinking, as if he had fallen asleep.

Then Ruta's mother went away. Ruta poked in the earth with a stick.

"She likes you. She's always asking about you."

"About me?"

"You have no idea how strong she is. She can lift huge stones."

"No woman can be stronger than a man," said Izydor, who had woken up now.

"She knows all the secrets."

"If she were how you say she is, you wouldn't be living in a tumbledown cottage in the forest, but on the market square in Jeszkotle. You'd go about in shoes and dresses, you'd have hats and rings. Then she'd really be important."

Ruta lowered her head.

"I'll show you something, though it's a secret."

They went beyond Wydymacz, passed the young oak wood, and were walking through a birch copse. Izydor had never been here before. They must have been very far from home.

Suddenly Ruta stopped.

"It's here."

Izydor looked about in surprise. There were birch trees growing around them. The wind was rustling in their slender branches.

"This is the boundary of Primeval," said Ruta, stretching her hand out ahead.

Izydor didn't understand.

"This is where Primeval ends, there's nothing beyond here."

"What do you mean? What about Wola, Taszów, and Kielce? The road to Kielce must be somewhere near here."

"There's no Kielce, and Wola and Taszów belong to Primeval. This is where it all ends."

Izydor burst out laughing and spun on his heel.

"What sort of nonsense are you talking? Some people go to Kielce, you know. My father goes there. They brought Misia's furniture from Kielce. Paweł's been to Kielce. My father's been to Russia."

"They all just thought they were there. They set off on a journey, they reach the boundary, and here they come to a standstill. Maybe they dream they're travelling onwards, that Kielce or Russia are there. My mother once showed me some of those who looked like they'd turned to stone. They stand on the road to Kielce. They don't move, their eyes are open and they look terrible. As if they're dead. Then, after a while, they wake up and go home, and they take their dreams for memories. That's what really happens."

"Now I'll show you something!" cried Izydor.

He stepped back a few paces and started running towards the spot where, according to Ruta, the boundary ran. Then he suddenly stopped. He himself did not know why. Something here wasn't right. He stretched his hands out ahead of him, and his fingertips disappeared.

Izydor felt as if he had split inside into two different boys. One of them was standing with his hands held out ahead, and they clearly lacked any fingertips. The other boy was next to him, and couldn't see the first boy, or moreover his lack of fingers. Izydor was both boys at once.

"Izydor," said Ruta. "Let's go home."

He came to and put his hands in his pockets. Gradually his duality disappeared. They set off for home.

"The boundary runs just beyond Taszów, beyond Wola, and beyond the Kotuszów tollbooth. But no one knows exactly. The boundary can give birth to ready-made people, and we think they've come from somewhere. What I find most frightening is that it's impossible to get out of here. As if we're sitting in a pot."

Izydor didn't say a word the whole way. Only when they came onto the Highway did he say:

"We could pack a rucksack, take some food, and set off along the boundary to investigate it. Maybe there's a hole somewhere."

Ruta jumped over an anthill and turned back to the forest.

"Don't worry about it, Izydor. What do we need any other worlds for?"

Izydor saw her dress flashing among the trees, and then the girl vanished.

It is strange that God, who is beyond the limits of time, manifests Himself within time and its transformations. If you don't know "where" God is — and people sometimes ask such questions — you have to look at everything that changes and moves, that doesn't fit into a shape, that fluctuates and disappears: the surface of the sea, the dances of the sun's corona, earthquakes, the continental drift, snows melting and glaciers moving, rivers flowing to the sea, seeds germinating, the wind that sculpts mountains, a foetus developing in its mother's belly, wrinkles near the eyes, a body decaying in the grave, wines maturing, or mushrooms growing after a rain.

God is present in every process. God is vibrating in every transformation. Now He is there, now there is less of Him, but sometimes He is not there at all, because God manifests Himself even in the fact that He is not there.

People — who themselves are in fact a process — are afraid of whatever is impermanent and always changing, which is why they have invented something that doesn't exist — invariability, and recognised that whatever is eternal and unchanging is perfect. So they have ascribed invariability to God, and that was how they lost the ability to understand Him.

In the summer of 1939 God was in everything all around, so rare and unusual things happened.

At the beginning of time God created all possible things, but He Himself is the God of impossible things, things that either do not happen at all, or happen very rarely.

God appeared in blueberries the size of plums that ripened in the sun just below Cornspike's house. Cornspike picked the ripest one, wiped the dark blue skin on her handkerchief, and saw another world reflected in it. The sky there was dark, almost black, the sun was hazy and distant, the forests looked like clusters of bare sticks driven into the earth, and the Earth, drunken and reeling, was suffering from holes. People were slipping off it into a black abyss. Cornspike ate the ominous blueberry and tasted its sour flavour on her tongue. She realised she must stock up for the winter, storing more food than ever before.

Now every morning Cornspike dragged Ruta from bed at dawn, and together they went to the forest and brought all sorts of riches home from it — baskets of mushrooms, churns of strawberries and blueberries, young hazelnuts, bilberries, dogwood, barberry, bird cherry, elderberry, hawthorn and sea-buckthorn. They spent days drying it all in the sun and the shade, and watched anxiously to see if the sun was still shining as before.

God also worried Cornspike physically. He was present within her breasts, which suddenly and miraculously filled with milk. When people found out about it, they secretly came to Cornspike and placed sick parts of their bodies under her nipples, and she squirted a white stream on them. The milk cured young Krasny's eye infection, the warts on Franek Serafin's hands, Florentynka's ulcer, and a skin rash on a Jewish child from Jeszkotle.

Everyone who was cured was killed during the war. That is how God manifests Himself.

THE TIME OF SQUIRE POPIELSKI

God manifested Himself to Squire Popielski through the Game the little rabbi had given him. The squire tried over and over to start the Game, but he found it hard to understand all the bizarre instructions. He took out the little book and read the rules until he knew them just about by heart. To start the Game, you had to throw a one, but every time he tried the squire threw an eight. It was contrary to all the principles of probability, and the squire thought he had been cheated. The strange, eight-sided die could have been distorted. But as he wanted to play honestly, he had to wait until the next day — those were the rules of the Game — to have another throw. And once again he was unsuccessful. This went on all spring. The squire's amusement changed into impatience. In the unsettled summer of 1939 the stubborn number one finally appeared, and Squire Popielski could breathe again. The Game had started.

Now he needed a lot of spare time, peace and quiet — the Game was absorbing. It demanded concentration even during the day when he wasn't playing it. In the evenings he shut himself in the library, laid out the board, and spent a long time rolling the eight-sided die in his hands. Or he carried out the Game's instructions. It annoyed him to be wasting such a lot of time, but he couldn't stop.

"There's going to be a war," said his wife.

"There are no wars in the civilized world," he replied.

"Indeed, there might not be any in the civilized world, but there is going to be a war here. The Pełskis are leaving for America."

On hearing the word "America" Squire Popielski fidgeted nervously, but nothing had the same meaning as it had before — before the Game.

In August the squire enrolled for conscription, but he was discharged in view of his state of health. In September they listened to the radio until it started to speak in German. In the night the squire's wife buried the silver in the park. The squire spent whole nights sitting over the Game.

"They didn't even fight. They came home. Paweł Boski didn't

even pick up a weapon," wept the squire's wife. "We've lost, Felix."

He nodded pensively.

"Felix, we've lost the war!"

"Leave me in peace," he said and went into the library.

Every day the Game revealed something new to him, something he didn't know and hadn't sensed. How was it possible?

One of the first instructions was to dream. To move on to the next square, the squire had to dream he was a dog. "How bizarre," he thought in disgust. But he went to bed, thought about dogs, and that he himself could be a dog. In these visions before falling asleep he imagined himself as a dog, a hound that hunts waterfowl and chases around the common land. But in the night his dreams did what they wanted. It was hard to stop being a man in them. A certain degree of progress appeared with a dream about the ponds. Squire Popielski dreamed he was an olive-green carp. He was swimming in green water, where the sun was nothing but blurred light. He had no wife, he had no manor house, nothing belonged to him and nothing mattered to him. It was a beautiful dream.

That day, when the Germans turned up at his manor house, at dawn the squire finally dreamed he was a dog. He was running about the market square in Jeszkotle looking for something, he himself did not know what. He dug up some food scraps from under Szenbert's shop and ate them with relish. He was attracted to the smell of horse manure and human faeces in the bushes. Fresh blood smelled like ambrosia.

The squire woke up amazed. "It's irrational, quite absurd," he thought, but he was pleased the Game would be able to move onwards.

The Germans were very polite. Captain Gropius and another

one. The squire came out of the house to meet them. He tried to keep his distance.

"I understand you," Captain Gropius interpreted the sour look on his face. "Unfortunately we are here before you as invaders, an occupying force. But we are civilized people."

They wanted to buy a lot of wood. Squire Popielski said he would take care of supplying the wood, but deep down he had no intention of tearing himself away from the Game. At that the entire conversation between the occupants and the occupied came to an end. The squire went back to the Game. He was glad he had already been a dog, and now he could move onto the next square.

That night the squire dreamed he was reading the instructions for the Game. The words jumped before his sleeping vision, because the part of the squire that was dreaming was not a fluent reader.

The Second World was made by the young God. He did not yet have experience, and so in this world everything is faded and indistinct, and things crumble to dust more quickly. War goes on eternally. People are born, love desperately, and soon die of sudden death, which is everywhere. But the more suffering life brings them, the more they want to live.

Primeval does not exist. It has not even come into being, because hordes of starving troops are constantly trailing from east to west across the land where someone might have founded it. Nothing has a name. The earth is full of bomb holes, both rivers, sick and wounded, churn their turbid water, and it is hard to tell them apart. Stones fall apart in the fingers of hungry children.

In this world Cain met Abel in the field and said: "There is no law and no judge! There is no world beyond, no reward for the righteous and no punishment for the evildoers. This world was not created in good grace, it is not governed by sympathy. For why was your sacrifice accepted and mine rejected?" Abel replied: "Mine was accepted because I love God, and yours was rejected because you hate Him. People like you should not exist at all." And Abel killed Cain.

THE TIME OF KURT

Kurt saw Primeval from the lorry that brought the Wehrmacht soldiers. For Kurt, Primeval was no different from the other foreign villages they had passed in this foreign, enemy country. And the villages were not much different from the ones he knew from his holidays. They may have had narrower streets, poorer houses, funny lopsided wooden fences, and whitewashed walls. Kurt was no expert on villages. He came from a big city and he missed it. He had left his wife and daughter in the city.

They did not try to set up billets in the peasant houses. They requisitioned Cherubin's orchard and started building themselves wooden barracks. One of them was going to house the kitchen, which Kurt ran. Captain Gropius took him by jeep to Jeszkotle and the manor house, to Kotuszów and the neighbouring villages. They bought wood, cows, and eggs for prices they set themselves — very low, or else they didn't pay at all. This was when Kurt saw the defeated enemy country close up, came eye to eye with it. He saw baskets of eggs brought out of cubbyholes, with streaks of hen's droppings on the creamy-white shells, and the hostile, malevolent glances of the peasants. He saw ungainly, scrawny cows and admired the affection with which they were tended. He saw hens scratching in heaps of manure, apples dried in attics, round loaves baked once a month, bare-foot, blue-eyed children whose shrill voices reminded him of his daughter. But it was all alien to him. Maybe because of the primitive, harsh language they spoke here, maybe because the facial features were strange. Sometimes, when Captain Gropius sighed and said this entire country should be razed to the ground and a new order built on this spot, Kurt thought the captain was right. It would be cleaner and nicer here. At other times, the unbearable thought occurred to him that he should go home and leave these stretches of sandy ground, these people, cows, and baskets of eggs in peace. At night he dreamed of his wife's smooth, fair body, and in the dream everything smelled safe and familiar, completely different from here.

"Look, Kurt," said Captain Gropius, when they went on their next expedition for supplies. "Look what a big work force there is here, what a lot of space and land. Look at these stout rivers of theirs. You could set up hydroelectric power stations instead of these primitive mills, bring in power lines, build factories and get them to work at last. Look at them, Kurt, they're not so bad after all. I even like the Slavs. Do you know that the name of this race comes from the Latin word *sclavus*, a servant? This is a nation with servility in its blood . . ."

Kurt wasn't listening to him properly. He was feeling homesick.

They took everything they could lay their hands on. Sometimes when they entered a cottage, Kurt got the impression the people there had only just finished hiding the food. Then Captain Gropius would draw his pistol and shout angrily:

"Confiscation for the needs of the Wehrmacht!"

At such moments Kurt felt like a thief.

In the evenings he would pray "that I won't have to go further east. That I can stay here, and then take the same road home. That the war will end."

Gradually Kurt got used to this foreign land. He knew more or less where each farmer lived, and even acquired a taste for their peculiar names, as he had for the local carp. As he liked animals, he had all the kitchen leftovers taken to their neighbour's house — she was a skinny old woman with at least a dozen emaciated dogs. Eventually he got the old woman to greet him by smiling at him toothlessly and in silence. The children from the last, new house by the forest also came to see him. The boy was a little older than the girl. They both had very fair hair, almost white, like his daughter's. The little girl raised a chubby arm and mumbled:

"Hi-hitla!"

Kurt gave them some sweets. The soldiers on guard duty smiled.

At the beginning of 1943 Captain Gropius was sent to the Eastern Front. He clearly hadn't been saying his evening prayers. Kurt was promoted, but he wasn't at all pleased. Promotion was a dangerous thing now — it distanced you from home. It was harder and harder to get supplies, and every day Kurt travelled around the local villages with a unit of men. In the voice of Captain Gropius he said:

"Confiscation for the needs of the Wehrmacht!" and took away whatever could be taken.

His men helped the SS troops to pacify the Jews from Jeszkotle. Kurt oversaw the loading onto trucks. He was sorry, though he knew they were going to a place that was better for them. He found it unpleasant when they had to seek out Jewish runaways in cellars and attics, chase terror-crazed women around the common and tear their children from their arms. He gave orders to shoot at them, because there was no other way. He fired, too; he didn't wriggle out of it. The Jews refused to board the trucks, they ran away and shouted. He preferred not to dwell on it. After all, there was a war on. In the evenings he prayed "that I won't have to go east from here, that I can stay here to the end of the war. God, make it so they don't take me to the Eastern Front." And God heeded his prayers.

In the spring of 1944 Kurt received an order to transfer everything to Kotuszów, one village further west, one village nearer home. It was said that the Bolsheviks were coming, though Kurt couldn't believe it. Then, once they had all their belongings packed on trucks, Kurt survived a Russian raid, when the German garrisons at Taszów were bombarded. Several bombs hit the ponds. One hit the barn belonging to the old woman with the dogs. The maddened dogs went running around the Hill. Kurt's soldiers started shooting. Kurt didn't try to stop them. It wasn't them shooting. It was their terror, in a foreign country, and their homesickness. It was their fear of death. Infuriated by terror, the dogs lunged at the loaded trucks and bit the rubber tires. The soldiers aimed at them straight between the eyes. The force of the shots sent the dogs' bodies flying, and it looked as if they were turning somersaults. Splashes of dark blood appeared as they did back flips in slow motion. Kurt saw his familiar old lady run out of her house and try to drag away the live dogs. She picked up the wounded ones and carried them to the orchard. Her grey apron abruptly went red. She was shouting something that Kurt couldn't understand. As the commander he should have stopped the stupid shooting, but the sudden thought possessed him that here he was witnessing the end of the world, and that he belonged to the angels that have to cleanse the world of dirt and sin. That something had to end, in order for something new to begin. That it was dreadful, but it had to be like that. That there was no turning back, that this world was condemned to death.

And then Kurt shot the old woman, who had always smiled at him in greeting, toothlessly and in silence.

The troops from the entire district assembled in Kotuszów. They occupied any buildings that had survived the air raids and built an observation point. Now Kurt's task was the observation of Primeval. As a result, despite the move, Kurt was still in the village.

Now he saw Primeval from a certain distance, above the line of the forest and the river, as a community of scattered cottages. He also had a fairly precise view of the new house by the forest, where the fair-haired children lived.

In late summer Kurt saw the Bolsheviks through his binoculars. The size of peas, their vehicles were gliding along ominously in total silence. Kurt thought it looked like an invasion of small, lethally dangerous insects. He shuddered.

From August to the next January he watched Primeval several times a day. In this time he came to know every tree, every path, and every house. He could see the lime trees on the Highway and Maybug Hill, the meadows, the forest, and the copses. He could see people abandoning the village on carts and disappearing beyond the wall of the forest. He could see single, nighttime robbers, who looked like werewolves from a distance. He could see how day by day, hour by hour, the Bolsheviks were amassing more and more troops and equipment. Sometimes they fired at each other, not to do any harm — the time had not yet come — but to remind each other of their presence.

After dusk he drew maps and transferred Primeval to paper. He enjoyed doing it, because, amazingly, he was starting to miss Primeval. He even thought of how, once the world was cleansed of all the mess, he could fetch his two women and settle here, farm carp and run the mill.

As God could read Kurt's thoughts like a map and was in the habit of fulfilling his wishes, He allowed him to stay in Primeval forever. He set aside for him one of those single, random bullets that they say are carried by God.

Before the people from Primeval dared to bury the corpses left after the January offensive, spring had set in, and so no one recognised Kurt in the decaying corpse of a German soldier. He was buried in an alder grove right by the priest's meadows and lies there to this day.

THE TIME OF GENOWEFA

Genowefa was washing her white linen in the Black River. Her hands were going numb with cold. She raised them high towards the sun. Between her fingers she could see Jeszkotle. She saw four army trucks drive past Saint Roch's chapel and enter the market square. Then they disappeared behind the chestnut trees by the church. As she plunged her hands into the water again, she heard shots. The current tore the sheet from her grip as the single shots changed into a rattle, and Genowefa's heart began to pound. She ran along the riverbank, chasing the drifting white cloth, until it disappeared around a bend.

A cloud of smoke appeared over Jeszkotle. Genowefa stood helplessly on the spot, which was equidistant to her home, to the bucket full of linen, and to burning Jeszkotle. She thought of Misia and the children. Her mouth went dry as she ran to fetch the bucket.

"Virgin Mary of Jeszkotle, Virgin Mary of Jeszkotle . . ." she repeated over and over, glancing in despair at the church on the other side of the river. It was still there as before.

The trucks drove onto the common land. Soldiers poured out of one and formed a double file. Then the others appeared, their tarpaulin covers flapping. A column of people emerged from the shadow of the chestnut trees. They were running, stumbling and getting up, carrying suitcases and pushing barrows. The soldiers started pushing the people into the vehicles. It was all happening so quickly that Genowefa couldn't comprehend the events she was witnessing. She raised a hand to her eyes because the setting sun was dazzling her, and only then did she see old Szlomo in an unbuttoned gabardine, the Gertzes' and Kindels' fair-haired children, Mrs Szenbert in a sky-blue dress, her daughter carrying a baby, and the little rabbi, who was being held up by the arms. And she saw Eli, as clear as day, holding his son by the hand. And then there was some confusion and the crowd broke through the line of soldiers. People started running in all directions, and those who were already in the trucks jumped out of them. From the corner of her eye Genowefa saw fire emerging from the barrels, then at once she was deafened by the thunder of multiple bursts of machine-gun fire. The figure of a man, from which she had not dropped her gaze, staggered and fell, just like others, like most of the others. Genowefa dropped the bucket and waded into the river. The current tugged at her skirt and tried to trip her feet. The machine guns fell silent, as if they were exhausted.

Once Genowefa was on the other bank of the Black River, one loaded truck was already driving towards the road. People were silently getting into another one. She saw them giving each other a helping hand. One of the soldiers was finishing off the people lying there with single shots. The next truck set off.

A figure got up from the ground and tried to run towards the river. Genowefa knew at once that it was Rachela, the Szenberts' daughter, Misia's friend. She was carrying a baby. One of the soldiers knelt down and unhurriedly aimed at the girl. She tried to dodge awkwardly. The soldier fired and Rachela stopped. For a moment she rocked sideways, and then fell. Genowefa watched as the soldier ran up to her and turned her on her back with his foot. Then he fired into the white bunting and went back to the trucks.

Genowefa's legs gave way beneath her, so she had to kneel down.

Once the trucks had driven off, she struggled to get up and walk across the common land. Her legs were heavy, like stone, refusing to obey her. Her wet skirt kept dragging her to the ground.

Eli was lying nestled into the grass. For the first time in many years Genowefa saw him close up once more. She sat down beside him, and never stood on her own legs again.

THE TIME OF THE SZENBERTS

The next night Michał woke Paweł, and the two of them went off somewhere. Misia could not go back to sleep. She thought she could hear shots, faraway, anonymous, sinister. Her mother was lying still on the bed with her eyes open. Misia checked to see if she was breathing.

At dawn the men came back with some people. They led them down to the cellar and locked it.

"They'll kill us all," she said into Paweł's ear when he came back to bed. "They'll stand us against the wall and burn down the house."

"It's the Szenberts' son-in-law and his sister and her children. No one else survived," he replied.

In the morning Misia went down to the cellar with some food. She opened the door and said "Good day." She saw them all: a stout woman, a teenage boy, and a little girl. She didn't know them. But she knew the Szenberts' son-in-law, Rachela's husband. He was standing with his back to her, monotonously banging his head against the wall.

"What's going to happen to us?" asked the woman.

"I don't know," replied Misia.

They lived in the fourth, darkest cellar until Easter. Only once did the woman and her daughter come upstairs to bathe. Misia helped the woman to comb her long black hair. Michał went down to them each evening with food and maps. On the second day of the holiday he took them to Taszów by night.

A few days later he was standing by the fence with Krasny, the neighbour. They were talking about the Russkies, and the reports that they weren't far off. Michał didn't ask about the Krasnys' son, who was in the partisans. No one spoke about that. Right at the end, Krasny turned around and said:

"The news is there are some murdered Jews lying by the road to Taszów."

THE TIME OF MICHAŁ

In the summer of 1944 the Russians arrived from Taszów. All day they trailed along the Highway. Everything was covered in dust: their trucks, tanks, guns, wagons, and rifles, their uniforms, hair, and faces — they looked as if they'd emerged from under the ground, as if a fairy-tale army put to sleep in the lands of the ruler of the East had risen again.

People lined up along the road and joyfully greeted the head of the column. The soldiers' faces didn't respond. Their gazes travelled indifferently across the faces of their welcomers. The soldiers had bizarre uniforms, overcoats with ragged hems, from under which there was the occasional flash of a surprising colour — magenta trousers, the black of evening-dress waistcoats, and the gold of trophy watches.

Michał wheeled Genowefa's Bath chair onto the porch.

"Where are the children? Michał, fetch the children," Genowefa kept mumbling.

Michał went out beyond the fence and seized Antek and Adelka tightly by the hand. His heart was pounding.

He was seeing not this, but that other war. Once again the vast stretches of the country he had once crossed appeared before his eyes. It must have been a dream, because only in dreams does everything keep recurring like a refrain. He kept dreaming the same dream, vast, silent and terrible, like columns of troops, like explosions muffled by pain.

"Granddad, when's the Polish army coming?" asked Adelka, raising a flag she had made from a stick and a rag.

He took it away from her and threw it into the lilac tree, then took the children home. He sat down by the kitchen window and gazed at Kotuszów and Papiernia, where the Germans were still stationed. He realised that the Wola Road was now the front line. Exactly.

Izydor came rushing into the kitchen.

"Papa, come quickly! Some officers have stopped here and they want to talk to you. Come now!"

Michał went stiff. He let Izydor lead the way down the front steps. He saw Misia, Genowefa, the Krasnys from next door, and a small group of children from all over Primeval. In the middle stood an open-topped army car with two men sitting in it. A third was talking to Paweł. As usual, Paweł looked as if he understood everything. When he saw his father-in-law, he livened up.

"This is our father. He knows your language. He fought in your army."

"In our army?" said the Russian in amazement.

Michał saw the man's face and felt himself flush. His heart was in his throat, beating fast. He knew he had to say something now, but his tongue was tied. He turned it in his mouth like a hot potato, trying to make it form some words, if only the simplest, but he knew nothing, he had forgotten.

The young officer stared at him in curiosity. The black hem of a tailcoat was sticking out from under his soldier's greatcoat. A joyful glint appeared in his slanting eyes.

"Well, Father, what's up with you? What's up with you?" he said in Russian.

Michał felt as if all this, the slant-eyed officer, this road, these columns of dusty soldiers, all this had already happened before, that even the "what's up with you?" had happened before. He felt as if time had gone into a spin. He was seized with horror.

"My name is Mikhail Jozefovich Niebieski," he said, his voice trembling, in perfect Russian.

THE TIME OF IZYDOR

The young, slant-eyed officer was called Ivan Mukta. He was adjutant to a gloomy lieutenant with blood-shot eyes.

"The lieutenant likes your house. It'll be his quarters," he said cheerfully in Russian, and took the lieutenant's things into the house. As he did so, he pulled faces that made the children laugh, but not Izydor.

Izydor took a close look at him and thought here he was seeing someone truly foreign. Although they were evil, the Germans looked the same as the people from Primeval. If it weren't for the uniforms, it would be impossible to tell them apart. The same went for the Jews from Jeszkotle — maybe they had slightly browner skin and darker eyes. But Ivan Mukta was different, not like anyone. His face was round and chubby, a strange colour — like looking into the stream of the Black River on a sunny day. Ivan's hair sometimes seemed dark blue, and his lips were like mulberries. Strangest of all were his eyes — narrow as chinks, hidden under elongated eyelids, black and piercing. And no one could have known what they were expressing. Izydor found it hard to look at them.

Ivan Mukta accommodated his lieutenant in the largest, nicest room on the ground floor, where the clock stood.

Izydor found a way to watch the Russian — he climbed into the lilac tree and peeped into the room from there. The gloomy lieutenant stared at maps spread out on the table, or sat still, leaning over his plate.

Whereas Ivan Mukta was everywhere. Once he had given the lieutenant his breakfast and polished his boots, he set about helping Misia in the kitchen: he chopped wood, took food out for the hens, picked currants for jam, played with Adelka, and drew water from the well.

"It's very nice of you, Mr Ivan, but I can manage by myself," said Misia to begin with, but evidently she came to like it.

Over the first few weeks Ivan Mukta learned to speak Polish.

Izydor's most important task was not to lose sight of Ivan Mukta. He watched him the whole time, and was afraid that if he let him out of sight the Russian would become lethally dangerous. He was also worried about Ivan's advances to Misia. His sister's life was in danger, so Izydor sought excuses to be in the kitchen. Sometimes Ivan Mukta tried to accost Izydor, but the boy was so affected by this that he slobbered and stammered with redoubled energy.

"He was born like that," sighed Misia.

Ivan Mukta would sit at the table and drink vast amounts of tea. He brought sugar with him — either loose, or in soiled lumps that he kept in his mouth as he drank the tea. At these times he would tell the most interesting stories. Izydor's manner displayed complete indifference, but on the other hand the Russian said such interesting things . . . Izydor had to keep pretending he had something important to do in the kitchen. It was hard to spend a whole hour drinking water or laying the fire. The infinitely resourceful Misia would shove a bowl of potatoes her brother's way, and put a knife in his hand. One day Izydor drew air into his lungs and spluttered:

"The Russkies say God doesn't exist."

Ivan Mukta put down his glass and looked at Izydor with those impenetrable eyes of his.

"It's not about whether God exists or not. It's not like that. To believe, or not to believe, that is the question."

"I believe God exists," said Izydor, boldly thrusting out his chin. "If He does, then it matters to me that I believe. If He doesn't, it doesn't cost me anything to believe."

"You think well," Ivan Mukta praised him. "But it's not true that believing costs nothing."

Misia started furiously stirring the soup with a wooden spoon and cleared her throat.

"What about you? What do you think? Does God exist, or not?"

"It's like this." Ivan splayed four fingers at face height, and Izydor thought he winked at him. He put out the first finger.

"Either God exists and has always existed, or" — here he added the second finger — "God doesn't exist and never has. Or else" — the third appeared — "God used to exist, but no longer does. And finally," — here he poked all four fingers at Izydor — "God doesn't yet exist and has yet to appear."

"Izek, go and fetch some wood," said Misia in the same tone as when the men were telling filthy jokes.

Off went Izydor, thinking about Ivan Mukta the whole time, and that Ivan Mukta must have a lot more to say.

A few days later he finally managed to catch Ivan all on his own. He was sitting on a bench outside, cleaning a rifle.

"What's it like where you live?" Izydor asked boldly.

"Exactly the same as here. Except there's no forest. There's one river, but it's very big and very far off."

Izydor did not take this topic further.

"Are you old or young? We can't guess how old you might be."

"I've clocked up a few years."

"But could you be . . . seventy, say?"

Ivan burst out laughing and put down the gun. He didn't answer.

"Ivan, do you think there's a chance that God might not exist? Then where would all this have come from?"

Ivan rolled a cigarette, then inhaled and pulled a face.

"Look around you. And what can you see?"

"I can see the road, and fields and plum trees beyond it, and grass in between them . . ." Izydor gave the Russian an inquiring look. "And further on the forest, and there are sure to be mushrooms there, except you can't see them from here . . . And I can also see the sky, blue underneath, and white and swirling on top."

"And where's this God?"

"He's invisible. He's underneath it. He guides and runs it all, He makes the laws and adapts everything to fit Him . . ."

"Very good, Izydor. I know you're clever, though you don't look it. I know you've got an imagination." Ivan lowered his voice and began to speak very slowly. "So now imagine there isn't any God, as you say, underneath. That no one takes care of it all, that the whole world is just one big mess, or, even worse, like a sort of machine, a broken chaff-cutter that only works on blind impulse . . ."

And Izydor looked again, just as Ivan Mukta had told him to. He strained his entire imagination and opened his eyes wide, until they started to water. Then for a brief moment he saw everything completely differently. Open space, empty and end-less, stretched away in all directions. Everything within this dead expanse, every living thing was helpless and alone. Things were happening by accident, and when the accident failed, automatic law appeared — the rhythmical machinery of nature, the cogs and pistons of history, conformity with the rules that was rotting from the inside and crumbling to dust. Cold and sorrow reigned everywhere. Every creature was trying to huddle up to some-thing, to cling to something, to things, to each other, but all that resulted was suffering and despair.

The quality of what Izydor saw was temporality. Under a colourful outer coating everything was merging in collapse, decay, and destruction.

THE TIME OF IVAN MUKTA

Ivan Mukta showed Izydor all the important things.

He started by showing him the world without God.

Then he took him to the forest, where the partisans shot by the Germans were buried. Izydor had known many of these men. Afterwards he came down with a fever and lay in the cool bedroom on his sister's bed. Misia refused to let Ivan Mukta in to see him.

"It amuses you to show him all those dreadful things. But he's still a child."

In the end, however, she let Ivan sit by Izydor's bed. He put his rifle at the foot of it.

"Ivan, tell me about death and about what happens after it. And tell me if I have an immortal soul that will never die," asked Izydor.

"There's a tiny spark in you that will never go out. And I've got one in me, too."

"Have we all got one? The Germans, too?"

"Everyone. Now sleep. When you get better, I'll take you to our place in the forest."

"Please go now," said Misia, looking in from the kitchen.

Once Izydor was better, Ivan kept his promise and took Izydor to the Russian units that were stationed in the forest. He also let him look through his binoculars at the Germans in Kotuszów. Izydor was amazed to see that through them the Germans looked no different from the Russians. They had uniforms of a similar colour, similar trenches, and similar helmets. So he found it even harder to understand why they shot at Ivan, as he carried orders from the gloomy lieutenant in his leather shoulder bag. They also shot at Izydor when he accompanied him. Izydor had to swear he wouldn't tell anyone about this. If his father found out, he would tan his hide.

Ivan Mukta showed Izydor another thing that he couldn't tell anyone about. Not because he wasn't allowed, or Ivan had forbidden him, but because the memory of it made him feel anxious and ashamed — too strongly to say anything about it, but not too strongly to stop him thinking about it.

"Everything couples. It has always been like that. The need to couple is the most powerful need of all. You only have to look around."

He knelt down on the path they were walking along, and pointed at the coupled abdomens of two insects.

"It's instinct, in other words, something you can't control."

Suddenly Ivan Mukta unbuttoned his flies and shook his penis.

"That's the tool for coupling. It fits in the hole between a woman's legs, because there's order in the world. Each thing fits into another."

Izydor went as red as a beetroot. He didn't know what to say. He looked down at the path. They went out into the fields beyond the Hill, out of range of the German fire. A goat was grazing by some abandoned buildings.

"When there aren't many women, like now, the tool fits into your hand, into the backsides of other soldiers, into holes dug in the ground, or into various animals. Stay here and watch," said Ivan Mukta quickly, and handed Izydor his cap and map case. He ran up to the goat, shifted his gun onto his back, and dropped his trousers.

Izydor saw Ivan press against the goat's rump and start rhythmically moving his hips. The faster Ivan's movements became, the more Izydor was rooted to the spot.

When Ivan came back for his cap and map case, Izydor was crying.

"Why are you crying? Feeling sorry for the animal?"

"I want to go home."

"Of course. Off you go! Everyone wants to go home."

The boy turned and ran into the forest. Ivan Mukta wiped

his sweating brow, put on his cap and, whistling a sad tune, went on his way.

THE TIME OF RUTA

Cornspike was afraid of the people in the forest. She watched them secretly as they disturbed the peace of the forest with their foreign jabber. They had thick clothing that they never took off, even in hot weather. They lugged weapons about with them. They hadn't yet reached Wydymacz, but she sensed that sooner or later it would happen. She knew they were tracking each other down to kill one another, and she wondered where she and Ruta could go to escape them. They often stayed the night at Florentynka's house, but Cornspike felt nervous in the village. At night she dreamed the sky was a metal cover that no one was able to lift.

Cornspike hadn't been to Primeval for a long time, and she didn't know the Wola Road had become the border between the Russians and the Germans. She didn't know Kurt had shot Florentynka, and that the wheels of the army vehicles and the soldiers' rifles had killed her dogs. She dug a shelter under the house, so they would both have somewhere to hide when the men in uniforms came. She was so absorbed in digging the shelter that she was careless, and let Ruta go to the village alone. She packed her a basket of blackberries and potatoes stolen from the field. Only when Ruta had left did Cornspike realise she had made a terrible mistake.

Ruta walked from Wydymacz to the village, to Florentynka's, taking her usual route through Papiernia, then down the Wola Road that ran along the edge of the forest. In the wicker basket she was carrying food for the old woman. She was to bring home a dog from Florentynka's to warn them of people coming. Her mother told her that as soon as she saw any person, regardless whether it was someone from Primeval or a stranger, she was to go into the forest and run away.

Ruta was only thinking about the dog, when she saw a man pissing against a tree. She stopped and slowly began to retreat. Then someone very strong grabbed her by the arms from behind and twisted them painfully. The man who'd been pissing ran up to her and hit her in the face so hard that Ruta wilted and fell to the ground. The men put down their rifles and raped her. First one, then the second, and then a third one came along.

Ruta lay on the Wola Road, which was the border between the Germans and Russians. Beside her lay the basket of blackberries and potatoes. That was how the second patrol found her. Now the men had uniforms of a different colour. Each in turn they lay down on her, as each in turn they handed their rifles to the other to hold. Then, standing over her, they smoked cigarettes. They took the basket and the food.

Cornspike found Ruta too late. The girl's dress was pulled up to her little face and her body was injured. Her belly and thighs were red with blood, which had attracted flies. She was unconscious.

Her mother picked her up and put her in the hole she had dug under the house. She laid her on some burdock leaves — their fragrance reminded her of the day her first child had died. She lay down beside the girl and listened closely to her breathing. Then she got up and, with trembling hands, mixed herbs. There was a scent of masterwort.

One day in August the Russians told Michał to gather all the people from Primeval and take them into the forest. They said Primeval was going to be on the front line any day now.

He did as they wanted. He went round all the cottages and said:

"Any day now Primeval will be on the front line."

On impulse he dropped in at Florentynka's house, too, but only when he saw the empty dog bowls did he remember that Florentynka was no longer there.

"What will happen to you?" he asked Ivan Mukta.

"We're at war. For us this is the front."

"My wife is sick. She can't walk. We're both staying."

Ivan Mukta shrugged.

Misia and Mrs Papuga were sitting on the cart, hugging the children. Misia's eyes were swollen with tears.

"Papa, come with us. Please, I beg you."

"We're going to take care of the house. Nothing bad will happen. I've survived worse things."

They left one cow for Michał and tied one to the cart. Izydor led all the rest out of the barn and took the halters off their necks. They didn't want to go, so Paweł picked up a stick and whacked them on the rumps. Then Ivan Mukta gave a long whistle and the startled cows set off at a trot across Stasia Papuga's vegetable patches into the fields. Later they saw them from the cart, standing there, stupefied by their unexpected freedom. Misia cried the whole way.

The cart drove off the Highway into the forest, and its wheels fitted into the ruts carved out by the carts of those who had driven this way earlier. Misia walked after the cart, leading the children. By the road there were masses of chanterelles and ceps growing. Now and then she stopped, knelt down, and pulled mushrooms from the ground along with moss and turf.

"You have to leave the foot, a bit of the foot in the ground," worried Izydor. "Otherwise they'll never grow back again."

"Too bad," said Misia.

The nights were warm, so they slept on the ground, on quilts brought from home. The men spent all day making dugouts and chopping wood. As in the village, the women cooked and lent each other salt for the potatoes.

The Boskis took up residence between some big pine trees. There were diapers hung out to dry on their branches. Next to the Boskis the Malak sisters had their quarters. The younger one's husband had joined the Home Army. The older one's had joined the "Little Andrews" resistance fighters. Paweł and Izydor built the women a dugout.

Without any verbal agreement, the villagers arranged themselves just as they lived in Primeval. They even left an empty space between the Krasnys and Cherubin. In Primeval, Florentynka's house stands there.

One day at the beginning of September, Cornspike and her daughter came to this forest settlement. The girl was evidently sick. She could hardly drag her feet along. She was bruised and had a high temperature. Paweł Boski, who performed the duties of a doctor in the forest, went up to them with his bag, in which he had iodine, bandages, pills for diarrhoea, and sulfamide powder, but Cornspike wouldn't let him come near her daughter. She asked the women for hot water and brewed herbs for her. Misia gave them a blanket. It looked as if Cornspike wanted to stay with them, so the men cobbled together a home for her in the ground.

In the evening, when the forest was silent, everyone sat by

glimmering bonfires and listened. Sometimes the night flared up, as if a storm were raging nearby. Then they heard a low, terrifying rumble, muffled by the forest.

There were brave people who went to the village, for the potatoes that were ripening in the small home gardens, for flour, or simply because they couldn't stand living in uncertainty. Old Mrs Serafin, who no longer cared about life, went most often. Sometimes one of her daughters-in-law went with her, and it was from one of them that Misia heard:

"You haven't got a house any more. There's just a heap of rubble left."

THE TIME OF THE BAD MAN

Ever since the people from Primeval had run away into the forest and lived there in dugout shelters, the Bad Man could find no place for himself in the forest. People were pushing in everywhere, into every grove, into every clearing. They were digging up peat and looking for mushrooms and nuts. They wandered to one side of their hurriedly established camps to relieve themselves straight onto a strawberry bush or fresh grass. On warmer evenings he could hear them copulating in the bushes. He watched in amazement as they built miserable shelters, and was surprised how much time it took them.

Now he spent all day long watching them, and the longer he looked at them, the more he feared and hated them. They were noisy and deceitful. They never stopped moving their mouths, spouting noises that made no sense. It wasn't weeping, or shouting, or purring with satisfaction. Their speech didn't mean anything. Everywhere they left their tracks and their smells behind them. They were insolent and incautious. When the ominous booming noises came, and the sky was coloured red at night, they fell into panic and despair, they didn't know where to run or where to hide. He could smell their fear. They stank like a rat when it fell into the Bad Man's trap.

The smells that surrounded them irritated the Bad Man. But among them there were also pleasant, though new odours: the smell of roast meat, boiled potatoes, milk, sheepskins and furs, the smell of coffee made of chicory, ashes, and rye. There were also terrible smells, not animal, but purely human: of grey soap, carbolic, lye, paper, weapons, grease, and sulphur.

One day the Bad Man stood at the edge of the forest and gazed at the village. It was empty, gone cold like carrion. Some of the houses had smashed-in roofs, others had broken windows. There were no birds or dogs in the village. Nothing. This sight pleased the Bad Man. As the people had gone into the forest, the Bad Man went into the village.

THE TIME OF THE GAME

In the little book entitled *Ignis fatuus, or an instructive game for one player*, this is how the description of the Third World begins:

Between Earth and Heaven there are Eight Worlds. They hang motionless in space like eiderdowns hung out to air.

God created the Third World a very long time ago. He started with the seas and volcanoes, and finished with the plants and animals. Yet as there is nothing sublime about creating, just hard work and effort, God grew tired and disheartened. The newly made world seemed boring to Him. The animals couldn't understand His harmony, they didn't admire Him or praise Him. They ate and multiplied. They didn't ask

God why He had made the sky blue and the water wet. The hedgehog didn't wonder at his prickles or the lion at his teeth, the birds didn't give their wings a second thought.

This world went on for a very long time, and bored God to death.

So He went down to Earth and forcibly equipped each animal He met with fingers, hands, faces, soft skin, reason and the capacity to wonder — He changed the animals into people. But the animals didn't want to be changed into people at all, because people seemed to them as terrible as monsters. So they plotted, caught God, and drowned Him. And that is how it remained.

In the Third World there is no God and no people.

THE TIME OF MISIA

Misia put on two skirts and two sweaters and wrapped her head in a shawl. Silently, to avoid waking anyone, she crept out of the dugout. The forest was muffling the monotonous rumble of distant guns. She took a rucksack and was just about to set off when she saw Adelka. The child came up to her.

"I'm coming with you."

Misia was cross.

"Go back to the dugout. Right now. I'll be back in a moment."

Adelka clutched her skirt tightly and began to cry. Misia hesitated. Then she went back to the dugout for her daughter's little sheepskin coat.

Once they were standing at the edge of the forest, they thought they could see Primeval. But Primeval wasn't there. Against the dark sky not the thinnest trail of smoke was visible, there were no lights shining, and no dogs barking. Only in the west, somewhere over Kotuszów, low clouds showed as a brown glow. Misia shuddered and an old dream came back to her, in which it had looked just like this. "I'm dreaming," she thought. "I'm lying on the bunk in the dugout. I haven't gone anywhere. This is in my dream." And then she thought she must have fallen asleep even earlier. It seemed as if she were lying on her new double bed, with Paweł sleeping beside her. There was no war. She was having a long nightmare, about the Germans, the Russians, the front line, the forest, and the dugouts. That helped — Misia stopped feeling afraid and went out onto the Highway. Wet stones on the road crunched under her shoes. Then Misia had a hopeful thought that she had fallen asleep earlier still. Tired of monotonously turning the coffee grinder's handle, she had fallen asleep on the bench outside the mill. She was only a few years old, and now she was having a child's dream about adult life and war.

"I want to wake up," she said aloud.

Adelka looked at her in amazement, and Misia realised that no child would be capable of dreaming the shooting of the Jews, the death of Florentynka, the partisans, what they had done to Ruta, the bombardments, the displacement, or her mother's paralysis.

She looked upwards: the sky was like the lid of a can, in which God had shut the people.

They passed a dark silhouette, and Misia guessed it was their barn. She stepped onto the verge and stretched out a hand in the darkness. She touched the rough boards of the fence. She heard some faint noises, strange and muffled.

"Someone's playing the accordion," said Adelka.

They stood by the gate, and Misia's heart began to pound. Her house was standing, she could sense it, though she could not see it. She could feel its large, quadrangular mass, she could feel its weight and the way it filled space. Feeling her way, she opened the gate and went onto the porch.

The music was coming from inside. The door from the porch into the hall was boarded up, just as they had left it, so they went to the kitchen entrance. The music became clearly audible. Someone was playing jaunty songs on the accordion. Misia crossed herself, grabbed Adelka tightly by the hand, and opened the door.

The music fell silent. She saw her kitchen plunged in smoke and semi-darkness. There were blankets hanging over the windows. Soldiers were sitting at the table, by the walls, and even on the sideboard. Suddenly one of them aimed his rifle at her. Misia slowly raised her hands.

The gloomy lieutenant stood up from the table. He reached upwards for her hand and shook it in greeting.

"This is our landlady," he said in Russian, and Misia curtsied awkwardly.

Among the soldiers was Ivan Mukta. His head was bandaged. From him Misia learned that her parents were living in the mill with the cow. Apart from that there was no one left in Primeval. Ivan took Misia upstairs and opened the door into the south-facing room for her. There before her Misia saw the wintry night sky. The south-facing room had ceased to exist, but she found it strangely unimportant. As she had been expecting the loss of the entire house, what did losing just one room mean?

"Mrs Misia," said Ivan Mukta on the stairs, "you must take your parents away from there and hide in the forest. Straight after your Christmas the front will move. There's going to be a terrible battle. Don't tell anyone about it. It's a military secret."

"Thank you," said Misia, and only after a pause did the full horror of his words get through to her. "Oh God, what'll become of us? How will we manage in the forest in winter? What is this war for, Mr Ivan? Who's running it? Why are you people going to a certain death and killing others?"

Ivan Mukta gazed at her sadly and didn't reply.

Misia distributed knives to the tipsy soldiers for peeling potatoes. She fetched some lard that was hidden in the cellar and fried a big bowl of chips. They weren't familiar with fried potato chips. At first they inspected them mistrustfully, but finally they started to eat them, with increasing relish.

"They don't believe they're potatoes," explained Ivan Mukta.

More bottles of vodka appeared on the table, and the accordion started to play. Misia put Adelka to bed under the stairs, which seemed the safest place.

The presence of a woman excited the soldiers. They began to dance, first on the floor, and then on the table. The rest clapped to the beat of the music. They kept pouring vodka down their throats and were seized by a sudden madness — they stamped, shouted, and banged their rifles against the floor. Then a pale-eyed young officer drew a pistol from its holster and fired several shots into the ceiling. Plaster showered down into their glasses. Deafened, Misia covered her head with her hands. Suddenly it went quiet and Misia could hear herself screaming. From under the stairs the child's terrified crying joined in with her.

The gloomy lieutenant yelled at the pale-eyed officer and touched his holster. Ivan Mukta knelt down beside Misia.

"Don't be afraid, Misia. It's just a bit of fun."

They let Misia have a whole room. Twice she checked to make sure she had locked the door.

In the morning, when she went to the mill, the pale-eyed officer came up to her and said something apologetically. He showed her the ring on his finger and some documents. Out of nowhere as usual, Ivan Mukta appeared.

"He has a wife and child in Moscow. He says he's very sorry for yesterday evening. It's anxiety getting the better of him."

Misia didn't know what to do. On sudden impulse she went up to the man and hugged him. His uniform smelled of earth.

"Please try not to get killed, Mr Ivan," she said to Mukta in parting.

He shook his head and smiled. Now his eyes looked like two dark dashes.

"People like me don't die."

Misia smiled.

"So goodbye," she said.

THE TIME OF MICHAŁ

They were living in the kitchen with the cow. Michał had made it a place to lie down behind the door, where the buckets of water always used to stand. By day he ventured out to the barns for hay, then he fed the cow and threw out her manure. Genowefa watched him from her chair. Twice a day he took a bucket, sat on a stool and milked the animal as best he could. There wasn't much milk. Just as much as two people need. Michał saved the cream from the milk to take it to the children in the forest one day.

The days were short, as if they were sick and had no strength to keep going to the end. It went dark early, so they sat at the table, on which an oil lamp flickered. They covered the windows with blankets. Michał lit the stove and opened the little door — the fire cheered them up. Genowefa asked him to turn her towards the fire.

"I can't move. I am dead while still alive. I am a terrible burden to you that you don't deserve," she sometimes said in a sepulchral voice that emerged from somewhere deep in her belly.

Michał would reassure her.

"I like taking care of you."

In the evenings he sat her on a chamber pot, washed her and carried her to bed. He straightened out her arms and legs. He felt as if she were looking at him from the depths of her body, as if she were trapped in there. In the night she would whisper: "Hold me."

Together they heard the noises of guns, most often from somewhere near Kotuszów, but sometimes everything shook, and then they knew a shell had hit Primeval. At night some strange sounds reached them: squelching, mumbling, and then the rapid footsteps of a man or an animal. Michał was afraid, but he didn't want to show it. Whenever his heart began to beat too fast, he turned on his side.

Then Misia and Adelka came to fetch them. Michał no longer insisted on staying. The mill of the world had stopped, its mechanism was broken. They waded through the snow along the Highway to the forest.

"Let me take one more look at Primeval," asked Genowefa, but Michał pretended not to hear.

THE TIME OF DIPPER THE DROWNED MAN

Dipper the Drowned Man woke up and peeped out at the world's surface. He saw that the world was rippling — the air was sailing by in great gusts, billowing and shooting into the sky. The water was ruffled and cloudy, and heat and fire were beating down on it. What had been above was now below, and what had been below was pushing its way above.

The Drowned Man was prompted by curiosity and an urge to

take action. He tried his strength and pulled a fog of mist and smoke from the river. Now the grey cloud went drifting after him along the Wola Road towards the village.

By the Boskis' fence he saw an emaciated dog. He leaned down to it without any intention. The dog whimpered in terror, tucked its tail under and ran away. This annoyed Dipper, so he sent the cloud of mist and smoke over the orchard and tried to lower it down the smoking chimneys, as he usually did, but now the chimneys weren't warm. Dipper went around the Serafins' house, and then he knew there was no one there. There was no one in Primeval. The noise of the barn doors set in motion by the wind expanded in the air.

Dipper wanted to romp and move about among all the human equipment, to make the world react to his presence. He wanted to control the air, stop the wind against his misty body, play with the shape of the water, beguile and frighten people, and startle animals. But the violent movements of air ceased, and everything became empty and silent.

He stopped for a while and sensed somewhere in the forest the diffuse, feeble warmth that people exude. He was pleased and began to whirl. He went back along the Wola Road and frightened the same dog again. Low clouds were trailing across the sky, which gave the Drowned Man strength. There was no sun yet.

Just by the forest something stopped him. He didn't know what. He hesitated, then turned towards the river, not onto the priest's meadows, but beyond, to Papiernia.

The sparse pine forest was smashed and smoking. Huge holes gaped in the earth. The end of the world must have passed this way yesterday. In the tall grass lay hundreds of human bodies going cold. Their blood was steaming redness into the grey sky, until it began to go a crimson colour in the east.

The Drowned Man could see something moving among all this lifelessness. Then the sun broke free of the fetters of the horizon and began to release the souls from the soldiers' dead bodies.

The souls were emerging from the bodies confused and stupefied. They flickered like shadows, like transparent balloons. Dipper the Drowned Man was almost as overjoyed as a live person. He headed into the sparse forest and tried to set the souls whirling, to dance with them, startle them and drag them after him. There was a huge number of them, hundreds or maybe thousands. They got up and wavered unsteadily above the ground. Dipper glided among them, snorting, stroking and whirling, as eager to play as a puppy, but the souls took no notice of him, as if he didn't exist. They swayed for a while between the layers of morning wind, and then, like untied balloons, they soared upwards and disappeared.

Dipper couldn't understand that they were leaving, and that there was a place you could go to when you die. He tried to chase after them, but they were already subject to a different law from Dipper the Drowned Man's law. Deaf and blind to his courtship, they were like tadpoles driven by instinct, knowing only one direction.

The forest went white with them, then suddenly emptied, and once again Dipper the Drowned Man was alone. He was angry. He spun around and crashed into a tree. A frightened bird let out a shrill scream and blindly flew off towards the river.

The Russians collected their dead from Papiernia and transported them on carts to the village. They dug a large hole in Cherubin's field and buried the soldiers' bodies there. They laid the officers to one side.

Everyone who came back to Primeval went to watch this hurried burial with no priest, no words, and no flowers. Michał went, too, and incautiously let the gaze of the gloomy lieutenant rest on him. The gloomy lieutenant clapped Michał on the back and had the officers' bodies taken to the Boskis' house.

"No, don't dig here," asked Michał. "Is there so little ground for your soldiers' graves? Why in my daughter's garden? Why are you pulling up the flower bulbs? Go to the graveyard, I'll show you other places, too . . ."

The gloomy lieutenant, always polite and courteous until now, pushed Michał aside, and one of the soldiers aimed a rifle at him. Michał moved away.

"Where is Ivan?" Izydor asked the lieutenant.

"Dead," he said in Russian.

"No," said Izydor, and for a moment the lieutenant fixed his gaze on him.

"Why not?"

Izydor turned and ran away.

The Russians buried eight officers in the garden under the bedroom window. They covered them all with earth, and once they had driven away, snow fell.

From then on no one wanted to sleep in the bedroom overlooking the garden. Misia rolled up the eiderdowns and took them upstairs.

In spring Michał nailed a cross together out of wood and

erected it under the window. Then he carefully made rows in the earth with a stick and sowed snapdragons. The flowers grew lush and colourful, with their little mouths open to heaven.

Towards the end of 1945, when the war was already over, a military jeep drove up to the house, and out got a Polish officer and a man in civilian clothes. They said they were going to exhume the officers. Then a truck full of soldiers appeared and a hayrack wagon, on which the bodies removed from the earth were laid. The earth and the snapdragons had sucked the blood and water out of them. Best preserved were the woollen uniforms, and it was they that held the decaying corpses together. The soldiers who shifted them onto the cart tied handkerchiefs over their mouths and noses.

People from Primeval stood on the Highway and tried to see as much as possible over the fence, but when the cart set off for Jeszkotle, they withdrew in silence. Boldest of all were the hens — they bravely ran after the cart as it bounced on the stones and greedily devoured whatever fell from them to the ground.

Michał vomited into the lilac bushes. He never put a hen's egg in his mouth again.

THE TIME OF GENOWEFA

Genowefa's body had frozen solid like a clay pot scorched in the embers. It was propped in a Bath chair. Now it was at the mercy of others. It was put to bed, washed, sat up, and taken out onto the porch.

Genowefa's body was one thing, and Genowefa was another. She was stuck inside it, trapped and deafened. She could only move the tips of her fingers and her face, but she could no longer smile or cry. Her words, hoarse and angular, fell from her mouth like pebbles. Words like these had no power. Sometimes she tried to scold Adelka, who was hitting Antek, but her granddaughter didn't take much notice of her threats. Antek took refuge in his grandmother's skirts, and Genowefa could do nothing to hide him or even hug him. She watched helplessly as the bigger, stronger Adelka pulled her brother's hair, and she felt a burst of anger that immediately died away, however, because it had no chance of finding any sort of outlet.

Misia talked to her mother a lot. She moved her chair from near the door to the warm stove tiles and prattled on. Genowefa didn't listen very carefully. The things her daughter talked about bored her. She was less and less curious about who was left and who had perished, she didn't care about the masses being said, Misia's girlfriends from Jeszkotle, new ways of bottling peas, the radio news that Misia always commented on, her nonsensical doubts and questions. Genowefa preferred to focus on what Misia was doing and what was happening in the house. So she saw her daughter's belly growing for the third time, the miniature snow-fall of flour that fell from the pastry board to the floor as Misia kneaded dough for noodles, a fly drowning in the milk, a poker left on the hotplate that had gone red-hot, the hens trying to pull out bootlaces in the hall. This was the concrete, tangible life that was drifting away from her day by day. Genowefa saw that Misia couldn't cope with the large house they had given her. So she dug a few sentences out of herself and persuaded her daughter to take on a girl to help. Misia brought home Ruta.

Ruta had grown into a beautiful girl. Genowefa's heart ached as she looked at her. She watched out for the moments when both of them, Misia and Ruta, were standing next to each other — then she compared them. And — had no one noticed? — they were so alike. Two versions of the same thing. One was smaller and darker, the other taller and fuller. One had chestnut-brown eyes and hair, the other's were honey-coloured. Apart from that, everything was just the same. Or so it seemed to Genowefa.

She watched Ruta washing the floors, shredding large heads of cabbage, and grating cheese in a mixing bowl. And the longer she looked at her, the more certain she was. Sometimes, when they were doing the laundry or cleaning the house, and Michał was busy, Misia told the children to take Granny to the forest. The children took the chair outside carefully, and then, past the lilac, once they were no longer visible from the house, they raced down the Highway, pushing the chair that carried Genowefa's stiff, majestic body. They would leave her, with windswept hair and a hand fallen helplessly over the armrest, while they ran into clearings looking for mushrooms or strawberries.

On one such day, from the corner of her eye Genowefa saw Cornspike coming out of the forest and onto the Highway. Genowefa could not move her head, so she waited. Cornspike came up to her and curiously walked right round the chair. She knelt down before Genowefa and peered into her face. For a while they eyed each other. Cornspike no longer resembled the girl who had walked through the snow barefoot. She had become stout and even bigger. Her thick plaits were white now.

"You switched my child for yours," said Genowefa.

Cornspike burst out laughing and took her lifeless hand in her warm palm.

"You took the girl and left me the boy. Ruta is my daughter."

"All young women are the daughters of older women. Anyway, you don't need daughters or sons any more."

"I'm paralysed. I can't move."

Cornspike raised Genowefa's lifeless hand and kissed it.

"Get up and walk," she said.

"No," whispered Genowefa and, without feeling her own movement, shook her head.

Cornspike laughed and set off towards Primeval.

After this encounter Genowefa lost the desire to speak. She just said "yes" or "no." One time she heard Paweł whispering to Misia that the paralysis was attacking her mind, too. "Let them think that," she thought. "The paralysis is attacking my mind, but even so I still exist somewhere."

After breakfast Michał took Genowefa outside. He set the chair on the grass by the fence, and sat down on a bench. He took out a cigarette paper and spent a long time crumbling tobacco in his fingers. Genowefa gazed ahead of her at the Highway, staring at the smooth cobblestones that looked like the tops of thousands of heads of people buried in the ground.

"Aren't you cold?" asked Michał.

She shook her head.

Then Michał finished his cigarette and walked away. Genowefa remained in her chair, gazing at Mrs Papuga's garden, at the sandy field road that wound its way between splashes of green and yellow. Then she looked at her own feet, knees, hips — they were just as far away and just as much not part of her as the sand, fields, and gardens. Her body was a broken figurine made of fragile human material.

She was surprised she could still move her fingers, that she still had feeling in the tips of her pale hands, which had known no work for months. She laid those hands on her insensible knees and fumbled with the folds of her skirt. "I am a body," she said to herself. And in Genowefa's body, like cancer, like mould, the image of killing people was growing. Killing involves taking away the right to move, as after all, life is motion. A killed body has stopped moving. A person is a body. And everything a person experiences has its beginning and end in the body.

One day Genowefa said to Michał:

"I feel cold."

He brought her a woollen shawl and gloves. She moved her fingers, but she couldn't feel them any more, so she didn't know if they were moving or not. When she looked up at the Highway, she saw the dead returning. They were heading down the Highway from Czernica to Jeszkotle in a large procession, like the pilgrimage to Częstochowa. But pilgrimages always involve a hubbub, monotonous songs, mournful litanies, and boot-soles shuffling over the stones. Here silence reigned.

There were thousands of them. They were marching in uneven, broken ranks. They walked in icy silence, at a rapid pace. They were grey, as if deprived of blood.

Genowefa sought Eli among them and the Szenberts' daughter with the baby in her arms, but the dead were moving too fast for her to look at them closely. Only later did she see the Serafins' son, and that was only because he was walking nearest to her. He had a huge, brown hole in his forehead.

"Franek," she whispered.

He turned his head and, without slowing his pace, glanced at her. He stretched out a hand to her. His lips were moving, but Genowefa couldn't hear any words.

She saw them all day, until evening, and the procession did not dwindle. They still went gliding past when she closed her eyes. She knew God was watching them, too. She could see His face — it was black, terrible, covered in scars.

In 1946 Squire Popielski was still living in the manor house, though everyone knew it wouldn't last much longer. His wife had taken the children to Kraków and was now to-ing and fro-ing, getting ready to move out.

The squire didn't seem to care what was going on around him. He was playing the Game. He spent days and nights in the library. He slept on a couch. He didn't change his clothes or shave. When his wife went off to the children, he didn't eat, sometimes for three or four days. He didn't open the windows, he didn't speak, he didn't go for walks, he didn't even go downstairs. Once or twice people from the district administration came to see him about the nationalisation. They had briefcases full of writs and official stamps. They banged on the door and pulled at the bell. Then he went up to the window, looked at them from above, and rubbed his hands.

"It all fits," he said in a hoarse voice unaccustomed to speaking. "I'm moving onto the next square."

Sometimes Squire Popielski needed his books.

The Game required him to find various bits of information, but he had no trouble with that — he could find it all in his own library. As dreams played a crucial role in the Game, Squire Popielski taught himself to dream to order. More than that, he gradually gained control of his dreams, doing in them what he wanted, completely differently from in life. He consciously dreamed on the prescribed topic, and at once just as consciously awoke on the other side, as if he had gone through a hole in the fence. It took him a while to come to his senses, and then he began to act.

And so the Game gave him everything he needed, and even more. Why should he have to leave the library?

Meanwhile, the officials from the district administration took away his forests, clearings, arable land, ponds, and meadows. They sent a letter in which he was informed, as a citizen of the young socialist state, that the brickworks, sawmill, distillery, and water mill no longer belonged to him. Nor in the end did the manor house. They were polite, they even set out a deadline for handing over his property. First his wife cried, then she prayed, and finally she began to pack their things. She looked like a votive candle, she was so thin and wax-pale. Suddenly gone white, her hair shone in the gloom of the manor house with a cold, equally pale light.

Squire Popielski's wife bore no grudge against her husband for going mad. She was worried that she would have to decide on her own what could be taken and what left behind. When the first vehicle drove up, however, Squire Popielski, pale and unshaven, came downstairs with two suitcases in his hands. He refused to show what he had in them.

His wife ran upstairs and spent a while scanning the library with a keen eye. She did not think anything was missing. There were no empty spaces on the shelves, not a single painting or ornament had been moved, nothing. She summoned the removal men, and they threw the books into cardboard boxes any old how. Then, to be quicker, they started scooping them off the shelves in entire rows. The books spread their flightless wings and torpidly fell in a heap. When they ran out of boxes, they left it at that, took the full boxes and went. Only later did it turn out that they had taken everything from A to L.

Meanwhile Squire Popielski was standing by the car, enjoying inhaling the fresh air, which intoxicated him after months of being shut indoors. He felt like laughing, rejoicing, dancing — the oxygen blazed in his thick, sluggish blood and dilated his clogged arteries.

"Everything is exactly as it should be," he told his wife in the car as they were driving along the Highway towards the Kielce road. "Everything that's happening is turning out well."

Then he added something else that made the driver, and the removal men, and his wife give each other meaningful looks:

"The eight of clubs has been shot dead."

THE TIME OF THE GAME

In the book entitled *Ignis fatuus, or an instructive game for one player*, which is the instruction manual for the Game, the description of the Fourth World includes the following story:

God created the Fourth World in a passion that brought Him relief in His divine suffering.

When He created man, He came to His senses — such an impression did he make on Him. So He stopped creating the world any further — for could there have been anything more perfect? — and now, in His divine time, He admired His own work. The deeper God's vision reached into the human inside, the more ardently God's love for man intensified.

But man proved ungrateful — he was busy cultivating the land and begetting children, and took no notice of God. Then in His divine mind arose sorrow, from which darkness seeped.

God's love for man was unrequited.

Divine love, like any other, can be oppressive. Meanwhile man matured and decided to free himself from his importunate lover. "Let me leave," he said. "Let me get to know the world in my own way and give me provisions for the journey."

"You won't manage without me," God told man. "Don't go."

"Oh, come on," said man, and regretfully God leaned the branch of an apple tree towards him.

God was left alone and He pined. He dreamed that it was He who had driven man out of paradise, so painful was the thought that He had been abandoned.

"Come back to me. The world is terrible and it can kill you. Look at the earthquakes, the volcanic eruptions, the fires and the floods," He thundered from the rain clouds.

"Oh, come on, I'll manage," man replied, and was gone.

THE TIME OF PAWEŁ

"You have to live," said Paweł. "You have to bring up children, earn a living, keep on studying and climbing upwards."

And so he did.

He and Aba Kozienicki, who had survived the concentration camp, went back to trading in timber. They bought a forest for felling and organised the cutting and transport of the wood. Paweł bought a motorbike and drove around the district in search of orders. He got himself a pigskin briefcase in which he kept a receipt book and several copying pencils.

As business was going quite well and there was a steady stream of cash flowing into his pocket, Paweł decided to continue his education. Studying to be a doctor was no longer very realistic, but he could still improve his qualifications as a health worker and paramedic. Now he spent his evenings fathoming the mysteries of how flies multiplied and the complex sequences in the life of tapeworms. He studied the vitamin content in nutritional products and the ways illnesses spread, such as tuberculosis and typhoid. Over several years of courses and training he became convinced that medicine and hygiene, once liberated from the power of ignorance and superstition, would be capable of transforming human life, and the Polish village would change into an oasis of sterilised pots and yards disinfected with Lysol. So Paweł was the first in the district to devote one room in his house to a bathroom and medical treatment room in one. It was spotlessly clean in there, with an enamelled bathtub, scrubbed taps, a metal waste bin with a lid, glass containers for cotton wool and wadding, and a glazed cabinet with a padlock, in which he kept all his medicines and medical instruments. Once he had finished the next course, he had nursing qualifications, and now in this room he gave people injections, without forgetting at the same time to give them a short lecture on the subject of everyday hygiene.

Then the business with Aba collapsed, because the forests were nationalised. Aba went away. He came to say goodbye. They embraced like brothers. Paweł Boski realised that a new stage in his life was beginning and that from now on he must manage on his own, on top of that in completely new conditions. He could not keep a family merely on giving injections.

So he packed all his certificates into his leather briefcase and rode his motorbike to Taszów to look for work. He found it at the health centre, which was the district kingdom of sterilisation and stool samples. From then on, especially after joining the Party, he gradually and irrevocably began to gain promotion.

His job involved travelling on his noisy motorbike around the neighbouring villages and inspecting the cleanliness in shops, restaurants, and bars. In all these places, his appearance, with his leather briefcase full of documents and test tubes for excrement, was regarded like the coming of a rider of the Apocalypse. If he wanted, Paweł could have any shop or eatery closed down. He was important. He was given presents, treated to vodka and the freshest jellied pig's feet.

This was how he met Ukleja, who was the owner of a cake shop in Taszów and several other, less official businesses. Whereas Ukleja introduced Paweł to the world of secretaries and lawyers, drinking sprees and hunting, willing busty barmaids and alcohol, which provided the courage to get as much out of life as possible.

In this way, Ukleja took the place vacated by Aba Kozienicki, the place assigned in the life of every man for a friend and guide, without whom a man would be just a lonely, misunderstood warrior in a world of chaos and darkness, which creeps out from every corner the moment his back is turned.

THE TIME OF THE MUSHROOM SPAWN

The mushroom spawn grows under the entire forest, or maybe even under the whole of Primeval. In the earth under the soft forest floor, under the grass and stones, it creates a tangle of slender threads, strings and bundles, which it twines around everything. The threads of the mushroom spawn have great strength and push their way in between every clod of earth, tangle around tree roots and restrain huge boulders in their infinitely gradual onward motion. The mushroom spawn is like mould — cold, white, and delicate — underground lunar lace, damp, hem-stitched mycelia, the world's slimy umbilical cords. It overgrows meadows and wanders under human roads, climbs the walls of people's houses, and sometimes in surges of power it imperceptibly attacks their bodies.

The mushroom spawn is not a plant or an animal. It cannot gain strength from the sun, because its nature is alien to the sun.

It is not drawn to the warm and the living, because its nature is neither warm nor alive. The mushroom spawn lives thanks to the fact that it sucks up the remains of juices from whatever dies, whatever is decaying and soaking into the earth. The mushroom spawn is the life of death, the life of decay, the life of whatever has died.

All year the mushroom spawn bears its cold, wet children, but the ones that come to light in the summer and autumn are the most beautiful. Along human paths, marasmius mushrooms grow on slender legs, near-perfect puffballs and earthballs show white in the grass, and slippery jacks and bracket fungi take crippled trees into their possession. The forest is full of yellow chanterelles, olive-green russulas, and suede boletus.

The mushroom spawn does not separate or single out its children, it gives them all the strength to grow and the power to spread their spores. To some it gives a scent, to others the capacity to hide from the human eye, yet others have shapes that are breathtaking.

Deep under the ground, at the very centre of Wodenica, there is a great, white tangled mycelium ball pulsing away, the heart of the mushroom spawn. From here the spawn spreads out to all corners of the world. The forest here is dark and damp. Luxuriant brambles hold the tree stumps prisoner. Everything is covered in lush moss. People instinctively avoid Wodenica, though they don't know that here, underneath, the heart of the mushroom spawn is beating.

Of all the people, only Ruta knows about it. She guessed it from the most beautiful amanitas, which grow here every year. The amanitas are the spawn's guards. Ruta lies down on the ground among them and examines the underside of their foaming, snow-white petticoats.

Ruta once heard the life of the mushroom spawn. It was an

underground rustling that sounded like a dull sigh, and then she could hear the gentle crackle of clumps of earth as the thread of the mycelium pushed its way between them. Ruta heard the spawn's heartbeat, which happens once every eighty human years. Ever since she has been coming to this damp spot in Wodenica, and always lies down on the wet moss. If she lies there for a while, she starts to sense the mushroom spawn in another way, too — because the spawn slows down time. Ruta falls into a waking sleep, and sees everything in a completely different way. She can see individual gusts of wind, the slow and graceful flight of insects, the fluent movements of ants, and particles of light that settle on the surfaces of leaves. All the high-up noises — the warbling of birds, the squealing of animals — change into booming and rumbling, and glide along just above the ground, like mist. Ruta feels as if she has been lying like that for hours, though only a moment has passed. So the mushroom spawn takes time into its possession.

THE TIME OF IZYDOR

Ruta was waiting for him under a lime tree. The wind was blowing, and the tree was creaking and moaning.

"It's going to rain," she said instead of a greeting.

They walked in silence along the Highway, then turned into their forest beyond Wodenica. Izydor walked half a pace behind, stealing a glance at the girl's naked shoulders. Her skin looked ever so thin, almost transparent. He felt like touching and stroking it.

"Do you remember how I once showed you the border, ages ago?"

He nodded.

"We were going to investigate it one day. Sometimes I don't believe in the border. It let in the foreigners . . ."

"From the scientific point of view that sort of border is impossible."

Ruta burst out laughing and grabbed Izydor by the hand. She pulled him after her among the small pine trees.

"I'll show you something else."

"What? How many more things do you have to show me? Show me all of them at once."

"It can't be done like that."

"Is it alive or dead?"

"Neither the one nor the other."

"Is it an animal?"

"No."

"A plant?"

"No."

Izydor stopped and asked anxiously:

"A person?"

Ruta didn't answer. She let go of his hand.

"I'm not going," he said and squatted on the ground.

"No is no. After all, I'm not forcing you."

She knelt down beside him and stared at the trails of big forest ants.

"Sometimes you're so clever. And sometimes so stupid."

"But more often stupid," he said sadly.

"I wanted to show you something strange in the forest. Mama says it's the centre of Primeval, but you don't want to go."

"All right, let's go."

In the forest they couldn't hear the wind, and it had gone muggy. Izydor could see tiny drops of sweat on the back of Ruta's neck.

"Let's have a rest," he said from behind. "Let's lie down here and rest."

"It's just about to start raining, come on."

Izydor lay on the grass and folded his hands under his head.

"I don't want to look at the centre of the world. I want to lie here with you. Come here."

Ruta hesitated. She walked a few steps away, then came back. Izydor narrowed his eyes, and Ruta changed into a blurred shape. The shape came up to him and sat down on the grass. Izydor stretched out a hand and found Ruta's leg. He could feel tiny hairs under his fingers.

"I'd like to be your husband, Ruta. I'd like to make love with you."

She pulled her leg away. Izydor opened his eyes and gazed straight into Ruta's face. It looked cold and determined. Not as he knew it.

"I'm never going to do that with someone I love. Only with those I hate," she said and got up. "I'm going. Come with me if you want."

He hurriedly got up and headed after her, half a pace behind as usual.

"You've changed," he said quietly.

She turned round abruptly and stopped.

"Of course I've changed. Are you surprised? The world is evil. You've seen it for yourself. What sort of a God created a world like this? Either He's evil Himself, or He allows evil to happen. Or else He's got it all messed up."

"You're not allowed to talk like that . . ."

"I am," she said and ran ahead.

It became very quiet. Izydor couldn't hear the wind or the birds or the buzzing of insects. It was hollow and empty, as if he had fallen into feathers, into the very middle of a huge eider-down, or into a bank of snow.

"Ruta!" he shouted.

He saw her flash among the trees, and then she vanished. He rushed in that direction. He looked all round, feeling helpless, because he realised that without her he would never be capable of getting home.

"Ruta!" he shouted even louder.

"I'm here," she said, and emerged from behind a tree.

"I want to see the centre of Primeval."

She dragged him into some bushes — raspberries and wild blackberries. The plants caught on Izydor's sweater. Before them lay a small glade among huge oak trees. The ground was covered in acorns, old ones and this year's. Some were crumbling to dust, others were sprouting, and yet others were shining a fresh green colour. In the very middle of the glade stood a tall, oblong rock made of white sandstone. Another one, broader and more solid, lay on top of this obelisk. It looked like a hat. Izydor could see the outline of a face under the stone hat. He went nearer, to take a closer look, and then he noticed that the same face appeared on either side, too. So there were three faces. And suddenly Izydor was aware of a deep sense of incompleteness, a lack of something extremely important. He felt as if he knew all this from somewhere already, as if he had seen the glade and the stone in the middle of it, and its three faces before. He sought Ruta's hand, but that didn't reassure him. Ruta's hand pulled him after it and they began to walk around the glade, on the bed of acorns. Then Izydor saw a fourth face, just the same as the others. He kept walking faster, and then let go of Ruta's hand, because he was starting to run, with his eyes glued to the stone. He could always see one face turned towards him and two in profile. And now he realised where his sense of lack was coming from, the sorrow that underlay everything, the sorrow that was present in every single thing, in every phenomenon, and always had been — it is impossible to grasp everything at once.

"It's impossible to see the fourth face," said Ruta, as if reading his thoughts. "That is the very centre of Primeval."

It began to pour, and when they reached the Highway they were completely soaked. Ruta's dress was clinging to her body.

"Come to our place. You can dry off," he suggested.

Ruta stood opposite Izydor. She had the whole village behind her.

"Izek, I'm going to marry Ukleja."

"No," said Izydor.

"I want to leave here for the city, I want to travel, I want to have earrings and smart shoes."

"No," repeated Izydor and began to tremble. Water poured down his face and blurred his view of Primeval.

"Yes," said Ruta and took a few steps backwards.

Izydor's legs gave way under him. He was afraid he would fall over.

"I'll only be in Taszów. It's not far away!" she cried and turned towards the forest.

THE TIME OF CORNSPIKE

The Bad Man came to Wydymacz in the evening. He would emerge from the forest at dusk, and it looked as if he had come unglued from its wall: he was dark, on his face he had the shadow of the trees which never disappeared. Cobwebs shone in his hair, earwigs and maybugs roamed in his beard — it disgusted

Cornspike. And he smelled different. Not like a man, but like wood, like moss, like a wild boar's hair, like a hare's fur. Whenever she allowed him to enter her, she knew she wasn't copulating with a human. He wasn't a human being, despite his human form, despite the two or three human words he was able to say. When she realised this, she was seized with terror, but excitement, too, at the idea that she herself was changing into a doe, a sow, an elk, that she was nothing more than a female animal, like billions of female creatures the world over, and that she had in her a male like billions of males the world over. Then the Bad Man let out a long, piercing howl that must have been heard all over the forest.

At dawn he would leave her, and on his way out he always pinched some of her food. Many times Cornspike tried to follow him through the forest to spot his hideout. If she knew where it was, she would have more power over him, because in his hiding place an animal or a man reveals the weak sides of his nature.

She never succeeded in tracking the Bad Man further than to the big lime tree. If she turned her gaze for just a moment from his hunched shoulders flashing between the trees, the Bad Man vanished, as if the earth had swallowed him.

Finally Cornspike realised that she was betrayed by her human, female smell, and so the Bad Man knew he was being followed. So she gathered some mushrooms and tree bark, took some pine needles and leaves, and put it all in a stone pot. She poured in rainwater and waited a few days. And when the Bad Man came to her, and then at dawn went off into the forest with a bit of pork fat between his teeth, she quickly undressed, smeared the mixture on herself and set off after him.

She saw him sit down on the grass at the edge of a meadow and eat the pork fat. Then he wiped his hands on the ground and went into the long grass. In an open space he looked around fearfully and sniffed. Once he even fell to the ground, and only a little later did Cornspike hear the rattle of a cart on the Wola Road.

The Bad Man went into Papiernia. Cornspike threw herself down in the grass now and, bending close to the earth, ran after him. When she found herself at the edge of the forest, she couldn't see him anywhere. She tried sniffing, just as he did, but she couldn't smell anything. She hung about helplessly under a large oak tree, when suddenly a branch fell beside her, then another, and a third. Cornspike realised her mistake, and looked up. The Bad Man was sitting on a branch of the oak tree, baring his teeth. She felt terrified of her nocturnal lover. He didn't look like a human being. He growled at her in warning, and Cornspike realised she must go away.

She went straight to the river, where she washed off the odours of the earth and forest.

THE TIME OF RUTA

Ukleja's Warszawa car went as far as it was possible to go. Then he had to get out and walk the last few metres on foot. He tripped on the ruts in the forest road and cursed. Finally he was standing outside Cornspike's half tumbledown cottage, spitting with rage.

"Good woman, if you please, I've business to discuss with you!" he called.

Cornspike came outside and stared straight into Ukleja's bloodshot eyes.

"I won't give her to you."

For a moment he lost his confidence, but instantly pulled himself together again.

"She's already mine," he said calmly. "She merely insists that you have to bless her. I am to ask you for her hand."

"I won't give her to you."

Ukleja turned towards the car and shouted:

"Ruta!"

A moment later the door opened and Ruta got out of the car. Her hair was short now, with curls of it escaping from under a little hat. In a narrow skirt and heels she seemed very slender and very tall. In those shoes of hers she hobbled along the sandy road. Cornspike looked at her possessively.

Ruta stopped beside Ukleja and hesitantly put her arm through his. This gesture gave Ukleja the courage he needed.

"Bless your daughter, woman, because we haven't much time."

He gently pushed the girl forwards.

"Go home, Ruta," said Cornspike.

"No, Mama, I want to marry him."

"He'll do you wrong. I'll lose you because of him. He's a werewolf."

Ukleja laughed.

"Ruta, let's go . . . this is pointless."

The girl abruptly turned to face him and threw her handbag at his feet.

"I'm not going until she lets me!" she cried in anger.

She walked up to her mother. Cornspike hugged her, and they stood like that until Ukleja began to grow impatient.

"Let's go, Ruta. You don't have to convince her. No means no. What a fine lady of the manor . . ."

Then Cornspike spoke to him over her daughter's head.

"You can take her, but on one condition."

"Well?" said Ukleja, intrigued. He liked bargaining.

"From October to the end of April she is yours. From May to September she is mine."

The amazed Ukleja looked at her as if he didn't understand. Then he started counting the months on his fingers, and found that this division was not even, and that he profited by it. He had more months than Cornspike. He smiled slyly.

"All right, so be it."

Ruta took her mother's hand and laid it on her own cheek.

"Thank you, Mama. I'll be fine. I've got everything I could wish for there."

Cornspike kissed her brow. She didn't even glance at Ukleja as they left. Before it got going, the car emitted clouds of grey smoke, and for the first time in their lives the trees in Wydymacz got a taste of exhaust fumes.

THE TIME OF MISIA

For his family and colleagues from work, for the secretaries and lawyers, Paweł gave a name-day party in June, on Saint Peter's and Saint Paul's day. But for his birthday he only ever invited Ukleja. Birthdays are for close friends, and Paweł had one close friend.

When the children heard the dull whirr of the Warszawa car, they ran away in panic to the hideout under the stairs. Unaware that he caused terror, Ukleja brought the children a large thermos of ice cream and wafers in a cardboard box.

In a blue maternity dress, Misia asked them to come and sit at table in the living room, but they were reluctant to take their places. Izydor stopped Ruta in the doorway.

"I've got some new stamps," he said.

"Izydor, don't pester the guests," Misia scolded him.

"You look lovely in that fur coat, like the Snow Queen," Izydor whispered to Ruta.

Misia began to serve the food. There were jellied pig's feet and two kinds of salad. There were plates of cold meat and stuffed egg shells. There was bigos stew heating up and chicken thighs sizzling in the kitchen. Paweł filled the shot glasses with vodka. The men sat opposite each other and talked about the prices of animal hides in Taszów and Kielce. Then Ukleja told a dirty joke. The vodka kept disappearing down their throats, and the glasses seemed too small to slake their bodies' monstrous thirst. And the men still seemed sober, though their faces had gone red and both had undone their collars. Finally their eyes misted over, as if they had frozen from the inside. Then Ruta followed Misia into the kitchen.

"I'll help you," she said, and Misia handed her a knife. Ruta's large hands sliced the cake, her red fingernails flashing against the whiteness of the cream like drops of blood.

The men started singing, and Misia glanced anxiously at Ruta.

"I must put the children to bed. Take them the cake," she asked her.

"I'll wait for you. I'll do the dishes."

"Ruta!" the drunken Ukleja suddenly screamed from the living room. "Come here, you floozy!"

"Come on," said Misia quickly, and took the tray with the cake.

Ruta put down the knife and reluctantly followed Misia. They sat down by their husbands.

"Look what a nice bodice I bought my wife!" cried Ukleja, and tugged at her blouse, revealing a freckly cleavage and a snow-white lacy brassiere. "French!"

"Stop it," said Ruta quietly.

"What do you mean, stop it? Aren't I allowed? You're mine, all of you and everything you've got on." Ukleja looked at the amused Paweł and repeated:

"She's all mine! And so's everything she's got on! I've got her all winter. In summer she fucks off to her mother."

Paweł pointed at his guest's full shot glass. They took no notice when the women went back into the kitchen. Ruta sat down at the table and lit a cigarette. Then Izydor, who was lying in wait for her, took the opportunity to bring out his box of stamps and postcards.

"Look," he said encouragingly.

Ruta picked up the postcards and looked at each one for a while. She blew streams of white smoke from her mouth, and her lipstick left mysterious marks on the cigarette.

"I can give them to you," said Izydor.

"No. I prefer to look at them at your place, Izek."

"You'll have more time in the summer, won't you?"

Izydor saw that a big tear had settled on Ruta's stiff, mascara-coated eyelashes. Misia handed her a glass of vodka.

"I'm so unlucky, Misia," said Ruta, and the tear trapped in her lashes rolled down her cheek.

THE TIME OF ADELKA

Adelka didn't like her father's friends, all those men whose clothes stank of cigarettes and dust. The most important of them was Ukleja — surely because he was so big and fat. But even Ukleja was nice and polite and spoke in a less booming voice when Mr Widyna came to see her father.

Widyna was brought by a chauffeur, who then waited all evening outside in his car. Widyna had a green hunter's uniform and a feather in his hat. He clapped Paweł on the shoulder in greeting and gave Misia's hand a long, disgusting kiss. Misia told Adelka to look after little Witek while she fetched the best provisions from the larder. The knife flashed in her hand as she sliced dry sausage and ham. Paweł talked of Widyna with pride, saying: "In this day and age it's good to have such acquaintances."

These particular acquaintances of her father's were keen on hunting, and would arrive from the forest laden with hares or pheasants. They would put it all on the table in the hall, and before sitting down to dinner they would knock back half a tumbler of vodka. The house smelled of bigos stew.

Adelka knew that on this sort of evening she would have to play. She also made sure Antek was on hand with his accordion. There was nothing she feared as much as her father when he got angry.

When the time came, her mother told them to fetch their instruments and go into the living room. The men would be smoking cigarettes, and silence would fall. Adelka struck the key note, and then she and Antek began to play together. For *In the Trenches of Manchuria* Paweł fetched his violin and joined their duet. Misia stood in the doorway and watched them proudly.

"I'm buying a double bass for the youngest one," said Paweł.

Witek hid behind his mother whenever people looked at him.

The whole time she played, Adelka kept thinking about the dead animals on the hall table.

They all had their eyes open. The birds' eyes looked like glass stones from rings, but the hares' eyes were terrible somehow. They seemed to follow her every move. The birds lay tied by the legs in bunches, like radishes. The hares lay singly. She looked for bullet wounds in their fur and feathers, but she only occasionally managed to find congealed round scabs. The dead hares' blood dripped from their noses onto the floor. They had sweet little muzzles similar to a cat's. Adelka would adjust their heads to make sure they were on the table.

One day, among the shot pheasants she noticed another kind of bird. It was smaller and had beautiful blue feathers. Their colour thrilled her, and she longed to have them. She didn't yet know what she would do with them, but she knew she wanted them. She carefully pulled out the feathers, one after another, until she was holding a feathery bouquet. She tied it with a white hair ribbon and went to show her mother. In the kitchen she ran straight into her father.

"What's this? What have you done? Do you know what you've done?"

Adelka shrank back against the dresser.

"You've plucked Mr Widyna's jay! And he shot it specially."

Misia stood next to Paweł, and the guests' curious heads appeared in the doorway.

Her father grabbed Adelka by the arm with an iron grip and steered her into the living room. He pushed her angrily, so that she stopped in front of Widyna, who was talking to someone.

"What is it?" he asked vacantly. His eyes were cloudy.

"She's plucked your jay!" cried Paweł.

Adelka held out the bouquet of feathers. Her hands were shaking.

"Give those feathers back to Mr Widyna," Paweł snapped at her. "Misia, fetch me some peas. We'll punish her as an example. You have to be tough with children . . . And keep them on a tight rein."

Misia reluctantly handed him a bag of peas. Paweł scattered

the peas in a corner of the room and told his daughter to kneel down on them. Adelka knelt down, and there was a short silence. She could feel everyone looking at her. She thought she was going to die now.

"To hell with the jay. Pour us a drink, Paweł," gurgled Widyna in this silence, and the hubbub started up again.

THE TIME OF PAWEŁ

Paweł lay on his back and knew he'd never fall asleep now. Outside it was getting grey. His head ached and he was terribly thirsty. But he was too tired and downcast to get up and go to the kitchen. So he brooded on the whole of the previous evening, the big drinking spree, the first few toasts, because he couldn't remember the rest, Ukleja's vulgar jokes, the displeased expressions on some of the women's faces and some of their grievances. And then he considered the fact that he had turned forty, and that the first part of his life was over. He had reached the peak, and now, lying on his back with a monstrous hangover, he was watching time go by. He started recalling other days and other evenings, too, watching them like a film when it is run from end to beginning — ludicrous, funny, and nonsensical, like his life. He could see all the images in detail, but they seemed trivial and meaningless. Like this he saw his entire past, and found nothing in it to be proud of, nothing to gladden him, or stir any kind of positive emotions. In this entire, bizarre tale there was nothing certain or permanent, nothing to get a grip on. There was just an endless struggle, some unfulfilled dreams and unsatisfied desires. "I've had no success at all," he thought. He felt like crying, so he tried, but he must have forgotten how, because he hadn't cried since childhood. He swallowed thick, bitter saliva and tried to emit a childish sob from his throat and lungs. But nothing came of it, so he cast his mind into the future and forced himself to think about what was going to happen, what he still had to do: a training course and certainly a promotion, the children going to middle school, building an extension for the house and some rooms to let — not just rooms but a boarding house, a holiday cottage for summer vacationers from Kielce and Kraków. For a while he cheered up inside and forgot about his headache, his bone-dry tongue and his suppressed tears. But the dreadful grief came back. He felt as if his future would be the same as his past — various things would happen in it that meant nothing and led nowhere. This idea made him feel fear, because after all that, after the course and the promotion, after the boarding house and the extension, after all sorts of ideas or any kind of activity came death. And Paweł Boski realised that on this sleepless, hung-over night he was staring helplessly at the birth of his own death — that in his life the hour of noon had already struck, and now, gradually, deviously, and imperceptibly the twilight was closing in.

He felt like an abandoned child, like a clod of earth thrown on the roadside verge. He lay on his back in the rough, elusive present, and felt that with every passing second he was dissolving into non-existence.

THE TIME OF RUTA

Ruta was even ready to love Ukleja. She could treat him like a large, sick animal. But Ukleja didn't want her love — he wanted power over her.

Sometimes Ruta felt as if the shaggy Bad Man were sitting inside Ukleja — he lay on top of her the same way as the Bad Man lay on her mother. But whereas her mother let it happen with a smile on her face, it made Ruta feel anger and hatred that grew and swelled like dough. Ukleja always fell asleep on top of her afterwards, and his body gave off a stink of alcohol. Ruta would slide out from under it and go into the bathroom. She would fill the bathtub with water and lie in it until the water went cold.

Ukleja would lock Ruta in the house alone. He left lots of good food for her in the kitchen, from the "Cosy Corner" restaurant: cold chicken, pork knuckle, fish in aspic, vegetable salad, egg mayonnaise, herrings in sour cream — whatever there was on the menu. In Ukleja's house she lacked nothing. She went from room to room, listened to the radio, changed into her dresses, and tried on shoes and hats. She had two wardrobes filled with clothes, a casket full of gold jewellery, about fifteen hats and dozens of pairs of shoes, so she had been given everything she wanted. To begin with she really thought she would be able to walk about the streets of Taszów in these outfits and parade outside the church in the market square, hear the sighs and catch the glances full of admiration. But Ukleja never let her go out alone. She could only go out with him. And he took her to see his pals and lifted her silk skirts to show off her thighs. Or he took her to the Boskis' house in Primeval, or to play bridge with the lawyers and secretaries, where she got bored and spent hours staring at her nylon stockings.

Then Ukleja took possession of a camera on a stand and some darkroom equipment from a photographer who owed him money. Ruta soon realised what taking photographs involved. The camera stood in the bedroom, and before getting into bed, Ukleja always set the automatic shutter release. Then in the red light of the darkroom Ruta saw Ukleja's mounds of flesh, his backside, genitals, and fat breasts bulging like a woman's, covered in black bristles. She also saw herself crushed and fragmented into breasts, thighs, and belly. So when she was left alone, she put on her dresses and stood perfumed and elegant before the eye of the camera lens.

"Click," said the camera in admiration.

THE TIME OF MISIA

The passage of time worried Misia in May in particular. May abruptly forced its way into its place in the rank of months and burst forth. Everything began to grow and flower — all at once.

Familiar with the early-spring, tawny-grey view from the kitchen window, Misia couldn't get used to the day-to-day changes in which May abounded. First of all, in just two days, the meadows went green. Then the Black River shone olive-green and let the light into its waters, which from then on assumed different shades daily. The woods at Papiernia went willow-green, then grass-green, and finally darkened and plunged into shadow.

In May Misia's orchard blossomed, and that was a sign that she could launder all the clothes, curtains, bedding, mats, napkins, and bedspreads that had gone musty over the winter. She stretched washing lines between the blossoming apple trees and filled the pink-and-white orchard with bright colours. The children, hens, and dogs came toddling after her. Sometimes Izydor came, too, but he always talked about things that didn't interest her.

In the orchard she thought about the fact that it was impossible to stop the trees from blossoming, and that the petals would inevitably fall, while in time the leaves would go brown and then drop. She wasn't comforted by the thought that next year the same thing would happen again, because she knew it wasn't true. Next year the trees would be different — bigger, their branches weightier, the grass would be different, and so would the fruits. This blossoming branch would never be repeated. "Hanging out the washing like this will never be repeated," she thought. "I shall never be repeated."

She went back into the kitchen and set about making the dinner, but everything she did seemed to her crude and clumsy. The pierogi were shapeless, the dumplings uneven, the pasta thick and coarse. Peeled clean, the potatoes suddenly got eyes that had to be dug out with the tip of a knife.

Misia was just like the orchard, and like everything in the world that is subject to time. After her third child she grew fat, her hair lost its shine and went straight. Now her eyes were the colour of bitter chocolate.

She was pregnant for the fourth time, and for the first time she thought it was too much for her. She didn't want this child.

A son was born, to whom she gave the name Marek. He was calm and quiet.

From the start he slept right through the night. He only came to life when he saw her breast. Paweł had gone on yet another course, so Michał looked after Misia in her confinement.

"Four children is a lot for you," he said. "You should be using some sort of protection. After all, Paweł knows a thing or two about it."

Soon Misia became certain that Paweł went whoring with Ukleja. Perhaps she shouldn't resent him for that. First of all she had been pregnant — fat and swollen — then in her confinement, which she took badly. But she did resent him.

She knew he was squeezing and screwing all those barmaids, butcher's shop girls, and waitresses from the restaurants he monitored as a state official. She found lipstick marks and single long hairs on his shirt. She started noticing alien smells on his things. Finally she found an open packet of condoms, which he never used when they made love.

Misia called Izydor upstairs to the bedroom, and together they divided the big double bed in half. She could see that Izydor liked this idea. He even added something of his own to this new arrangement — he put a flowerpot with a big palm tree in the middle of the room between the beds. Michał watched it all from the kitchen as he smoked a cigarette.

When Paweł came home rather tipsy, Misia went up to him with all four children.

"I'll kill you if you ever do it again," she said.

He blinked, but didn't try pretending not to know what was the matter. Then he threw his boots in the corner and laughed merrily.

"I'll kill you," repeated Misia so grimly, that the baby in her arms began to cry pitifully.

In late autumn Marek fell sick with whooping cough and died.

THE TIME OF THE ORCHARD

The orchard has two times that are interwoven, succeeding each other year after year. These are the time of the apple tree and the time of the pear tree.

In March, when the ground becomes warm, the orchard

begins to vibrate and digs its claw-like, underground paws into the earth's flesh. The trees suck the earth like puppies, and their trunks become warmer.

In the year of the apple, the trees draw from the earth the sour waters of underground rivers that have the power of change and motion. These waters contain the need to push, to grow and spread.

The year of the pear is completely different. The time of the pear trees involves sucking sweet juices from the minerals, as inside the leaves they gently and gradually merge with the rays of the sun. The trees come to a stop in their growing and relish the sweetness of sheer existence, without moving, without developing. Then the orchard seems unchanging.

In the year of the apple tree the flowers bloom briefly, but most beautifully. Often the frost beheads them or violent winds shake them off. There are lots of fruits, but they are small and not very impressive. Seeds roam far from the place of their birth: dandelion clocks cross the stream, grasses fly over the forest to other meadows, and sometimes the wind even carries them across the sea. Animal litters are weak and not large, but those that survive the first few days grow into healthy, clever specimens. Foxes born during apple-tree time do not hesitate to approach henhouses, and the same is true of falcons and martens. Cats kill mice not because they are hungry, but for the sake of killing, aphids attack people's gardens and butterflies assume the brightest colours on their wings. Apple-tree summers give birth to new ideas. People tread new paths. They fell forests and plant young trees. They build weirs on rivers and buy land. They dig the foundations for new houses. They think about journeys. Men betray their women, and women their men. Children suddenly become adult and leave to lead their own lives. People cannot sleep. They drink too much. They take important decisions and start doing whatever they have not done until now. New ideologies arise. Governments change. Stock markets are unstable, and from one day to the next you can become a millionaire or lose everything. Revolutions break out that change regimes. People daydream, and confuse their dreams with what they regard as reality.

In a pear-tree year nothing new happens. Things that have already begun continue. Things that do not yet exist gather their strength in non-existence. Plants strengthen their roots and trunks, and do not soar upwards. Flowers bloom slowly and idly, until they are large. There are not many roses on a rose bush, but each of them is as big as a human fist. So are the fruits in the time of the pear tree — sweet and fragrant. The seeds fall where they grew, and instantly put down strong roots. The ears of corn are fat and heavy. If it weren't for man, the weight of the seeds would crush them to the ground. Animals and people grow a layer of fat, because the barns are bursting with crops. Mothers give birth to big babies, and twins are born more often than usual. Animals, too, have large litters, and so much milk in their teats that they are able to feed their young. People think about building houses, or even entire cities. They draw plans and measure the ground, but they do not get down to work. The banks show enormous profits, and the warehouses of large factories are full of products. Governments grow stronger. People daydream, and finally notice that each of their dreams is coming true — even once it is already too late.

Paweł had to take several days' leave from work because of his father's death. His father died on the third day. It looked as if the end had already come, but an hour later old Boski got up and walked to the Highway. He stood by the fence and nodded. Paweł and Stasia took him by the arms and led him back to bed. For those three days their father said nothing. Paweł thought he was looking at him beseechingly, as if he wanted something. But Paweł reckoned he had done everything he could. He was with him the whole time, giving him things to drink and changing his sheets. How else you can help a dying father he didn't know.

Finally old Boski died. Paweł dozed off at dawn, and when he awoke an hour later, he saw that his father was no longer breathing. The old man's small body had caved in, gone floppy like an empty sack. There was no doubt there was no longer anyone inside it.

But Paweł did not believe in the immortal soul, so he found this sight appalling. He was seized with horror that soon he, too, would change into a lifeless scrap of flesh, and that would be all that was left of him. Tears fell from his eyes.

Stasia behaved very calmly. She showed Paweł the coffin that their father had made for himself. It was leaning against a wall in the barn. It had a lid made of shingle.

Now Paweł had to arrange the funeral and — like it or not — go and see the parish priest.

He met him in the presbytery courtyard, by the car. The priest invited him into a cool, gloomy office, where he sat down at a shiny polished desk. He spent a long time looking for the right page in the registry of deaths, and painstakingly recorded old Boski's details there. Paweł stood by the door, but as he didn't enjoy feeling like a supplicant, he came up to a chair by the desk and sat down.

"How much is it going to cost?" he asked.

The priest put down his pen and looked at him closely.

"I haven't seen you in church for years."

"I'm an atheist, sir."

"Your father wasn't easy to find at mass either."

"He always went to Midnight Mass at Christmas."

The priest sighed and stood up. He started pacing the office, snapping his fingers.

"My God," he said, "he went to Midnight Mass. That's just not enough for a decent Catholic. 'Remember to keep the Sabbath day holy' — that's what the Scripture says, doesn't it?"

"I've never bothered with all that, sir."

"If in the past ten years the deceased had taken part in each Sunday holy mass and put the proverbial zloty on the collection plate, do you know how much would have accumulated?"

The priest did some mental arithmetic and then said:

"The funeral will cost two thousand."

Paweł felt the blood rush to his head. He saw red spots before his eyes.

"Then fuck the whole thing," he said and sprang to his feet.

In a split second he was at the door, grabbing the handle.

"Well, all right, Boski," he heard from the desk. "Let's make it two hundred."

THE TIME OF THE DEAD

When old Boski died, he found himself in the Time of the Dead. In some way this time belonged to the cemetery in Jeszkotle. On the cemetery wall there was a plaque on which was clumsily engraved:

God sees
Time escapes
Death pursues
Eternity waits

When Boski died, he immediately realised he had made a mistake; he had died badly, carelessly, that he had made a mistake in dying and that he would have to go through the whole thing again. He also realised that his death was a dream, just like life.

The Time of the Dead imprisoned those who naively reckoned you don't have to learn death, those who had failed death like an exam. And the more the world moved forwards, the more it extolled life, the more firmly attached to life it was, the larger a crowd prevailed in the Time of the Dead and the noisier the cemeteries became. For only here did the dead gradually gain consciousness after life and find they had lost the time granted to them. Only after death did they discover the secret of life, and it was a futile discovery.

THE TIME OF RUTA

Ruta made bigos stew for Christmas and threw a handful of cardamom pods in it. She threw in cardamom because its seeds were beautiful — they had a perfect shape, they were shiny black and aromatic. Even their name was beautiful. It sounded like the name of a faraway country — the Kingdom of Cardamom.

In the stew the cardamom lost its black sheen, but its aroma pervaded the cabbage.

Ruta was waiting for her husband to come home for Christmas dinner. She lay on the bed and painted her nails. Then from under the bed she took out the German newspapers that Ukleja brought home, and looked through them with great interest. What she liked most were the pictures of faraway countries. They showed views of exotic beaches, beautifully sun-tanned men and slender, smooth women. Ruta understood just one word in the entire newspaper: "Brazil." This country was Brazil. In Brazil a great river flowed (a hundred times bigger than the Black and White Rivers combined) and a vast forest grew (a thousand times bigger than the Great Forest). In Brazil the cities enjoyed all kinds of riches, and the people looked happy and contented. Suddenly Ruta longed for her mother, though it was the middle of winter.

Ukleja came home late. As he stood on the threshold in a fur coat sprinkled in snow, Ruta instantly knew he was drunk. He didn't like the smell of cardamom and he didn't like the stew.

"Why didn't you make beetroot soup and ravioli? It's Christmas Eve!" he screamed. "You only know how to screw. You don't care who you do it with, whether it's Russkies or Germans or that halfwit Izydor. That's all you've got in your head, you bitch!"

He shakily went up to her and hit her in the face. She fell down. He knelt beside her and tried to get inside her, but his flaccid manhood refused to obey him.

"I hate you," she drawled through her teeth and spat in his face.

"Very good. Hatred is just as strong as love."

She managed to wriggle out from under his drunken bulk. She locked herself in the bedroom. Soon after, the pot of stew hit the door. Ruta took no notice of the blood flowing from her split lip. She tried on dresses in front of the mirror.

All night the aroma of cardamom seeped through cracks into her room. The furs and lipsticks smelled of it. It was the aroma of distant journeys and exotic Brazil. Ruta couldn't sleep. Once she had tried on all the dresses and matched all the shoes and hats to them, she pulled out two suitcases from under the bed and put all her most valuable things in them: two expensive fur coats, a silver fox collar, a box of jewellery, and the newspaper featuring Brazil. She dressed warmly, picked up her cases, and quietly, on tiptoes, crossed the dining room, where Ukleja lay sprawled on the sofa, snoring.

She came out past Taszów and reached the Kielce road. She had a hard time wading through the snow for a few kilometres, dragging the suitcases, until finally in the darkness she recognised the spot where there was a way into the forest. The wind rose, and a snow shower began.

Ruta walked to the border of Primeval, turned around, stood facing north and found in herself the feeling that makes it possible to pass through all borders, locks, and gates. For a while she savoured it inside her. Then the snowstorm really took hold, and Ruta walked into it with her entire being.

THE TIME OF THE GAME

When the Player finally finds the way out into the Fifth World, wonders what to do next, and seeks help in the instruction manual, *Ignis fatuus, or an instructive game for one player*, he finds the following story:

In the Fifth World God talks to Himself whenever He is particularly beset by loneliness.

He takes pleasure in watching people, especially one of them named Job. "If I were to take away everything he has, all the foundations of his confidence, if I were to strip him of all his goods, layer by layer, would he still be the man he is now? Wouldn't he start to curse and blaspheme against Me? Would he respect Me and love Me in spite of all?"

God gazes at Job from on high and tells Himself: "Definitely not. He only esteems Me because I bestow goods on him. I'll take away everything I have given him."

And God strips Job like an onion. And He weeps over him in sympathy. First He deprives Job of every possession he had: his house, land, herd of goats, labourers, groves, and woods. Then He takes away every person he loved: his children, women, closest friends, and relatives. Finally He removes everything that made Job the man he was: his physical health, mental health, habits and special interests.

Now He looks upon His work, and has to narrow His divine eyes. Job is shining with the same light that makes God glow. Or Job's brilliance may be even greater, because God has to narrow His divine eyes. Terrified, He hurriedly returns everything to Job in turn, and even gives him some extra new goods. He institutes money for their exchange, and along with the money safes and banks, He gives beautiful objects, fashions, wishes, and desires. And constant fear. He showers all this on Job, until gradually his light begins to fade and finally vanishes.

THE TIME OF LILA AND MAJA

The girls were born the year Michał died of heart disease in Taszów hospital, and Adelka started going to high school. She resented them for being born. She could not sit and read to her heart's content, as she wanted to. Instead, her mother's shaking voice would call her from the kitchen and ask her to help.

Those were lean years, like the prewar jackets with frayed seams that were worn now instead of an overcoat, poor, like pantries where there is never anything but a pot of lard and a few jars of honey.

Adelka could remember the night her mother gave birth to the twins and wept. Her grandfather, already ill then, sat by her bed.

"I'm almost forty. How am I going to bring up two little girls?"

"The same as the other children," he had said.

But the entire burden of bringing up this double trouble fell on Adelka. Her mother had lots of other things to do — the cooking, the laundry, and cleaning the yard. Her father only appeared in the evenings. They spoke to each other angrily, as if they couldn't bear the sight of each other, as if they suddenly hated each other. He would go straight down into the cellar, where he illegally tanned hides. That was how they survived. So after coming home from school Adelka had to fetch the pram and take the girls for a walk. Then she and her mother fed them and changed them, and in the evening she helped her mother to give them a bath. Only once she had watched to see they were asleep could she finally sit down to read. So when they fell ill with scarlet fever she thought it would be better for everyone if they died.

They lay in their little double bed unconscious with fever — identical, two-fold child suffering. The doctor came and said they must be wrapped in wet sheets to bring the fever down. Then he packed his bag and left. At the garden gate he told Paweł that he could find antibiotics on the black market. The word sounded miraculous, like a magic potion from a fairy tale, so Paweł got on his motorbike. In Taszów he learned that Stalin had died.

He waded through the melting snow to Ukleja's house, but he didn't find anyone there. So he went to the marketplace, to the district committee, to look for Widyna. The assistant's eyes were swollen from crying, and she told him the secretary wasn't receiving. She refused to let him go further inside. So Paweł went back outside, and looked around the town helplessly. "Whoever has already died and whoever is yet to die, Taszów is full of death," he thought. Then he decided he should just go and drink some vodka. Right away, at once. His legs took him of their own accord to the "Cosy Corner" restaurant. There he went straight up to the bar, where Basia was flaunting her wasp waist and enormous breasts. She had pinned a piece of lace in her thick hair.

Paweł wanted to go behind the counter and cuddle up to her fragrant cleavage. She poured him a double vodka.

"You've heard what happened?" she asked.

He knocked back the vodka in one gulp, and Basia offered him a plate of herring in sour cream.

"I need antibiotics. Penicillin. Do you know what that is?"

"Who's sick?"

"My daughters."

Basia emerged from behind the counter and threw her coat over her shoulders. She led him along the back streets downhill, to the river, and in among some small cottages where the Jews used to live. Her strong legs in their nylon stockings hopped across the soggy piles of horse manure. She stopped outside one of these cottages and told him to wait. A minute later she came back and named a sum of money. It was staggeringly high. Paweł gave her a roll of banknotes. Soon he was holding a small cardboard box. The only words he understood of the message on the lid were, "Made in the United States."

"When are you coming to see me?" she asked as he got on his motorbike.

"Not now," he said and kissed her on the lips.

That evening the girls' temperature dropped, and next day they were well. Misia prayed to the Virgin Mary of Jeszkotle, Queen of Antibiotics, for this sudden recovery. In the night, once she had checked to see if their foreheads were cool, she slid under Paweł's quilt and cuddled up to him as close as she could.

THE TIME OF THE LIME TREES

There are lime trees lining the Highway leading from Jeszkotle to the Kielce road. They looked the same at the beginning, and they will look the same at the end. They have thick trunks and roots that reach deep into the earth, where they meet the foundations of everything that lives. In winter their mighty boughs cast sharp shadows onto the snow and measure the hours of the short day. In spring the lime trees put out millions of green leaves that bring sunlight down to the earth. In summer their fragrant flowers attract swarms of insects. In autumn the lime trees add red and brown to the whole of Primeval.

Like all plants, the lime trees live an eternal dream, whose origin lies in the tree's seeds. The dream does not grow or develop along with it, but is always exactly the same. The trees are trapped in space, but not in time. They are liberated from time by their dream, which is eternal. Feelings do not grow in it, as they do in animals' dreams, nor do images appear in it, as they do in people's dreams.

Trees live thanks to matter, by absorbing juices that flow from deep in the ground and by turning their leaves to the sunlight. The tree's soul rests after going through many existences. The tree only experiences the world thanks to matter. For a tree, a storm is a warm-and-cold, idle-and-violent stream. When it gathers, the whole world becomes a storm. For the tree there is no world before or after the storm.

In the fourfold changes of the seasons the tree is unaware that time exists and that the seasons come in succession. For the tree all four qualities exist at once. Winter is part of summer, and autumn is part of spring. Cold is part of hot, and death is part of birth. Fire is part of water, and earth is part of air.

To trees people seem eternal — they have always been walking through the shade of the lime trees on the Highway, neither frozen still nor in motion. For trees people exist eternally, but that means just the same as if they had never existed.

The crash of axes and the rumble of thunder disturb the trees' eternal dream. What people call their death is just a temporary disruption of the dream. What people call the death of trees involves coming closer to the anxious existence of animals. For the clearer and stronger consciousness becomes, the more fear there is in it. But the trees never reach the kingdom of anxiety occupied by animals and people.

When a tree dies, its dream that has no meaning or impression is taken over by another tree. That is why trees never die. In ignorance of their own existence, they are liberated from time and death.

THE TIME OF IZYDOR

When Ruta left Primeval and it became clear she wasn't coming back, Izydor decided to enter a monastery.

There were two monastic orders in Jeszkotle — a women's and a men's. The nuns ran an old people's home. He often saw them taking their shopping home by bicycle. They tended the neglected graves at the cemetery. Their contrasting black-and-white habits stood out against the washed out greyness of the rest of the world.

The male order was called the Reformers of God. For a long time Izydor watched the sad, bleak building hidden behind a crumbling stone wall before setting off there. He noticed that the same two monks spent the whole time working in the garden. In silence they grew vegetables and white flowers. Only white ones — lilies, snowdrops, anemones, white peonies, and dahlias. One of the monks, who must have been the most important, made trips to the post office and did the shopping. The rest had to be shut in the mysterious interior forever. They devoted themselves to God. That was what Izydor liked best — to be separated from the world, deeply immersed in God. To get to know God, examine the order of the works He created, and finally answer the questions why Ruta had left, why his mother had fallen ill and died, why his father had died, why people and animals were killed in the war, and why God allowed evil and suffering.

If Izydor were accepted into the order, Paweł would no longer call him a scrounger. He would stop sneering at him and mocking him. Izydor wouldn't have to keep seeing all the places that reminded him of Ruta.

He confided his plans to Misia. She burst out laughing.

"Give it a try," she said, wiping a child's bottom.

Next day he went to Jeszkotle and rang the old-fashioned bell at the monastery door. For a long time nothing happened — maybe it was a test of his patience. Finally, however, the bolt grated and an old man in a dark-grey habit, whom he had never seen before, opened the door to him.

Izydor said why he had come. The monk was not surprised and did not smile. He nodded and told Izydor to wait. Outside.

The door grated shut. A quarter of an hour later it opened again, and Izydor was allowed to come inside. Now the monk led him along corridors, down stairs and up, all the way to a spacious, empty hall, where there was a desk and two chairs. After another ten minutes or so a different monk came into the hall, the one who went to the post office.

"I'd like to join the order," declared Izydor.

"Why?" the monk simply asked.

Izydor cleared his throat.

"The woman I wanted to marry has left. My parents have died. I feel lonely and I yearn for God, although I don't understand Him. I know we could have a closer relationship if I got to know Him better. I'd like to do that by reading books, in foreign languages, on various theories. However, the local library is poorly stocked . . ." Izydor had to refrain from complaining about the library. "But please do not think I would do nothing but read. I'd like to do something useful, and I know that this order, the Reformers of God, is exactly what I need. I'd like to make change for the better, to redress all manner of evil . . ."

The monk interrupted Izydor in mid-sentence.

"To change the world . . . you say. That's very interesting, but unrealistic. The world is impossible to make better or worse. It is bound to remain just as it is."

"Yes, but you are called reformers, aren't you?"

"Oh, you have misunderstood, my dear boy. We have no intention of reforming the world in anybody's name. We reform God."

There was a moment's silence.

"How can you reform God?" asked the surprised Izydor at last.

"You can. People change. Times change. Cars, satellites . . .

God might sometimes seem . . . how should I put it, anachronistic, and He is too big, too mighty, and thus a touch indolent as well, to fit people's imaginations."

"I thought God was unchanging."

"Each of us is wrong about something essential. That is a purely human trait. Saint Milo, the founder of our order, proved that if God were unchanging, if He came to a standstill, the world would cease to exist."

"I don't believe that," said Izydor with conviction.

The monk stood up, so Izydor got up, too.

"Come back to us when you feel the need."

"I don't like it," said Izydor to Misia when he went into the kitchen.

Then he lay down on his bed, which stood right in the centre of the attic, just under the skylight. The small rectangle of sky was like a picture, a holy picture that could hang in a church.

Whenever Izydor saw the sky and the four points of the compass he felt like praying, but the older he got, the harder it was for the words of the familiar prayers to come to his mind. Instead thoughts appeared in his head that made holes in his prayers and tore them to pieces. So he tried to concentrate and imagine the figure of an unchanging God in the starry picture. But his imagination always produced an image that his mind could not accept. Once it was an old man sprawling on a throne with such a cold, severe look on his face that Izydor instantly blinked and drove him out of the skylight frame. Another time God was a sort of wavering, fluttering spirit, so volatile and indefinite as to be unbearable. Sometimes underneath the figure of God there was someone real impersonating him, most often Paweł, and then Izydor lost the desire to pray. He sat on his bed and swung his legs in the air. And then he discovered that what he found difficult about God was God's gender.

And then, not without a sense of guilt, he saw Him in the frame of the skylight as a woman, She-God, or whatever She should be called. It brought him relief. He found it far easier to pray to Her than it had ever been before. He spoke to Her as to a mother. This went on for some time, but finally along with his prayers he started feeling a vague anxiety, which expressed itself by sending waves of heat through his body.

God was a woman, large, powerful, damp, and steaming like the earth in spring. She-God existed somewhere in space, like a storm cloud full of water. Her power was overwhelming, and reminded Izydor of some childhood experience that he feared. Every time he addressed Her, She answered him with a comment that gagged him. He couldn't go on speaking, the prayer lost any thread it had, any intention. It was impossible to want anything from She-God, it was only possible to imbibe Her, breathe Her, or dissolve in Her.

One day, when Izydor was staring at his piece of sky, he had a revelation. He realised that God is neither a man nor a woman. He knew it as he uttered the words "O God." Here lay the solution to the problem of God's gender. By making it into one word, "Ogod," it sounded neither masculine or feminine, but neutral, just like "oak tree," "opal," "ocean," "odour," "oatmeal," "omen," "open," . . . Izydor excitedly repeated the real divine name that he had discovered, and every time he did, he knew more and more. So Ogod was young, and at the same time had existed since the beginning of the world or even earlier, without cease (because "Ogod" reminded him of "over and over"), it was unique and unrepeatable ("only"), and it was the start and finish of everything ("omega"), though if you tried to find it, it wasn't there ("n-owhere"). Ogod was full of love and joy, but could also be cruel and dangerous. It contained all the features and attributes that are present in the world, and took on the form of every thing, every event, every time. It created and destroyed, or allowed what It created to destroy itself. It was unpredictable like a child, like someone insane. In a way It was a bit like Ivan Mukta. Ogod existed in such an obvious way that Izydor wondered how he could ever have failed to realise it.

This discovery brought him genuine relief. Whenever he thought about it, somewhere inside he felt a burst of laughter. Izydor's soul was chuckling away. He stopped going to church, too, which met with Paweł's approval.

"Though I don't think they'd let you join the Party," he said one day at breakfast, to dispel any hopes his brother-in-law might have.

"Paweł, you don't have to chew porridge," Misia pointed out to him.

Izydor couldn't care less about either the Party or going to church. Now he needed time for thinking, remembering Ruta, for reading, for learning German, for writing letters, collecting stamps, staring at his skylight, and gradually, idly sensing the order of the universe.

THE TIME OF MRS PAPUGA

Old Boski had built a house, but he hadn't dug a well, and so Stasia Papuga had to go next door to her brother for water. She put a wooden yoke on her shoulders and attached buckets to it. As she walked along, the buckets creaked steadily.

Mrs Papuga drew water from the well and took a furtive look around the yard. She saw bedding hung out to air — the limp bodies of plump eiderdowns cast across poles. "I'd hate to have eiderdowns like that," she thought. "They're too warm and the feathers fall to the bottom. I prefer my nice light blankets with the linen covers." Cold water spilled from the buckets onto her bare feet. "I wouldn't like to have such large windows either. How much cleaning they must need! Or net curtains — you can't see anything through them. I wouldn't want that many children, and high-heeled shoes are bad for your feet."

Misia must have heard the yoke creaking, because she came out onto the steps and invited Stasia inside. Stasia put the buckets down on the concrete and went into the Boskis' kitchen, where it always smelled of burnt milk and dinner. She sat on a small table by the stove, never on a chair. Misia shooed away the children and ran under the stairs.

She always brought something useful out of there: trousers for Janek, a little sweater or some shoes Antek had grown out of. Stasia had to alter Misia's hand-me-downs, because they were too small for her. But she liked sewing in bed when she woke up. So she added gores, gussets, and frills, and unstitched all the tucks.

Misia treated Stasia to Turkish coffee.

The coffee was well made and had a thick skin on which the sugar sat for a moment before sinking to the bottom. Stasia couldn't take her eyes off Misia's nimble fingers as she tipped coffee beans into the grinder and then turned the handle. Finally the grinder's little drawer was full, and the aroma of freshly ground coffee floated about the kitchen. She liked the smell, but she found the actual coffee bitter and unpalatable. So she tipped a few spoonfuls of sugar into her glass until the sweetness overcame the bitterness. From the corner of her eye she watched the way Misia savoured the coffee, stirred it with her spoon, picked up the glass in two fingers and raised it to her lips. And then she did the same.

They talked about children, kitchen gardens and cooking. But there were times when Misia was inquisitive, too.

"How do you live without a man?"

"I've got Janek, haven't I?"

"You know what I mean."

Stasia didn't know what to say. She stirred her coffee.

"Living without a man is bad," she thought that evening in bed. Stasia's breasts and belly wanted to cuddle up to a man's body, solid and smelling of work in the sunshine. Stasia rolled up a pillow and hugged it as if it were another body, and fell asleep like that.

There were no shops in Primeval. All the shopping was done in Jeszkotle, and Stasia had an idea. She borrowed a hundred zlotys from Misia and bought several bottles of vodka and some chocolate. And then it just took off on its own. There was always someone needing a half litre in the evening. Sometimes on a Sunday someone felt like having a drink with a neighbour under a lime tree. The people from Primeval soon learned that Stasia Papuga had a bottle or two, and would sell it for not much more than in the shop. They would also buy some chocolate for the wife, so she wouldn't be annoyed.

In this way Stasia got a business going. At first Paweł resented her for it, but then he started sending Witek to her for vodka himself.

"You know what the penalty for that is?" he asked her, frowning, but Stasia was sure that if, God forbid, something were to happen, her brother had acquaintances, and he wouldn't let her come to harm.

She soon started going to Jeszkotle for goods two or three times a week. She also widened the range. She had baking powder and vanilla — things any housewife might suddenly run out of while doing the Saturday baking. She had various brands of cigarettes, oil and vinegar, and after a year when she bought herself a refrigerator, she started bringing home butter and margarine, too. She kept it all in the annex which, like everything, her father had built. There stood the refrigerator, and a couch on which Stasia slept, a tiled stove, a table, and some shelves behind a curtain of faded calico. Ever since Janek left to go to school in Silesia she hadn't used the main room.

The illicit sale of alcohol, as Stasia's business was called in official language, greatly enriched her social life. Various people came to see her, sometimes even from Jeszkotle and Wola. On Sunday mornings, hung-over forestry workers came on bicycles. Some bought whole half-litre bottles of vodka, others bought quarters, and others asked for a hundred grams on the spot. So Stasia would pour it for them and offer them pickled gherkins for free as a chaser.

One day a young forester turned up at Stasia's place in search of vodka. There was a heatwave, so she invited him to sit down and have some fruit juice. He thanked her and immediately downed two glasses.

"What delicious juice. Do you make it yourself?"

Stasia said yes, and for some reason her heart began to pound. The forester was a handsome man, though still very young. Too young. He wasn't tall but he was burly. He had a fine black moustache and lively hazel eyes. She carefully wrapped a bottle for him in newspaper. After that the forester came by again, and once again she gave him some fruit juice. They chatted for a while. And later on, one evening, he knocked as she was getting undressed for bed. He was tipsy. She quickly put on her dress. This time he didn't want a bottle to take away. He wanted to drink. She poured him a glass of vodka, sat on the edge of the couch and watched him knock it back. He lit a cigarette and looked around the annex. He cleared his throat, as if wanting to say something. Stasia sensed it was an unusual moment. She fetched another glass and filled both to the brim. They picked up the glasses and clinked them together. The forester drank, and shook the last few drops from his glass onto the floor in the traditional way. Then he suddenly put his hand on Stasia's knee. His mere touch was enough to make her feel so weak that she leaned back and lay supine on the couch. The forester fell on top of her and started kissing her neck. Just then it occurred to Stasia that she was wearing an old, patched and extended bra and some baggy knickers, so as he was kissing her she slipped them both off herself. The forester violently forced his way into her, and those were the finest minutes in Stasia's life.

Once it was all over, she was afraid to move underneath him. He got up without looking at her and buttoned his trousers. He muttered something and headed straight for the door. She watched as he struggled with the lock. He left, without even closing the door behind him.

THE TIME OF IZYDOR

Ever since he had learned to read and write, Izydor had been fascinated by letters. He collected them in an old shoe box — everything that came to the Boskis' house. Most of them were official letters, recognisable by the titles "Citizen" or "Comrade" on the envelope. Inside they were full of mysterious abbreviations such as "i.e.," "etc." and "e.g." There were also lots of postcards in the shoe box — black-and-white panoramas of the Tatra mountains, or black-and-white seas, with the same messages every year: "Warmest greetings from Krynica," or "Best wishes from the High Tatras," or "Merry Christmas and Happy New Year." Now and then Izydor took out the ever growing collection and saw how the ink was fading, and how the dates were getting funnily distant. What had happened to "Easter 1948"? Or "20 December 1949"? Or "Krynica, August '51"? What did it mean that they were past and gone? Were they gone in the same way as the views, which are left behind as people travel onwards, but which must still be somewhere and remain there for other people to see? Perhaps time prefers to erase all trace of itself, reduce the past to dust and destroy it forever?

Thanks to the cards Izydor discovered stamps. He could not get his head around the fact that they were so small, so fragile and perishable, and yet they contained miniature worlds. "Just like people," he thought, and carefully unstuck them from letters and postcards over a steaming kettle. He laid the stamps out on newspaper and spent hours examining them. There were animals and distant countries on them, precious stones and fish from far-away seas, ships and aeroplanes, famous people and historical events. Just one thing bothered Izydor — that their subtle draw-ings were spoiled by the ink from the postmarks. Before he died, his father showed him a fairly simple way to remove the ink. All it took was some egg white and a little patience. It was the most important lesson he ever learned from his father.

In this way Izydor became the owner of a large collection of pretty decent stamps. Now he could write letters himself, if only he had someone to write to. He thought of Ruta, but every thought of her caused him pain. Ruta was not there, and he couldn't write her a letter. Like time, Ruta had passed him by and crumbled to dust.

Sometime around 1962, thanks to Ukleja, a very colourful

German magazine full of advertisements ended up at the Boskis' house. Izydor spent days on end looking at it, and was amazed by all the long, unpronounceable words. In the local library he dug out a pre-war German-Polish dictionary, containing far more German words than just *raus*, *schnell*, and *Hände hoch*, which everyone in Primeval had learned during the war. Then one of the summer vacationers gave Izydor a small dictionary to keep, and Izydor wrote his first letter ever. In German: "Please send me car catalogues and tourist brochures. My name is Izydor Niebieski. This is my address." He stuck several of his finest stamps on the envelope and made his way to the post office in Jeszkotle. A lady clerk in a shiny black apron took the letter from him, examined the stamps, and placed it in a compartment.

"That's it. Thank you," she said.

Shifting from one foot to the other, Izydor went on standing at the window.

"It won't get lost, will it? It won't go astray, will it?"

"If you're in doubt, send it registered. But it costs more."

Izydor stuck on more stamps and spent a long time filling in a form. The clerk gave his letter a number.

A few weeks later a thick white envelope came, addressed to Izydor. It had foreign, completely different stamps, to which Izydor's eyes were unaccustomed. Inside there were advertisements for Mercedes-Benz cars and tourist brochures from various travel agencies.

Never in his life before had Izydor felt so important. And that evening as he looked at his brochures once more, he thought of Ruta again.

Mercedes-Benz and the German travel agencies gave Izydor so much courage that he started sending several registered letters a month. He also asked Adelka and Antek, who were at boarding schools somewhere beyond Kielce, to bring him all their old stamps. After removing the postmarks he stuck them on his letters. Sometimes he managed to sell some brochures to someone for a small amount. He kept receiving new brochures and new addresses.

Now he got in touch with German, Swiss, Belgian, and French tourist firms. He was sent colour photos of the Côte d'Azure, folders full of the sombre landscapes of Brittany and crystal-clear views of the Alps. He spent nights on end looking at them in delight, though he knew that for him they only existed on smooth paper smelling of ink. He showed them to Misia and his nieces. Misia said:

"How beautiful."

Then a small thing happened that changed Izydor's life: a letter got lost.

It was a registered one that Izydor had sent to a camera company in Hamburg, with a request for brochures, of course. This company always wrote back to him, but this time there was no reply. All night Izydor wondered how his registered letter could have got lost, as a receipt had been made out for it and a number assigned to it. Wasn't that meant to be a guarantee of indestructibility? Maybe it had been stopped in Poland? Maybe the drunken postman had lost it? Maybe there was a flood, or the train bringing the post had derailed?

Next morning Izydor went to the post office. The clerk in the black apron advised him to register a complaint. On a form with two carbon copies he filled in the name of the company, and in the box marked "sender" he put his details. He went home, but he couldn't think about anything else. If letters got lost in the post, it wasn't the same postal service that he regarded with such admiration. He thought of the post as a mysterious, mighty organisation that had its people in every place on the face of the earth. The post was a powerhouse, the mother of all stamps, the queen of all the navy-blue postmen in the world, the guardian of millions of letters, the Sovereign of Words.

Two months later, when the psychological wounds inflicted on Izydor by the postal service were starting to heal, an official letter came, in which the Polish Post Office apologised to "Citizen Niebieski Izydor" for the fact that it had failed to find the lost letter. At the same time, the German photography firm declared that it had not received a registered letter from "Citizen Niebieski Izydor," and so the postal services of both countries felt responsible for the lost letter and were offering "the aggrieved Citizen Niebieski Izydor" compensation of two hundred zlotys. At the same time, the Polish Post Office apologised for the ensuing incident.

That was how Izydor came into possession of a large sum of money. He immediately gave Misia a hundred zlotys, and with the rest he bought himself a stamp album and several sheets of stamps for registered letters.

Now, whenever there was no answer to a letter, he went to the post office and registered a complaint. If the letter turned up, he had to pay 1 zloty and 50 groszy for the cost of the complaint. That wasn't much. Meanwhile he was always finding that one of the dozens of letters he sent had got lost — either they had forgotten to deliver it, or the foreign addressees had forgotten they had received it and, baffled by the forms the Polish post had sent them, had answered *non, nein, no.*

So Izydor kept receiving money. He became a legitimate member of the family. He was capable of earning a living.

In Primeval, like everywhere in the world, there are places where matter creates itself, coming into being on its own out of nothing. They are always just small chunks of reality, not essential to the whole, and as a result they are no threat to the balance of the world.

There is a place like that on the embankment by the Wola Road. It looks inconspicuous, like a molehill, like an innocent little graze on the earth's flesh that never heals. Only Cornspike knows about it and stops on the way to Jeszkotle to watch the world creating itself. There she finds strange things and non-things: a red stone not like any other stone, a piece of gnarled wood, some prickly seeds that later produce some feeble little flowers in her garden, an orange fly, and sometimes just an odour. Cornspike sometimes gets the feeling that the inconspicuous molehill also creates a space, and that the roadside embankment is gradually getting bigger. In this way each year Malak's field gets bigger, where in complete ignorance he plants potatoes.

Cornspike dreamed up the idea that one day she would find a child there, a little girl, and would take her home to fill the gap left by Ruta. But one autumn the molehill disappeared. For the next few months Cornspike tried to catch empty space in the act of bubbling forth, but nothing happened, so she realised the self-creation outlet had gone off somewhere else.

For a while the fountain in the Taszów market square seemed to be another such place. The fountain produced noises, whispers and rustles, and sometimes a sort of jelly-like substance was found in its water, matted balls of hair, and the green parts of a large plant. People realised the fountain was haunted, so they demolished it and built a parking lot.

And of course there is a place in Primeval, as everywhere in the world, where reality rolls up and leaks from the world like air from a balloon. It appeared in the fields beyond the Hill just after the war, since when it has been growing more and more distinctly. A crater has formed in the ground, which sucks down yellow sand, tufts of grass, and field stones into nowhere.

THE TIME OF THE GAME

The *Instructive game for one player* is strange, and so are its rules. Sometimes the player feels as if he has experienced all this before, that he has already played something like it or that he knows the Game from his dreams, or maybe from the books in a local library he visited when he was a child. This is what it says in the instructions about the Sixth World:

God created the Sixth World by accident, and then went away. He made it any old how, haphazardly. His work was full of holes and mistakes. Nothing was obvious, nothing permanent. Black ran into white and evil sometimes seemed to be good, just as good often looked like evil. So once left to its own devices, the Sixth World began to create itself. Tiny acts of creation appeared out of nowhere in time and space. Matter managed to sprout into things of its own accord. By night objects replicated, stones and veins of metals grew in the ground, and new rivers began to flow in the valleys.

People learned to create by the force of their own will, and called themselves gods. Now the world was filled with millions of gods. But their will was subordinate to impulse, and so chaos returned to the Sixth World. There was too much of everything, though something new was always coming into being. Time started gathering speed, and people started dying from the effort of trying to make something that did not yet exist.

Finally God came back and, vexed by all the mess, destroyed the entire creation with a single thought. Now the Sixth World stands empty and silent as a concrete tomb.

THE TIME OF IZYDOR

One day, when Izydor went to the post office with a wad of letters, the clerk in the shiny apron suddenly put her face to the window and said:

"The postmaster is very pleased with you. He says you're our best customer."

Izydor froze, with his copying pencil poised above a complaint form.

"How come? I'm always exposing the post office to losses. But it's all in keeping with the law, I don't do anything wrong . . ."

"Oh, Izydor, you don't understand a thing." Sliding her chair forward with a scraping noise, the woman leaned halfway out of the window. "The post office earns money because of you. That's why the postmaster is pleased there's someone like you at our office. You see, the way the contracts between countries work, for every lost international letter the postal services of both countries pay half the cost each. We pay you in zlotys, and they pay in marks. We convert those marks for you according to the state exchange rate, all in keeping with the rules. We make a profit, and so do you. Nor does anyone lose by it either. Well, aren't you pleased?"

Izydor nodded half-heartedly.

"Yes."

The clerk backed away again. She took Izydor's complaint form and began to stamp it automatically.

When he got home, there was a black car outside the house. Misia was waiting for him in the doorway. Her face was grey and immobile. At once Izydor realised something terrible had happened.

"These gentlemen have come to see you," said Misia in a wooden tone.

Two men were sitting at the table in the living room wearing light raincoats and hats. It was about the letters.

"To whom do you write letters?" asked one of the men, and lit a cigarette.

"Well, to tourist firms."

"That sounds like spying."

"What on earth would I have to spy on? Thank God, when I saw the car I thought something had happened to the children . . ."

The men exchanged glances, and the one with the cigarette gave Izydor an ominous look.

"Why do you need so many colour magazines?" asked the other one out of the blue.

"I'm interested in the world."

"You're interested in the world . . . What are you so interested in the world for? Do you know what you can get for spying?"

The man drew his hand swiftly across his neck.

"Your throat cut?" asked Izydor in terror.

"Why don't you work? What do you live off? What's your occupation?"

Izydor felt his hands sweating and began to stammer.

"I wanted to join the monastery, but they wouldn't take me. I help my sister and my brother-in-law. I chop wood, I play with the children. Maybe I'll get a pension . . ."

"He's got a screw loose," muttered the man with the cigarette.

"Where do you send letters to? To Radio Free Europe, perhaps?"

"Only to car firms or travel agencies . . ."

"What was your connection with Ukleja's wife?"

It took Izydor a while to realise they meant Ruta.

"You could say everything and nothing."

"Leave out the philosophy."

"We were born on the same day and I wanted to marry her . . . but she left."

"Do you know where she is now?"

"No. Do you?" asked Izydor hopefully.

"None of your business. I'm asking the questions."

"Gentlemen, I'm innocent. The Polish Post Office is pleased with me. They've just told me that."

The men got up and headed for the exit. One of them turned around again and said:

"Just remember you're under observation."

A few days later Izydor received a crumpled, soiled letter with foreign stamps of a kind he had never seen before. On impulse he glanced at the sender's name and read: "Amanita Muscaria."

These words seemed strangely familiar. "Maybe it's a German company," he thought.

But the letter was from Ruta. He guessed as soon as he saw the clumsy, childish handwriting. "Dear Izek," she wrote, "I am far, far away, in Brazil. Sometimes I can't sleep because I miss you all so much. And sometimes I don't think about you at all. I have a lot to do here. I live in an enormous city full of colourful people. How is your health? I hope my mama is well too. I miss her very much, but I know she couldn't live here. I have everything I wanted. Don't send anyone my love, not even my mother. Better they forget about me quickly. Amanita Muscaria."

Izydor had a sleepless night. He lay staring at the ceiling as images and odours came back to him from the days when Ruta was still here. He remembered her every word, every gesture. One by one he brought them back to mind. When the sun's rays reached the eastern window in the roof, tears rolled from Izydor's eyes. Then he sat up and looked for an address: on the envelope, on the piece of paper, even under the stamp and in its intricate drawing. But he couldn't find one.

"I'll go to her. I'll save up the money and go to Brazil," he said out loud to himself.

Then he thought of an idea that the secret police agents had unwittingly suggested to him. On a piece of paper torn from an exercise book he wrote: "Please send me some brochures. Best wishes, Izydor Niebieski." On the envelope he wrote the address: "Radio Free Europe, Munich, Germany."

The clerk at the post office went pale when she saw this address. Without a word she handed him a form for a registered letter.

"And a complaint form, too, please," said Izydor.

It was a very simple deal. Izydor sent a letter like that once a month. He knew it would not just never reach the addressee, but wouldn't even leave the boundaries of the county. Every month he received compensation for the letters. Finally he put a blank sheet of paper in the envelope. There was no point asking for brochures any more. This was extra income, which Izydor put aside in an old UNRRA tea tin — for a ticket to Brazil.

The next spring the secret police agents in raincoats took Izydor off to Taszów. They shone a lamp in his eyes.

"The code," said one of them.

"What's a 'code'?" asked Izydor.

The other one slapped him in the face.

"Give us the code. How do you code the information?"

"What information?" asked Izydor.

He was hit in the face again, harder this time. He could taste blood on his lips.

"We've checked every word, every square centimetre of the letter and envelope by all available methods. We've peeled the paper apart. We've checked the stamps. We've enlarged each one several dozen times. We've examined their serration and the composition of the glue under a microscope. We have analysed every letter, every comma and full stop . . ."

"We haven't found anything," said the other one, the one who had hit him.

"There's no code there," said Izydor quietly, wiping his bleeding nose with a handkerchief.

Both men burst out laughing.

"All right then," the first one began. "Let's agree to start again from the beginning. We won't do anything to you. We'll write in our report that you're not entirely normal. Everyone thinks of you like that anyway. And we'll let you go home. And in exchange you'll tell us how it all works. Where did we go wrong?"

"There's nothing there."

The other man was more nervous. He brought his face close to Izydor's. He stank of cigarettes.

"Listen, wise guy. You've sent twenty-six letters to Radio Free Europe. There were blank pieces of paper in most of them. You've been playing with fire. And now you've gone too far."

"Just tell us how you coded them. And that'll be it. Then you'll go home."

Izydor sighed.

"I can see it's very important to you, but I really don't know how to help you. There weren't any codes there. They were just blank sheets of paper, nothing more."

Then the second secret policeman jumped up from his chair and punched Izydor in the face. Izydor slid off his chair and lost consciousness.

"He's a loony," said the first one.

"Remember, pal, we're never going to let you alone," drawled the second, rubbing his fist.

Izydor was kept under arrest for forty-eight hours. Then a guard came for him, and without a word opened the door to let him out.

All week Izydor didn't come down from his attic. He counted the money in the tin and found he had a real fortune there. In any case, he didn't know how much a ticket to Brazil might cost.

"That's enough of the letters," he told Misia when he came down into the kitchen. She smiled at him and breathed a sigh of relief.

THE TIME OF DOLLY

The time of animals is always the present.

Dolly is a shaggy, red-haired dog. She has brown eyes that sometimes shine black. Dolly loves Misia best of all, so she always tries to have Misia within range of sight. Then everything is in its place. Dolly follows Misia to the well, into the garden, and goes out with her onto the Highway to take a look at the world. She never lets Misia out of her eyes' embrace.

Dolly doesn't think how Misia or any other person thinks. In this way there is a huge gulf between Dolly and Misia, because to think you have to swallow time, internalise the past, the present, the future and their constant changes. Time works inside the human mind. It is nowhere to be found on the outside. In

Dolly's small dog's brain there is no channel, no organ to filter the passage of time. So Dolly lives in the present. That is why when Misia gets dressed and goes out, Dolly thinks she is leaving forever. Every Sunday she goes to church forever. She goes down to the cellar for potatoes forever. When she disappears from Dolly's field of vision, she disappears forever. Then Dolly's grief is boundless, she lays her muzzle on the ground and suffers.

Man harnesses his suffering to time. He suffers as a result of the past and extends his suffering into the future. In this way he creates despair. Dolly only suffers here and now.

Human thinking is inseparably linked with swallowing time. It is a sort of choking. Dolly perceives the world as static images that some God has painted. For animals, God is a painter. He spreads the world before them in the form of panoramic views. The extent of these crude pictures lies in smells, touches, flavours, and sounds, which contain no meaning. Animals do not need meaning. People sometimes feel something similar when they dream. But when they are awake, people need meaning, because they are prisoners of time. Animals dream incessantly and for nothing. For them, waking up from this dream is death.

Dolly thrives on images of the world. She takes part in the images that people create with their minds. When Misia says "Let's go" and sees Dolly wagging her tail, she thinks Dolly can understand words like a person. But Dolly is wagging her tail not at the word, not at the concept, but at the image that has sprouted from Misia's mind. This image contains the anticipation of movement, and of landscapes that keep changing, grass swaying, the Wola Road leading to the forest, grasshoppers chirruping, and the rushing of the river. As she lies there staring at Misia, Dolly sees the images that a human unwittingly produces. They can be images full of sorrow or anger. Those images are even more distinct, because they pulsate with passion. Then Dolly is defenceless, because she has nothing in her to protect her from getting lost in those alien, gloomy worlds, there are no magic protective rings of identity, there is no "self" supplied with powerful energy. So she is subdued by them. That is why dogs regard man as their master. And why the lowliest man can feel like a hero in his dog's eyes.

The ability to experience emotion does not distinguish Dolly from Misia in any way.

An animal's emotion is even purer, not clouded by any thoughts.

Dolly knows that God exists. She perceives Him all the time, and not, like people, just in rare moments. Dolly can smell His odour in the grass, because she is not separated from God by time. That is why Dolly has more trust in the world than any man could ever have. The Lord Jesus had similar trust inside him as he hung upon the cross.

THE TIME OF POPIELSKI'S GRANDCHILDREN

Straight after the end of the school year, Squire Popielski's daughter, the one who used to walk about the park with a large dog, brought her children and her brother's children to Primeval. Misia fixed up three rooms for them upstairs, and if there was a need, a room downstairs, too. And so at the end of June Paweł Boski's dream guesthouse began to operate at full steam.

Squire Popielski's grandchildren were robust and noisy. They showed no resemblance to their grandfather. And, as always happens in good families, they were all boys, except for one single girl. They were cared for by a nanny, the same one every year. The nanny's name was Zuzanna.

The kids spent whole days by the Black River at a place called the Sluice, where young people came from all over the neighbourhood to bathe. Squire Popielski had once put flood-gates on the river to regulate the flow of water into his ponds. Now the ponds no longer existed, but skilful manipulation of the flood-gates made it possible to create a lake in summer and a metre-high waterfall. Grandfather Popielski cannot have imagined he would be giving his grandchildren so much joy.

The kids came home for lunch, which Misia often served in the garden under the apple trees. After lunch they went back to the river. In the evenings, Zuzanna organised games for them, either cards or "Categories" or anything else, as long as they were quiet. Sometimes Witek, who was not much older than them, made a bonfire for them behind the Hill.

Every year on Midsummer's Eve Squire Popielski's grandchildren headed off to the forest to look for the fern flower that was supposed to bloom that night. This expedition became a ritual, and one year Zuzanna let them go on their own. The squire's grandchildren took advantage of the opportunity, and so no one would know, they bought a bottle of cheap wine in Jeszkotle. They took sandwiches with them, bottles of orangeade, sweets, and flashlights. They sat on the bench outside the house and waited until it finally got dark. They laughed and were noisy, pleased about their hidden bottle.

Squire Popielski's grandchildren became quiet only in the forest, not because their mood had soured, but because in the darkness the forest seemed vast and scary. Their bold plan was to go to Wodenica, but the darkness put an end to that idea. Wodenica was a haunted place. They would go into an alder grove, where the most ferns grew. They would drink up the wine and smoke a forbidden cigarette, like the boys from Primeval.

The children walked towards the river in a line, holding each other by the shoulder.

It was so dark that the hands they stretched out ahead of them loomed in the blackness like barely recognisable smudges. Only the sky seemed clearer than the world enveloped in darkness — like a grand celestial colander with stars for holes.

The forest was behaving like an animal that keeps people away — it shook dew onto them, sent out a tawny owl, and told a hare to leap up suddenly under their feet.

The children went into the alder grove and groped in the dark, making themselves a picnic. The burning tips of the cigarettes glowed. The wine, which they drank straight from the bottle for the first time in their lives, gave them courage. Then they ran about in the ferns, until one of them found something shining among them. The alarmed forest began to whisper. The finder summoned the others. He was excited.

"I think I've got it, I think I've got it," he kept saying.

Among the tangled blackberry bushes, something silver was glittering in the dampness of the fern leaves. The children parted the large leaves with sticks, and by the light of their flashlights they saw a shining empty tin. The disappointed finder picked it up on the end of his stick and tossed it away into the bushes.

The squire's grandchildren sat down for a while longer to finish up the wine, and then went back to the road.

Only then did the empty tin blossom, casting an eerie, silvery brilliance all around it.

Cornspike saw it, who always gathered herbs on the night of the solstice, but was now too old to have any wishes, and she knew how much trouble you could bring on yourself with the fern flower. So she skirted round it at a distance.

"Won't you take a cup of tea with me, Misia, once you've finished?" asked the Popielskis' daughter, who still had a young girl's figure.

Misia stood up straight over the bowls full of dirty dishes and wiped her hands on her apron.

"Not tea, but I'd love a coffee."

They took a tray outside and sat on either side of the table under the apple tree. Lila and Maja finished washing the dishes.

"It must be hard for you, Misia, to serve so many dinners and wash so many dishes . . . We're very grateful to you for all this effort. If it weren't for you, we'd have nowhere to come to. After all, this is our family neighbourhood."

Miss Popielska, who once upon a time, long, long ago, used to run about the meadows with her big dogs, sighed sadly.

"And if it weren't for you, we'd never manage to survive on Paweł's wages. Letting out rooms is my contribution to keeping the family."

"You shouldn't think like that, Misia. After all, a woman works in the home, she bears children, she does the housekeeping, you know best of all . . ."

"But she doesn't earn a living, she doesn't bring home money."

Some wasps flew down to the table and started daintily licking up some chocolate sauce from the gingerbread. They didn't bother Misia, but Miss Popielska was afraid of them.

"When I was little, a wasp stung me on the eyelid. I was alone with my father at the time, my mother had gone to Kraków . . . it may have been 1935, or 1936. My father panicked and ran about the house yelling at me, and then took me somewhere in the car. I can hardly remember, to some Jews in town . . ."

Miss Popielska leaned her chin on her hand, and her gaze wandered somewhere among the apple and lime leaves.

"Squire Popielski . . . he was a distinguished man," said Misia. Miss Popielska's hazel eyes glazed over and looked like drops of honeydew. Misia guessed that her private, inner time stream, the kind each person carries inside them, had turned back, and in the empty space between the leaves she was now seeing images of the past.

When they left for Kraków, the Popielskis were poor as church mice. They lived by selling the silver with aching hearts. The Popielskis' large family, scattered about the entire world, helped their cousins a bit, as much as it was possible to provide them with some dollars or some gold. Squire Popielski was accused of collaborating with the Germans, for having traded in wood with them. He spent a few months in prison, but eventually he was released in view of his psychological problems, which the bribed psychiatrist exaggerated a little, but not much.

Then Squire Popielski spent days on end pacing from wall to wall in the cramped flat on Salwator Hill, and doggedly trying to lay out his Game on the only table. But his wife gave him such a look that he put it all back in its box and set off at once on one of his never-ending walks around the apartment.

Time went by, and the squire's wife left a little room in her prayers to thank it for passing, for continuing to move and, by doing so, introducing changes into people's lives. The family, the entire large Popielski family once again gradually gathered its strength and opened some small businesses in Kraków. Within the scope of an unwritten family agreement, Squire Popielski was assigned to overseeing shoe production, and specifically, the soles for the shoes. He supervised the work of a small plant, where a press imported from the West turned out plastic bases for sandals. At first he did it very reluctantly, but then the whole enterprise drew him in and, as usual for the squire, absorbed him totally. It fascinated him that an amorphous, indefinite substance could be given various shapes. He even began enthusiastically experimenting. He succeeded in making a completely transparent substance, and then gave it various shades and colours. And he turned out to have a good feel for the spirit of the times in the sphere of ladies' shoes — his plastic knee boots with shiny uppers sold like hot cakes.

"My father even set up a small laboratory. He was the sort of person who, whatever he did, did it with heart and soul, giving it absolute priority. In this respect he was unbearable. He behaved as if those soles and boots of his were going to save humanity. He kept playing around with test tubes and distillations, brewing and heating things.

"Finally because of all those chemical experiments of his he contracted a skin disease, maybe from burns or radiation. In any case, he looked dreadful. The skin flaked off him in whole pieces. The doctors said it was a type of skin cancer. We took him to the family in France, to the best doctors, but there's no cure for skin cancer, not here nor there. Or at least in those days there wasn't. The strangest thing was the way he regarded his illness, which we already knew at the time was fatal. 'I'm moulting,' he used to say, looking very pleased with himself, proud as Punch."

"He was a strange man," said Misia.

"But he wasn't a madman," Miss Popielska quickly added. "He had a restless soul. I think he suffered a shock because of the war and having to leave the manor. The world changed so greatly after the war. He couldn't find his place in it, so he died. He was conscious and cheerful to the very end. I couldn't understand that, I thought he'd got all confused because of the pain. You know, he suffered terribly, eventually the cancer attacked his entire body, but he kept repeating like a child that he was moulting."

Misia sighed and drank the remains of her coffee. At the bottom of the glass the brown lava of grounds had gone cold, and glints of sunlight were dancing on its surface.

"He gave instructions to be buried with that strange box, and in the whirl of preparations for the funeral we forgot about it . . . I have terrible pangs of conscience because we failed to carry out his wishes. After the funeral, Mama and I looked inside it, and do you know what we found? A bit of old cloth, a wooden die, and some little figures, of animals, people, and objects, like children's toys. And a tattered little book, some sort of incomprehensible nonsense. Mama and I tipped it out onto the table, and we couldn't believe these playthings were so valuable to him. I remember them as if it were yesterday: tiny brass figures of women and men, little animals, little trees, little houses, little manors, miniature objects, oh, tiny books the size of a little fingernail, for example, a coffee grinder with a handle, a red letterbox, a yoke with buckets — all precisely made . . ."

"And what did you do with it?" asked Misia.

"At first it all lay in the drawer where we keep the photo albums. Then the children played with it. It must still be in the house somewhere, maybe among the building blocks? I don't know, I must ask . . . I still feel guilty that we didn't put it in his coffin."

Miss Popielska chewed her lip, and her eyes glazed over again.

"I understand him," said Misia after a pause. "I used to have a special drawer where all the most important things were kept."

"But you were a child then. And he was a grown man."

"We have Izydor . . ."

"Maybe every normal family has to have a sort of normality

safety valve, someone who takes upon himself all those little bits of madness we carry inside us."

"Izydor isn't what he looks like," said Misia.

"Oh, I didn't mean anything bad by that . . . My father wasn't a lunatic either. Or maybe he was?"

Misia quickly denied it.

"What I fear most of all, Misia, is that his eccentricity could be hereditary and could happen to one of my children. But I take care of them. They're learning English, and I want to send them to the family in France to see a bit of the world. I'd like them to get good degrees — information technology, or economics, somewhere in the West, some practical specialities that give you something. They swim, they play tennis, they're interested in art and literature . . . See for yourself, they're normal, healthy children."

Misia followed Miss Popielska's gaze and saw the squire's grandchildren, who had just come back from the river. They were wearing colourful bathrobes, and they were holding snorkelling gear. They noisily pushed their way through the garden gate.

"Everything will be fine," said Miss Popielska. "The world is different now from how it once was. Better, bigger, brighter. There are inoculations against illnesses, there are no wars, people live longer . . . Don't you think so, too?"

Misia stared into her glass full of coffee grounds and shook her head.

THE TIME OF THE GAME

In the Seventh World the descendants of the first people wandered together from country to country, until they reached an extremely beautiful valley. "Come on," they said, "let's build ourselves a city and a tower reaching the sky, so that we can become a single nation and not let God break us up." And at once they got down to work, carrying stones and using tar instead of mortar. A vast city was built, in the middle of which a tower rose, until it was so high that from its top you could see what is beyond the Eight Worlds. Sometimes, when the sky was clear, the people working at the highest point raised their hands to their eyes to stop the sun from blinding them, and saw the feet of God and the outlines of the body of a great snake devouring time.

Some of them tried to reach even higher with sticks.

God looked at them and thought in alarm: "As long as they remain a single people speaking a single language they'll be able to do everything, anything that comes into their heads . . . So I'll mix up their languages, shut them inside themselves and make it so one cannot understand another. Then they'll turn against each other and give Me peace." And that was what God did.

People were scattered in all directions, and became enemies to each other. But the memory of what they had seen remained inside them. And he who has once seen the world's borders will suffer his imprisonment most painfully of all.

THE TIME OF MRS PAPUGA

Every Monday Stasia Papuga went off to the market in Taszów. On Mondays the buses were so packed that they went past the stop in the forest. So Stasia stood on the roadside verge and stopped cars. First Syrenkas and Warszawas, then big and small Fiats. She clambered awkwardly inside, and her chat with the driver always started the same way:

"Do you know Paweł Boski?"

Sometimes they did.

"He's my brother. He's an inspector."

The driver would turn round and look at her suspiciously, so she'd repeat:

"I'm Paweł Boski's sister."

They couldn't believe it.

In her old age Stasia had grown fat and had shrunk. Her nose, always prominent anyway, had got even bigger, and her eyes had lost their shine. Her feet were always swollen, and so she wore men's sandals. Only two of her lovely teeth were left. Time had not been kind to Stasia Papuga, and it was not surprising the drivers refused to believe she was Inspector Boski's sister.

One day, on just such a busy market Monday, she was knocked down by a car. She lost her hearing. A constant roaring in her head drowned out the sounds of the world. Sometimes voices appeared in the roaring, or snatches of music, but Stasia didn't know where they were from — whether they were coming through to her from the outside, or flowing from inside her. She would listen to them intently as she darned socks and endlessly altered Misia's hand-me-downs.

In the evenings she liked going to the Boskis'. Especially in summer there was something going on there. The vacationers lived upstairs. The children and grandchildren came. They would put up a table in the orchard under the apple trees and drink vodka. Paweł would get out his fiddle, and at once his children would fetch their instruments: Antek would get his accordion, Adelka — before she left — her violin, Witek his double bass, and Lila and Maja the guitar and flute. Paweł would give the signal with his bow and they would all start moving their fingers in rhythm, nodding and tapping out the beat with their feet. They always began with *In the Trenches of Manchuria*. She recognised the music from their faces. As they played *In the Trenches of Manchuria*, Michał Niebieski would briefly appear in the children's features. "Can it be possible," she wondered, "that the dead live on in the bodies of their grandchildren?" And would she, too, live on like that in the faces of Janek's children?

Stasia missed her son, who after finishing school had stayed on in Silesia. He rarely came to visit, and had inherited his father's trait of telling Stasia to wait and wait for him. In early summer she fixed up a room for him, but he never wanted to stay for long, not for the whole vacation like Paweł's children. He always left after a few days and forgot to take the fruit syrup she had spent all year making for him. But he did take the money his mother earned selling vodka.

She would accompany him to the bus stop on the Kielce road. At the crossroads lay a stone. Stasia picked up the stone and asked: "Put your hand here. I'll have it as a memento of you."

Janek looked around nervously, then allowed the imprint of his hand to remain under the stone at the crossroads for a year. Then, at Christmas and Easter, letters came from him that always started the same way: "At the start of my letter I can report that I am in good health, and I wish you the same."

His wishes had no force. As he wrote he must have been thinking about something else. One winter Stasia suddenly fell ill, and before the ambulance had managed to force its way through the snowdrifts, she died.

Janek came with some delay, when the grave was being filled in and everyone had already gone their ways. He went to his mother's house and spent a long time looking at the things. All those jars of fruit syrup, the calico curtains, crocheted bedspreads, and little boxes made out of the postcards he had sent his mother for holidays and namedays probably had no value for him. The furniture left by grandfather Boski was coarse and wouldn't have matched any high-gloss units at all. The cups had chipped rims and broken handles. Snow was pushing its way inside the annex through cracks in the door. Janek locked up the house and went to give it to his uncle.

"I don't want the house or anything that comes from Primeval," he told Paweł.

As he went back down the Highway to the bus stop, he stopped at the stone, and after a moment's hesitation did the same thing as every year. This time he pressed his hand deep into the chill, half-frozen ground and kept it there until his fingers went numb with cold.

THE TIME OF THINGS IN FOURS

From year to year Izydor became more and more aware that he would never leave Primeval. He remembered the border in the forest, that invisible wall. That border was for him. Perhaps Ruta knew how to cross it, but he hadn't the strength or the urge.

The house had emptied. Only in summer did it come to life because of the holiday guests, and then Izydor didn't leave his attic at all. He was afraid of strange people. Last winter Ukleja had often come to the Boskis'. He had grown old and even fatter. His face was grey and swollen, and his eyes were bloodshot from vodka. He would sit at the table, and then he looked like a mountain of spoiled meat, and in his croaky voice he would boast endlessly. Izydor hated him.

Ukleja must have sensed it, and being as generous as the devil himself, he gave Izydor a present — some photographs of Ruta. It was a premeditated present. Ukleja chose only those photographs where Ruta's naked body, fragmented by weird lighting, was covered by mounds of his great bulk. Only in a few of them was a woman's face visible — her mouth open, sweaty hair stuck to her cheeks.

Izydor looked at the photos in silence, then put them on the table and went upstairs.

"Why did you show him those pictures?" he heard Paweł ask.

Ukleja roared with laughter.

From that day Izydor had stopped going downstairs. Misia brought his food up to the attic and sat on the bed beside him. They would both be silent for a while, and then Misia would sigh and go back down to the kitchen.

He didn't feel like getting up. It was good to lie and dream. And he kept dreaming of the same thing — enormous spaces filled with geometric shapes, opaque polyhedrons, transparent pyramids, and opalescent cylinders. They floated above a broad plain that could have been called the earth, if it weren't for the fact that there was no sky above it. Instead there was a large, gaping black hole. Looking at it brought fear into the dream.

In the dream silence reigned. Even when the mighty solids came into contact with each other, there was no accompanying clash, not a whisper.

Izydor was not in the dream. There was only a sort of alien observer, a witness to the events of his life who lived inside Izydor, but wasn't him.

After this sort of dream Izydor's head ached and he had to keep fighting back the sobbing that came out of the blue and took up permanent residence in his throat.

One day Paweł came to see him. He said they would be playing in the garden and he should come down to join them. He looked about the attic appreciatively.

"You've got a nice place up here," he mumbled.

Winter accompanied Izydor's sorrow. Whenever he looked at the bare fields and the damp, grey sky, he was always reminded of the vision he had once seen because of Ivan Mukta, an image of the world without sense or meaning, without God. He blinked in terror, so eager was he to wipe this vision from his mind forever. But, nourished by sorrow, the image had a tendency to grow, seizing his body and soul. More and more often Izydor felt old, and his bones ached whenever the weather changed — the world was persecuting him in every possible way. Izydor didn't know what to do with himself, or where to hide.

This went on for several months, until an instinct awoke in him, and Izydor decided to save himself. When he appeared in the kitchen for the first time, Misia burst into tears and spent a long time hugging him to her apron smelling of dinner.

"You smell like Mama," he said.

Now once a day he slowly came down the narrow stairs and absent-mindedly put more twigs on the fire. Misia always had some milk boiling, or some soup, and the safe, familiar smell brought the rejected, empty world back to him. He would fetch himself something to eat and go back upstairs, muttering.

"You could chop some wood," Misia would call after him.

He chopped wood thankfully, filling the entire woodshed with logs for the fire.

"You could stop chopping wood," fumed Misia.

So he took Ivan's binoculars out of their box, and from his four windows he surveyed the whole of Primeval. He looked to the east and saw the houses of Taszów on the horizon, and in front of them the woods and meadows by the White River. He saw Mrs Niechciał, who lived in Florentynka's house, milking her cows in the meadow.

He looked to the south, at Saint Roch's chapel and the dairy, and the bridge to town, and a car that had lost its way, and the postman. Then he went across to the west window, where he had a view of Jeszkotle, the Black River, the manor-house roof, the church towers and the ever growing old people's home. Finally he went to the north-facing window and savoured the stretches of forest that were bisected by the ribbon of the Kielce road. He saw these same landscapes at each season of the year — snowy in winter, green in spring, colourful in summer, and faded in autumn.

That was when Izydor discovered that most of the things that matter in the world come in fours. He took a sheet of brown parcel paper and drew a table in pencil. The table had four columns. In the first row Izydor wrote:

West   *North*   *East*   *South.*

And right after that he added:

Winter   *Spring*   *Summer*   *Autumn.*

And he felt as if he had put down the first few words of an extremely important phrase.

This phrase must have had immense power, because now all Izydor's senses were focused on tracking down things in fours. He sought them in his attic room, but also in the garden when he was told to weed the cucumbers. He found them in everyday jobs, in objects, in his habits, and in the folk tales he remembered from childhood. He could feel himself recovering, coming out of the undergrowth onto a straight road. Wasn't everything starting to become clear? Didn't he just have to put his mind to it a bit to recognise the order that was right before his eyes, if he only bothered to look?

He started going to the local library again, and borrowed whole bagfuls of books, because he realised that lots of things in fours had already been recorded.

In the library there were many books with Squire Popielski's beautiful bookplates — above a heap of stones rose a bird with outspread wings, quite like an eagle. The bird's claws were resting on the letters FENIX. Above the bird ran the inscription: "Ex libris Felix Popielski."

Izydor borrowed nothing but books with the FENIX, and this sign became the hallmark of a good book. Unfortunately, he soon realised that the entire collection of books only began at L. On none of the shelves did he find authors with surnames from A to K. So he read Lao-tzu, Leibniz, Lenin, Loyola, Lucian, Martial, Marx, Meyrink, Mickiewicz, Nietszche, Origenes, Paracelsus, Parmenides, Plato, Plotinus, Poe, Porfirius, Prus, Quevedo, Rousseau, Schiller, Shakespeare, Sienkiewicz, Słowacki, Spencer, Spinoza, Suetonius, Swedenborg, Towiański, Tacitus, Tertulian, Saint Thomas Aquinas, Verne, Virgil, and Voltaire. And the more he read, the more he missed the authors from A to K: Augustine, Andersen, Aristotle, Avicenna, Blake, Chesterton, Clement, Dante, Darwin, Diogenes Laertius, Eckhart, Eriugen, Euclid, Freud, Goethe, the Brothers Grimm, Heine, Hegel, Hoffmann, Homer, Hölderlin, Hugo, and Jung. He also read an encyclopaedia at home, though it made him no wiser or better. But he did have more and more to write down in his tables.

Some foursomes were obvious — he only had to be observant:

| *Sour* | *Sweet* | *Bitter* | *Salty,* |

or:

| *Roots* | *Stem* | *Flower* | *Fruit,* |

or:

Green	Red	Blue	Yellow,

or:

Left	Up	Right	Down.

And also:

Eye	Ear	Nose	Mouth.

He found lots of these things in fours in the Bible. Some of them seemed more primitive, older, and these gave rise to others. He felt as if before his very eyes the foursomes were multiplying and duplicating into infinity. Finally he began to suspect that infinity itself must be fourfold, like the name of God:

Y	H	W	H

The four prophets of the Old Testament:

Isaiah	Jeremiah	Ezekiel	Daniel.

The four rivers of Eden:

Pison	Gihon	Tigris	Euphrates.

The faces of the cherubim:

Man	Lion	Ox	Eagle.

The four Evangelists:

Matthew	Mark	Luke	John.

The four cardinal virtues:

Courage	Justice	Prudence	Restraint.

The four horsemen of the Apocalypse:

Conquest	Murder	Famine	Death.

The four elements according to Aristotle:

Earth *Water* *Air* *Fire.*

The four aspects of consciousness:

Perception *Sensation* *Thought* *Intuition.*

The four kingdoms in the Kabbalah:

Mineral *Plant* *Animal* *Human.*

The four aspects of time:

Space *Past* *Present* *Future.*

The four alchemic ingredients:

Salt *Sulphur* *Nitrogen* *Mercury.*

The four alchemic processes:

Coagulatio *Solutio* *Sublimatio* *Calcinatio.*

The four letters of the holy syllable:

A *O* *U* *M.*

The four kabbalistic sephirot:

Mercy *Beauty* *Strength* *Rule.*

The four states of existence:

Life *Dying and death* *The time after death* *Rebirth.*

The four states of consciousness:

Lethargy *Deep sleep* *Shallow sleep* *Waking.*

The four qualities of creation:
Permanence *Fluidity*   *Volatility*   *Light.*

The four human capacities according to Galen:
Physical   *Aesthetic*   *Intellectual*   *Moral and spiritual.*

The four basic operations of algebra:
Addition   *Subtraction*   *Multiplication*   *Division.*

The four dimensions:
Width   *Length*   *Height*   *Time.*

The four states of concentration:
Solid   *Liquid*   *Gas*   *Plasma.*

The four bases that construct DNA:
T   *A*   *G*   *C*

The four humours according to Hippocrates:
Phlegmatic *Melancholic*   *Sanguine*   *Choleric.*

And still the list was not complete. It could never be complete, because then the world would end. So thought Izydor. He also thought he had come upon the trail of an order that is in force throughout the universe, a special divine alphabet.

With time, tracking down things in fours changed Izydor's mind. In every single thing, in even the most insignificant phenomenon he saw four parts, four stages, four processes. He saw foursomes following on from one another, multiplying into eights and sixteens, the constant transformation of the fourfold algebra of life. The blossoming apple tree in the orchard no longer existed for him, but a fourfold, cohesive structure consisting of roots, trunk, leaves, and flowers. And, curiously — the foursome was immortal — in autumn instead of flowers there were fruits. Izydor had to think hard about the fact that in winter only the trunk and roots were left. He discovered the law of reducibility of foursomes to twosomes — the twosome is a period of rest for the foursome. The foursome became a twosome when it was asleep, like a tree in winter.

Things that did not immediately reveal their inner fourfold structure presented Izydor with a challenge. One time he was watching Witek, who was trying to break in a young horse. The horse bucked and threw him to the ground. Izydor thought the configuration popularly known as "a man on a horse" only appeared to have two elements outwardly. Indeed, principally there is a man, and a horse. There is also a third whole, namely a man on a horse. So where is the fourth element?

It is the centaur, something more than a man and a horse, it is a man and a horse in one, the child of a man and a horse, a man and a goat, Izydor suddenly realised, and once again felt the same, long forgotten anxiety that Ivan Mukta had once left him with.

THE TIME OF MISIA

For ages Misia refused to cut her long grey hair. Whenever Lila and Maja came, they brought special dye with them and over an evening they restored her hair's original colour. They had an eye for colour — they chose exactly the right one.

One day something suddenly happened to her, and she had

her hair cut. As the dyed chestnut curls fell to the floor, Misia looked in the mirror and realised she was an old woman.

In spring she wrote back to the young squire's daughter to say she wasn't taking holiday guests, not this year, nor the next. Paweł tried to protest, but she wouldn't listen to him. At night she would wake up as her heart suddenly began to pound and her pulse to race. Her hands and feet became swollen. She looked at her feet, and didn't recognise them. "I used to have slender fingers and fine ankles. My calves tensed when I walked in high heels," she thought.

In summer, when the children came home, all except Adelka, they took her to the doctor. She had high blood pressure. She had to take pills and was not allowed to drink coffee.

"What's life without coffee?" muttered Misia, taking her grinder from the sideboard.

"Mama, you're like a child," said Maja, taking the grinder out of her hands.

Next day Witek bought a large tin of decaffeinated coffee at the hard-currency shop. She pretended to like it, but once she was alone, she ground some precious, rationed real coffee beans and made herself a glass of it. With a skin, just as she liked it. She sat at the kitchen window and gazed at the orchard. She could hear the rustle of the tall grass — there was no one left to mow it under the trees. From the window she could see the Black River, the priest's meadows, and beyond them Jeszkotle, where people were always building new houses out of white breeze blocks. The world was no longer as pretty as it used to be.

One day, as she was drinking her coffee, some people came to see Paweł. She found out that Paweł had hired them to build a family tomb.

"Why didn't you tell me about it?" she asked.

"I wanted to give you a surprise."

On Sunday they went to look at the deep excavation. Misia didn't like the spot — next to old Boski's and Stasia Papuga's grave.

"Why isn't it next to my parents?" she asked.

Paweł shrugged.

"Why, why, why," he mocked her. "It's too cramped there."

Misia remembered how she and Izydor had once divided her marital bed.

As they were on the way home, she cast a glance at the inscription at the graveyard exit.

"God sees. Time escapes. Death pursues. Eternity waits," she read.

The year that ensued was troubled. Paweł would switch on the radio in the kitchen and the three of them, including Izydor, listened to the reports. They didn't understand much of it. In summer the children and grandchildren came. Not all of them, as Antek hadn't got leave. They sat in the garden until late at night, drinking currant wine and discussing politics. Misia cast involuntary glances at the garden gate and waited for Adelka.

"She won't come," said Lila.

In September the house emptied again. For days on end Paweł drove his motorbike around the uncultivated fields and supervised the building of the tomb. Misia called Izydor downstairs, but he refused to come down. Instead he pored over the sheets of brown paper on which he drew his never-ending tables.

"Promise that if I die first you won't put him in the old people's home," she said to Paweł.

"I promise."

On the first day of autumn Misia ground some real coffee, tipped it into a glass, and poured on boiling water. She took some gingerbread from the sideboard. A wonderful aroma filled the kitchen. She pulled a chair up to the window and drank her coffee in small sips. Then the world exploded in Misia's head, and tiny shards of it scattered all around. Misia sank to the floor, under the table. The spilled coffee dripped onto her hand. She couldn't move, so she waited, like an animal caught in a snare, for someone to come and free her.

She was taken to the hospital in Taszów, where the doctors said she had had a stroke. Every day Paweł came to see her with Izydor and the girls. They sat by her bed and talked to her the whole time, though none of them was sure if Misia could understand. They asked questions, and sometimes she nodded to say "yes" or shook her head to say "no." Her face had caved in, and her gaze had turned inside and gone dull. They went into the corridor and tried to find out from the doctor what would happen to her, but the doctor looked preoccupied with something else. Red-and-white flags hung in every window of the hospital, and the staff were wearing strike armbands. So they stood at the hospital window and explained this misfortune to each other. Maybe she had hit her head and damaged all those centres, of speech, joie de vivre, interest in life, the will to live. Or maybe something else had happened: she had fallen and taken fright at the thought of her own fragility, at the miraculous fact of being alive, she had taken fright at the idea that she was mortal, and now, before their very eyes, she was dying of fear of death.

They brought her compote and oranges acquired at vast expense. Gradually they resigned themselves to the idea that Misia would die, that she was going somewhere else. But what they feared most was that in the fervour of dying, the separating of the soul from the body or the fading of the biological structure of the brain, Misia Boska would be gone forever, all her recipes would be gone, all the chicken liver and radish salads, her iced chocolate cakes, her gingerbread, and finally, her thoughts, her words, the events she had taken part in, as ordinary as her life, and yet — each of them was sure of it — lined in darkness and sorrow, because the world is not friendly to mankind, and the only thing to be done is to find a shell for yourself and your loved ones, and stay in there until you are released. As they looked at Misia sitting in bed, with her legs covered by a blanket and her face absent, they wondered what her thoughts were like — whether they were in shreds, ripped up, just like her words, or maybe hidden in the depths of her mind, preserving all their freshness and strength, or perhaps they had changed into pure images, full of colours and depth. They also reckoned on the fact that Misia may have stopped thinking. That would mean the shell was not airtight, and Misia had been struck down by chaos and destruction while still alive.

Meanwhile, until she died a month later, the whole time Misia saw nothing but the left side of the world, where her guardian angel was waiting for her, who always appeared at truly important moments.

THE TIME OF PAWEŁ

As the tomb still wasn't ready, Paweł buried Misia next to Genowefa and Michał. He thought she ought to like that. He himself was fully occupied with building the tomb, and kept giving the workmen more and more complicated orders, so the work dragged on. That was how Paweł Boski, inspector, kept putting off the time of his own death.

After the funeral, once the children had left, the house became very quiet. The silence made Paweł feel uneasy. So he switched on the television and watched all the programmes. The national anthem at the end of broadcasting was his cue to go to bed. Only then did Paweł hear that he was not alone.

Upstairs the floorboards creaked under the trailing, heavy footsteps of Izydor, who never came downstairs any more. His brother-in-law's presence got on Paweł's nerves. So one day he went upstairs to his room and encouraged him to go into the old people's home.

"You'll have proper care and hot meals," he said.

To his surprise Izydor didn't argue. The very next day he was packed to go. When Paweł saw the two cardboard cases and the carrier bag full of clothing, he felt pangs of conscience, but only for a moment.

"He'll have proper care and hot meals," he now told himself.

In November the first snow fell, and after that it kept falling and falling. A smell of damp arose in the house, and Paweł fetched out an electric heater from somewhere, which was hardly able to heat up the living room. The television crackled because of the damp and cold, but it did work. Paweł followed the weather forecasts and watched all the news reports, though he wasn't at all concerned about them. Some governments changed, some characters appeared and disappeared in the little silver window. Just before the holidays his daughters came and fetched him for Christmas Eve. He told them to take him home on the second day of the holiday, and then he saw that the roof of Stasia's cottage had collapsed under the weight of snow. Now the snow was falling inside, covering the furniture with a fleecy layer: the empty sideboard, the table, the bed in which old Boski used to sleep, and the bedside cabinet. At first Paweł wanted to save the things from the cold and frost, but then he thought he wouldn't be able to drag the heavy furniture out on his own. And what did he need it for?

"Dad, you made a shoddy roof," he said to the furniture. "Your shingle has rotted. My house is standing."

The spring winds knocked over two walls. The living room in Stasia's cottage changed into a heap of rubble. In summer nettles and dandelions appeared in Stasia's flower beds, with brightly coloured anemones and peonies blooming despairingly among them. There was a smell of strawberries gone wild. Paweł was astonished to see how quickly decay and destruction progress. As if building houses were contrary to the entire nature of heaven and earth, as if erecting walls and laying stones on top of each other went against the current of time. He found this thought appalling. On television the national anthem stopped and the screen turned to snow. Paweł switched on all the lights and opened the wardrobes.

He saw neatly folded piles of bedclothes, tablecloths, napkins, and towels. He touched their edges, and suddenly his entire body was filled with longing for Misia. So he took out a pile of duvet covers and buried his face in it. They smelled of soap, cleanliness and order, like Misia, like the world as it used to be. He started taking the entire contents out of the wardrobes: his clothes and Misia's, piles of cotton vests and pants, bags full of socks, Misia's underwear, her slips that he knew so well, her smooth stockings, suspender belts and bras, her blouses and sweaters. He took the suits off their hangers (lots of them, including the ones with padded shoulders, could still remember the war), trousers with belts trapped in the loops, shirts with stiff collars, dresses and skirts. He spent a long time examining a grey woman's suit made of thin woollen fabric, and he remembered buying that material, then taking it to the tailor. Misia had demanded wide lapels and inset pockets. He took hats and scarves from the top shelf, and handbags from the bottom shelf. He plunged his hand into their cool, slippery insides, as if gutting a dead animal. A pile of things grew on the floor, cast about in disorder. He thought he should distribute it all to his children. But Adelka had gone. So had Witek. He didn't even know where they were. Later, however, it occurred to him that only dead people's clothes are given away, and he was still alive.

"I'm alive and I don't feel bad. I'll manage," he said to himself and went to fetch his violin out of the grandfather clock. He hadn't played it for ages.

He took it outside onto the front steps and began to play, first *This Is Our Last Sunday*, then *In the Trenches of Manchuria*. Moths came flying down to the lamp and circled above his head — a moving halo full of tiny wings and feelers. He kept playing until the stiff, dusty strings snapped, one after another.

THE TIME OF IZYDOR

When Paweł took Izydor to the old people's home, he tried to explain the whole situation clearly to the nun who received him:

"He may not be all that old, but he is ailing, and also handicapped. Despite being a sanitation inspector," — Paweł put special stress on the word "inspector" — "and knowing about many things, I could not guarantee him proper care."

Izydor willingly agreed to the move. From here he had less of a distance to the graveyard, where his mother, father, and now Misia lay. He was glad Paweł hadn't managed to finish the tomb, and that Misia was buried with their parents. Every day after breakfast he got dressed and went to sit by them for a while.

But time flows differently in an old people's home from anywhere else; its stream is thinner. From one month to the next

Izydor lost strength, and finally he gave up the graveyard visits.

"I think I'm sick," he told Sister Aniela, who took care of him. "I think I'm going to die."

"But Izydor, you're still young and full of strength," she said, trying to cheer him up.

"I am old," he insisted.

He felt disappointed. He thought old age was going to open that third eye, which makes it possible to see right through everything, and to understand how the world works. But nothing became clear to him. Instead his bones ached and he couldn't sleep. No one came to visit him, neither the dead nor the living. At night he saw his images — Ruta just as he remembered her, and the geometrical visions — empty spaces with angular and oval shapes in them. More and more often these images seemed faded and blurred, and the shapes were twisted and inferior, as if they were aging along with him.

He no longer had the strength to work on his tables. He still dragged himself out of bed and roamed around the building to see his four points of the compass, and that took him all day. The old people's home had not been built honestly and didn't have windows facing north, as if its builders were trying to deny this fourth, darkest side of the world, to avoid upsetting the residents. So Izydor had to go out onto the terrace and lean over the railing. Then, around the corner of the building he could see the endless dark woods and the ribbon of the road. The winter completely deprived him of this view because the terraces were locked shut then. So he sat in an armchair in the so-called day room, where the television murmured non-stop, as he tried to forget about the north.

He learned how to forget, and forgetting brought him relief. It was simpler than he had ever expected it to be. It was enough not to think about the woods and the river for one single day, not to think about his mother and Misia combing her chestnut hair, it was enough not to think about the house and the attic with four windows, and the next day those images were paler and paler, more and more faded.

Finally Izydor could no longer walk. Despite all the antibiotics and irradiation, his bones and joints went stiff and refused to move at all. He was put to bed in an isolation ward, and there he gradually died.

Dying involved the systematic disintegration of what had been Izydor. It was a very rapid, irreversible process, self-perfecting and marvellously effective. Like deleting unnecessary information from the computer where the accounts were done at the old people's home.

First to disappear were the ideas, thoughts and abstract concepts that Izydor had made such an effort to acquire in the course of his life. All of a sudden the things in fours disappeared:

Lines	Squares	Triangles	Circles
Addition	Subtraction	Multiplication	Division
Sound	Word	Image	Symbol
Mercy	Beauty	Strength	Rule
Ethics	Metaphysics	Epistemology	Ontology
Space	Past	Present	Future
Width	Length	Height	Time
Left	Up	Right	Down
Struggle	Suffering	Sense of guilt	Death
Roots	Stem	Flower	Fruit
Sour	Sweet	Bitter	Salty
Winter	Spring	Summer	Autumn.

And finally:

West   *North*   *East*   *South.*

Then his favourite places faded, then the faces of those he loved best, then their names, and finally whole people yielded to oblivion. Next Izydor's emotions disappeared — some very old thrills (when Misia had her first child), some despair (when Ruta left), some joy (when the letter from her came), certainty (when he discovered the fourfold nature of things), fear (when he and Ivan Mukta were shot at), pride (when he got money from the post office), and many, many others. And finally, at the very end, when Sister Aniela said: "He has died," the open spaces that Izydor had inside him began to roll up, spaces that were neither earthly nor celestial — they fell apart into tiny pieces, caved in on each other and vanished forever. It was an image of destruction more terrible than any other, worse than war, fires, stars exploding or black holes imploding.

That was when Cornspike appeared at the old people's home.

"You're too late. He's dead," Sister Aniela told her.

Cornspike didn't answer. She sat down by Izydor's bed. She touched his neck. Izydor's body wasn't breathing any more, his heart wasn't beating inside it, but it was still warm. Cornspike leaned over Izydor and said into his ear:

"Go, and don't stop in any of the worlds. And don't be tempted to come back again."

She sat by Izydor's body until they took it away. Then she remained at his bedside all night and all day, mumbling continually. She only went when she was sure Izydor had gone forever.

THE TIME OF THE GAME

God has grown old. In the Eighth World He is now old. His mind is getting weaker and it is full of holes. The Word has become gibberish. So has the world, which arose from the Mind and the Word. The sky is cracking like desiccated wood, the earth has decayed in places and now falls apart under the feet of animals and people. The edges of the world are fraying and turning to dust.

God has tried to be perfect, and has come to a stop. Anything that does not move is at a standstill. Anything that comes to a standstill falls apart.

"Nothing comes of creating worlds," thinks God. "Creating worlds leads to nothing, nothing develops, or broadens, or changes. It is all in vain."

For God death does not exist, although sometimes God would like to die, as the people die, whom He has imprisoned in the worlds and entangled in time. Sometimes the people's souls escape from Him and disappear from His all-seeing eye. That is when God feels the greatest yearning. For He knows that apart from Him there exists an invariable order, joining everything variable into a single pattern. And in this order, which even contains God Himself, everything that seems transient and scattered in time starts to exist simultaneously and eternally, outside time.

THE TIME OF ADELKA

Adelka got out of the Kielce bus on the Highway and felt as if she had woken up, as if she had been asleep, and had dreamed about her life in some city, with some people, amid muddled, unclear events. She shook her head and saw the avenue through the forest to Primeval ahead of her, with the lime trees on either side, and the dark wall of Wodenica — everything was in its place.

She stopped to adjust her handbag on her shoulder. She glanced down at her Italian shoes and her camel-hair coat. She knew she looked beautiful, like someone from a fashion magazine, like someone from the big city. She walked ahead, teetering on her high stilettos.

As she came out of the woods, she was struck by the vastness of the sky, which suddenly unfurled in its entirety. She had forgotten the sky could be so large, as if it also contained other, unknown worlds. She had never seen a sky like that in Kielce.

She saw the roof of the house, and couldn't believe how much the lilac tree had grown. When she came closer, for a moment her heart sank — Aunt Stasia's house wasn't there. Instead the sky had flooded the place where it had always stood.

Adelka opened the garden gate and stopped in front of the house. The door and windows were shut. She went into the back yard. It was overgrown with grass. Some little bantam hens ran out towards her, as brightly coloured as peacocks. Then it occurred to her that her father and Uncle Izydor had died, but no one had told her, and now she had come to an empty house in her smart coat and her Italian stilettos.

She put down her suitcase, lit a cigarette, and walked across the orchard to the spot where Aunt Stasia's cottage used to stand.

"So you smoke now," she suddenly heard.

Instinctively she threw the cigarette to the ground and felt a lump in her throat, caused by her old, childhood fear of her father. She looked up and saw him. He was sitting on a kitchen stool in the heap of rubble that had once been his sister's house.

"What are you doing here, Dad?" she asked in surprise.

"I'm keeping an eye on the house."

She didn't know what to say. They looked at each other in silence.

She could see he hadn't shaved for weeks. His stubble was entirely white now, as if hoarfrost had settled on his face. She noticed that he had grown much older in all these years.

"Have I changed?" she asked.

"You've got older," he replied, turning his gaze on the house. "Like everyone."

"What's happened, Dad? Where's Uncle Izydor? Doesn't anyone help you?"

"Everyone demands money from me and wants to take over the house as if I weren't alive any more. But I am still alive. Why didn't you come to your mother's funeral?"

Adelka's hands were longing for a cigarette.

"I just came to tell you that I'm doing fine. I graduated, and I'm working. I have a big daughter already."

"Why didn't you have a son?"

Again the familiar lump rose to her throat, and once more she felt as if she had just woken up. Kielce did not exist, there were no Italian stilettos or camel-hair coat. Time was sliding downwards, like the undermined bank of a river, trying to carry them both off into the past.

"I just didn't," she said.

"You've all got girls. Antek has two, Witek has one, the twins have two each, and now you. I remember it all, I keep a rigorous count and I still haven't got a grandson. You've disappointed me."

She took another cigarette from her pocket and lit it.

Her father stared at the lighter flame.

"What about your husband?" he asked.

Adelka inhaled with relief and blew out a cloud of smoke.

"I haven't got a husband."

"Did he leave you?" he asked.

She turned and headed towards the house.

"Wait. The house is locked. This place is full of thieves and all sorts of riff-raff."

He slowly walked after her. Then he took a bunch of keys from his pocket. She watched him open the locks, one, two, three. His hands were shaking. She noticed to her surprise that she was taller than him.

She followed him into the kitchen and at once she smelled the familiar odour of the stove gone cold and burned milk. She inhaled it, like the cigarette smoke.

There were some dirty plates on the table, with flies walking idly about on them. The sun was drawing the pattern of the curtains on the waxed tablecloth.

"Dad, where's Izydor?"

"I took him to live at the old people's home in Jeszkotle. He was already old and doddery. Eventually he died. The same thing's in store for all of us."

She moved a pile of clothes from a chair and sat down. She felt like crying. Clods of earth and dry grass had stuck to her high heels.

"There's no need to feel sorry for him. They gave him proper care and full board. He was better off than I am. I have to see to everything, keep an eye on it all."

She stood up and went into the living room. He lumbered after her, not letting her out of sight. On the table she saw a pile of underwear that had gone grey: vests, underpants and knickers. On a newspaper there was an ink-pad and a seal with a wooden handle. She picked up a pair of underpants and read the print fuzzily stamped in ink: "Paweł Boski, Inspector."

"They steal," he said. "They even take underpants off the washing line."

"Dad, I'll stay here with you for a bit, I'll clean up for you and bake a cake . . ." Adelka took off her coat and hung it on a chair. She pulled up the sleeves of her sweater and began to clear the dirty cups from the table.

"Leave it." Paweł's tone was unexpectedly harsh. "I don't want anyone acting as though they own the place. I can manage fine."

She went into the yard for her suitcase, and then put some presents on the dirty table: a cream-coloured shirt and a tie for her father, a box of chocolates and some eau de Cologne for Izydor. For a while she held a photograph of her daughter.

"This is my daughter. Do you want to see?"

He took the photograph and cast an eye at it.

"She doesn't look like anyone. How old is she?"

"Nineteen."

"What have you been doing all this time?"

She took a deep breath, because she thought she had a lot to say, but suddenly it all flew out of her head.

Paweł picked up the presents in silence and took them to the sideboard in the living room. The bunch of keys jangled. She heard the rattle of patent locks forcibly set into the oak door of the sideboard. She looked around the kitchen and recognised things she had already forgotten. On a rack by the tiled stove there was a plate with a double bottom, where hot water was poured, so the soup wouldn't go cold too quickly. On a shelf there were some ceramic containers with blue lettering saying flour, rice, buckwheat, and sugar. For as long as she could remember the container for sugar had been cracked. There was a copy of the icon of the Virgin Mary of Jeszkotle hanging above the living-room door. Her lovely hands alluringly exposed her smooth neckline, but where there should have been a breast there was a small, blood-red piece of flesh — a heart. Finally Adelka's gaze landed on the coffee grinder with the porcelain belly and the neat little drawer. From the living room she heard the keys rattling as they opened the locks in the sideboard. She hesitated a moment, then quickly took the grinder from the shelf and hid it in her suitcase.

"You've come back too late," said her father in the doorway. "Everything's already over. Time to die."

He laughed, as if he had told an excellent joke. She saw that there was nothing left of his fine white teeth. Now they sat in silence. Adelka's gaze wandered along the pattern on the table-cloth and rested on some jars of blackcurrant juice that the fruit flies had got inside.

"I could stay . . ." she whispered, and the ash from her cigarette fell on her skirt.

Paweł turned to face the window and gazed through the dirty pane at the orchard.

"I don't need anything anymore. I'm not afraid of anything anymore."

She understood what he was trying to say to her. She got up and slowly put on her coat. She kissed her father awkwardly on both stubble-frosted cheeks. She thought he would see her to the gate, but at once he headed for the pile of rubble, where his stool was still standing.

She emerged onto the Highway, and only then did she notice that it had been surfaced in asphalt. The lime trees seemed smaller. Light gusts of wind were shaking the leaves off them, which were falling on Stasia Papuga's fields, overgrown with tall grass.

By Wodenica she wiped her Italian heels clean with a hand-kerchief and tidied her hair. She had to sit at the stop for another hour or so, waiting for the bus. When it came, she was the only passenger. She opened her case and took out the grinder. Slowly she began to turn the handle, and the driver cast her a look of surprise in the rear-view mirror.

Olga Tokarczuk was born in 1962 in Sulechów near Zielona Góra, Poland. A recipient of all of Poland's top literary awards, she is one of the most critically acclaimed authors of her generation. After finishing her psychology degree at the University of Warsaw, she initially practised as a therapist and often cites C.G. Jung as an inspiration for her work, in which mythmaking has become a hallmark.

Since the publication of her first book, a collection of poems, in 1989, Tokarczuk has published nine volumes of stories, novellas, and novels and one book-length essay (on Boleslaw Prus's novel *The Doll*). Her novel *House of Day, House of Night* has been translated into English. Awarded the Nike Prize, Poland's top book award, for *Bieguni* [The Runners] in 2008, she now divides her time between Wrocław and a small village near the Czech border.

Antonia Lloyd-Jones is among the leading translator of Polish prose into English. Having studied Russian and Ancient Greek at Oxford University, she has translated many works of Polish fiction, among them *House of Day, House of Night* by Olga Tokarczuk and Paweł Huelle's *Mercedes-Benz* and *Castorp*. She is the recipient of the 2009 Found in Translation Award for her translation of Huelle's *The Last Supper*. She lives in London.

PRIMEVAL AND OTHER TIMES

by Olga Tokarczuk

Translated by Antonia Lloyd-Jones from the Polish
Prawiek i inne czasy, originally published in 1996 by
WAB, Warsaw. The version used for this translation
was published in 2000 by Wydawnictwo Ruta, Wałbrzych

Design by Jed Slast
Set in Janson with Univers titles
Cover image and frontispiece by Markéta Vogelová

First published in 2010 by
TWISTED SPOON PRESS
P.O. Box 21 – Preslova 12
150 00 Prague 5, Czech Republic
twistedspoonpress@gmail.com
www.twistedspoon.com

THIRD PRINTING

Printed and bound in the Czech Republic by PB Tisk

Distributed to the trade by

SCB DISTRIBUTORS
www.scbdistributors.com

CENTRAL BOOKS
www.centralbooks.com